# A School
## for Sorcery

**TOR**®

A Tom Doherty Associates Book
New York

# A School for Sorcery

E. ROSE SABIN

A SCHOOL FOR SORCERY

Copyright © 2002 by E. Rose Sabin

Book design by Jane Adele Regina

A Tor Book
Published by Tom Doherty Associates, LLC
175 Fifth Avenue
New York, NY 10010

www.tor.com

Tor® is a registered trademark of Tom Doherty Associates, LLC.

Library of Congress Cataloging-in-Publication

Sabin, E. Rose.
        A school for sorcery / E. Rose Sabin.—1st ed.
        p. cm.
        "A Tom Doherty Associates book."
        ISBN 0-765-30289-6 (acid-free paper)
        1. Magic—Study and teaching—Fiction.    2. Teenage girls—
Fiction.    3. Good and evil—Fiction.    I. Title.

        PS3619.A27 S36 2002
        813'.6—dc21

                                                            2002068564


First Edition: September 2002

Printed in the United States of America

0   9   8   7   6   5   4   3   2   1

To Mom,
who has been, through the years and remains now,
not only mother, but also friend, supporter, confidante


and in memory of Dad,
for his love, and for the inspiration he provided

# ACKNOWLEDGMENTS

So many friends and mentors have helped make this book possible that it is impossible to name them all. I am quite certain that in naming some, I shall inadvertently omit others who should be included, and for that I ask their forgiveness.

First and foremost, I wish to thank Andre Norton for her encouragement and counsel since awarding the manuscript of this novel her prestigious Gryphon Award in 1992. A very special thanks to Ann Cripin of Writer Beware (www.sfwa.org/beware/—site maintained by Victoria Strauss), for her guidance and for her help in finding a legitimate agent. And thanks to my agent, Jack Byrne, for his invaluable aid, patience, and constant reassurance whenever self-doubt reared its head. Thanks, too, to my kind and patient editor, Jonathan Schmidt.

The members of PINAWOR (The Pinellas Authors and Writers Organization) helped more than they probably realize, and I am grateful for their perceptive critiques and most of all, for their friendship and support.

And, finally, a heartfelt thank-you goes to Diane Marcou for her indispensable assistance in critiquing the manuscript and for all that she has taught me about writing, and to that wonderful group of fellow writers and dear friends who found each other through Diane's writing classes and who have continued to meet and exchange critiques and encouragement for many years—Betty DeBate, Linda Harrell, Joyce Levesque, and Louise Miller—without whom this book would not have been possible.

ACKNOWLEDGMENTS

# LESLEY SIMONTON SCHOOL FOR THE MAGICALLY GIFTED

## HEADMISTRESS
Miryam Vedreaux

## FACULTY
Aletheia—Specialist in Interdimensional Concourse
Mistress Blake—Gifting Mistress, expert in the development
of all supernormal gifts
Mistress Dova—Professor of Arcane Rites and
Esoterica; Librarian
Master Hawke—Professor of Alchemy, the Mandala, and
the Healing Arts
Master San Marté—Professor of Ethics
Master Tumberlis—"Old Tumbles"—Professor of the History
and Philosophy of Metaphysics

## "MAID"
Veronica Crowell

## STUDENTS
First Year

| *Women:* | *Men:* |
|---|---|
| Bettina Barker | Tonyo Deste |
| Eula Claver | Jerrol Fyfe |
| Irel Lane | Davy Geer |
| Lina Mueller | Emory Knight |
| Coral Snow | Reece O'Shannon |

Petra Stratigeas
Tria Tesserell
Rehanne Zalos

Fenton Rhoze
Nevil Santomayor
Britnor Wythyn

## Second Year

*Women:*
Nubba Balder
Elspeth Carlin
Norietta Elden
Kathyn Klemmer
Taner Mayclan
Verin Savrile

*Men:*
Gray Becq
Oryon Brew
Kress Klemmer
Palmer Lawry
Salor Tribane
Wilce Riverman

## Third Year

*Women:*
Nan Evers
Helena Herrell
Rozelle Shepherd
Adeen Yont

*Men:*
Yosef Byne
Evyar Mason
Merjoe Pease
Cleance Vomai

# A School
## for Sorcery

# 1

## THE LETTER

"Tria! Tria, come into the house right away!"

Tria looked up from her egg gathering and saw her mother standing at the back door, shouting the summons. Whatever she wanted, it must be something serious. She never allowed Tria to leave her chores undone.

"Coming," she called back as she added two last eggs to those already in the basket.

She walked fast, carrying the basket carefully so as not to break the eggs.

"Run!" her mother called again.

Something terrible must have happened. With one hand over the eggs to keep them from bouncing, Tria ran.

"What is it?" she panted when she reached her mother. "What's wrong?"

"Nothing's wrong," her mother said, taking the basket of eggs. "Come inside, quickly, before your father sees us."

Her father was mending fences in the far field. She thought it unlikely that he would return for some time, and he certainly could not see the house from where he was working. Puzzled by her mother's unwarranted concern, she followed her in through the screen door and waited impatiently while her mother set the basket of eggs on the kitchen counter and led the way into the small living room.

"There!" Her mother pointed to a thick, white envelope that lay facedown on the small table by the sofa, a circle of red sealing wax closing its flap. "It's for you."

"For me?" Tria stared stupidly at the envelope and wondered who could be sending her a letter. She knew very few people outside of this small town where she had lived since her birth. In all her sixteen years she had never received a real letter, though friends had sent postcards, and farm-supply catalogs and quotes for hog and poultry prices arrived regularly for her father, while her mother occasionally got a letter from distant relatives in Wickton in Plains Province as well as a brief note from Kate, Tria's older sister, who lived in the next town.

"Pick it up and open it," her mother urged, her face alight with eagerness.

Tria reached for it slowly as though afraid it might vanish or dissolve when she touched it. She turned it over and saw her name written in elegant black script: Miss Tria Fay Tesserell. Below it was inscribed the name of the town. "Carey," it read, "Inland Province, Arucadi." The postal mark on the letter indicated that it came from Castlemount Province, and Tria was certain that no one in the family knew anyone from that far away.

She couldn't break the wax seal with her short fingernails. Her mother handed her a letter opener, and with it Tria lifted the seal, opened the flap, and drew out a letter and a colorful brochure. The letterhead said in fancy lettering, *The Lesley Simonton School for the Magically Gifted*.

Intrigued, she read the letter.

E. ROSE SABIN

*Dear Miss Tesserell,* it began formally.

*It has come to the attention of the Lesley Simonton School that you are among the minority of Arucadi's population who are Gifted with magical powers. You are surely aware of the importance of receiving training in the use of those powers. The Simonton School specializes in helping untrained Talents like yourself develop your powers within the ethical guidelines set forth by the Community of the Gifted. We prepare our students to take places of responsible leadership in a society that has all too frequently been intimidated by those with special Gifts. It is our earnest hope that you will consider joining our student body in the forthcoming academic year, which begins on the first day of Harvest Month.*

*The enclosed brochure will provide you with full information about the school, its distinguished faculty, the course offerings, and tuition costs, as well as an application form that you should complete and return immediately if you decide to take advantage of this unique opportunity.*

*Because an Adept who performs special services for us from time to time has determined through divination that you are a suitable candidate for Simonton School, you need only send with the application a down payment of 25 triums toward your first year's expenses, and your acceptance is assured.*

*Sincerely yours,*
*Miryam Vedreaux, Headmistress*

Tria looked up from the letter and saw her mother watching her with an odd intensity.

"Momma, did you know about this?" Holding back the brochure, she handed her mother the letter.

Her mother read through it quickly and nodded, smiling.

"I mentioned to a friend that I would so like to see you trained in your gifts, and she told me about the school and got me their address. I wrote without really expecting any response. But when the letter arrived, I knew—" She broke off and handed the letter back to Tria, her hand shaking. "This is what I've wanted for you. Tria, this is your chance, probably your only chance, to become what you are meant to be, what your gifts tell me that you should be."

Tria had never seen her mother so animated. Her careworn face suddenly acquired an unsuspected beauty. For the first time Tria caught a glimpse of her mother as she must have been long years ago, before she had married a farmer and set aside her own special talents to conform to her husband's expectations of what a farm wife should be—and should not be.

"Poppa will never let me go," she said. "He wouldn't even consider letting me go to the Harnor Trade School to study modern farming methods. He said he needed me here to help with the harvest. He won't change his mind about that."

"He might. Oh, not easily—I'll grant you that. But he can hire the Cromley boys to help with the harvest. They'd be glad to have the work. The yields have been exceptionally good this year, so the work would be too much for you anyway."

"Poppa always complains that the Cromley boys are careless."

"I know, I know." Her mother sighed, and her gnarled hands pleated her apron. "They really aren't, though. Your father is just too hard to please. Now wait here a minute."

Abruptly she let go of her apron and hurried off into her bedroom. She was back almost immediately, clutching a leather change purse and a pen.

"It is a saying among the gifted that when a door opens to you, you must go through it." She gazed downward, saying softly, "I wish I had taken that advice." Then, raising her eyes to Tria, she said resolutely, "Look, I have the twenty-five triums right here. It's money I've saved without your father's knowing."

She opened the purse and spilled out a mound of silver coins. Tria gaped, unable to imagine how her mother had hidden away so much money.

But the twenty-five triums was only a down payment. She'd have to pay far more for the full year's expenses. And as she glanced over the brochure, she saw that the school offered three years of instruction.

"Just get the application ready. I'll go to town this afternoon, get a bank draft, and send off the form and the draft. When your acceptance comes, it will be hard for your father to refuse."

Tria could not believe that her mother thought it would be so easy. Her father had never permitted her to use her special gifts, saying that a farm girl had no business putting on airs and doing what he termed "witchery" instead of tending to her rightful business. He would certainly never allow her to attend a school for the gifted.

But her mother pushed her toward the dining room table, shoved her into a chair, and placed the application form and pen in front of her. "Fill it out," she directed. "I know how unhappy you've been at the thought of spending your life on a farm. When you're trained in using your gifts, any number of opportunities will open to you. The gifted are in demand in law enforcement, in entertainment, in business, in education, even in government. You can go into just about any field you want."

Tria caught her mother's excitement. Yes, she did want to do more with her life than spend it on the farm. She'd tried to hide her discontent from her mother, but of course her mother, being gifted, *would* know how she had dreaded the thought of working with her parents, eventually marrying a local farmer's son, and then spending the rest of her life in

Carey as a farmer's wife, mother to children with no better prospects than she had.

She thrilled at the possibility of going away to school. She'd always been a good student, and most especially she'd loved learning about their vast country of Arucadi and its history. She'd dreamed of traveling across it some day, of finding a job that allowed her to visit the more remote and exotic parts of the country.

She'd shared her dreams and hopes with her school friends, but none had understood. She'd found no one like herself, no one with the special gifts that set her apart and made her hopes and dreams different from those of the other children in the school.

She'd finished the Carey Basic School in the spring. Several of her classmates planned to go on to trade school, but she, along with many others, expected to get no further schooling but to join their parents toiling on the farms and in the wheat fields. Most of her friends accepted their lot without complaint. Tria felt alone in her longing to do more with her life. Her sister, Kate, had seemed perfectly content to settle down to life as a farm wife. But Kate possessed no special gifts as Tria did.

Her mother stood behind her, her hands on Tria's shoulders. "I know you want this," she said. "And I want it for you. I want to be proud of you."

Tria blinked back sudden tears. "I'll make you proud, Momma, I promise I will." She picked up the pen and filled out the application. When she finished, she handed it to her mother.

"Now," her mother said, folding the paper, "go back and finish your chores. Say nothing at all about this to your father. When the acceptance comes, let me talk to him."

"He'll say no."

E. ROSE SABIN

18

"At first, but I have ways to persuade him. I haven't used my powers in a long time, but I haven't lost them—not completely."

Tria remembered evenings when her father was away, attending a farmers' meeting or drinking with his cronies at the town tavern, and she would sit with her mother by the fire, fascinated by her mother's tales of how, long ago, the gifted rode the winds and soared high over housetops and treetops to bathe in the clouds. Her mother, caught up in the enthusiasm of the old tales, would sometimes forget herself, stare into the fire, and shape the flames into the characters of her story, letting the fiery figures act out the drama. Tria would watch, entranced, until the heroes and heroines faded to ashes.

Those were only stories. Now the normals had their own form of magic in the steam engine and the railroads that crisscrossed Arucadi. The gifted traveled by train or bus as the normals did, and in the cities the recently invented automobiles had begun to proliferate. People claimed that someday engineers would build large winged machines to carry people through the air. Tria thought that idea more preposterous than the possibility of using magic to ride to the clouds.

But that sort of magic, if it still existed at all, would never be hers, even if she were to go to this marvelous school. And despite her mother's optimism, she foresaw a barrier she feared insurmountable.

"What about the rest of the money?" she asked. "What you showed me won't cover more than the down payment."

Her mother looked grim. "There's money set aside for your dowry," she said. "That will have to be enough."

# 2

## ARRIVAL

The bus pulled away from the Merritt General Store with Tria its sole remaining passenger. "Simonton School's the next stop," the driver shouted over the clacking motor. "Be another fifteen minutes."

The words breathed fresh energy into Tria. She smoothed the wrinkles from her long skirt and did her best to straighten and brush dirt from her white middy blouse and hide the frayed edges of its lace cuffs.

The two-and-a-half-day journey from Carey had taken her across a third of Arucadi. Her father had driven her to the Carey bus station by horse and wagon. She'd changed buses four times, twice to the new express buses with plush seats that leaned back and were almost comfortable, and finally to this bone-rattling local serving the farming communities beyond Millville, near the southern border of Castlemount Province. The Simonton School for the Magically Gifted was located in a rural area far from any large city.

The rumble of the tires on the potholed asphalt thumped promises. Tria repeated them softly in the uneven rhythm of the ride: *You'll meet people like you. You'll learn the use of your power. You'll meet people like you. You'll learn the use of your power.*

She'd always had to keep her talents hidden in order to fit in with her friends at school, knowing instinctively that if she revealed her abilities, the other children would either be afraid or jealous. At last she would be among people with whom such concealment would not be needed.

She leaned forward and peered out the window, eager for her first sight of the school, but saw only a dilapidated building up ahead, out of place among the fields and meadows shimmering in the midday sunlight.

The bus slowed and lurched to a stop before the old three-story building of faded yellow brick. "Simonton School, miss," the driver called over his shoulder. "End of the line."

Tria stared at the crumbling structure; anticipation turned to horror. She picked up her valise, pulled herself to her feet, and walked to the front. "You must have made a mistake," she said. "This can't be the School for the Magically Gifted."

"No mistake, miss. This is the place. I'll get your trunk."

"No, wait!" Tria laid a restraining hand on his blue-sleeved arm. "I have pictures." She dug frantically in her valise and pulled out the wrinkled and much-read recruitment brochure, opened it to the colored illustration spread across the center section, and waved it in front of the driver's face. "See? It shows new buildings, several of them, bright gold, beautiful."

He glanced at the picture and rolled his eyes. "Ads, miss. You can't trust 'em." He pushed past her and hopped out.

Tria followed, continuing her protest as he cranked open the baggage-compartment door. "If this is the school, shouldn't other students be arriving? I shouldn't be the only one."

Tria's battered leather trunk thudded to the ground. "I brought two others in on the morning run." The driver grasped the handrail, ready to climb back into the vehicle.

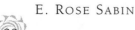

"Got another scheduled to arrive tonight. Aren't many of you anymore."

He settled into his seat and the door wheezed shut.

"Wait!"

Tria's desperate cry went unheeded. She had to jump out of the way as the engine coughed and the bus swerved onto the road, made a U-turn, and roared off in the direction from which it had come. Tria stared after it, the ache of abandonment swelling within her, pushing hot tears from her eyes. This ugly building couldn't be the place of her dreams.

She walked to the front entrance, ran a trembling hand over the chipped, cracked bricks around the door, and compared the façade with the illustration in the brochure. That building, like this one, had three stories, but it looked much wider, and its windows gleamed with light.

And the doors! Those in the picture were of polished wood covered with intricate carvings of marvelous scenes. She squinted at the doors in front of her. Double, like those in the picture. A finger rubbed over the gritty surface confirmed the presence of carvings under the layer of grime. So worn and damaged were they, Tria could not guess what they once depicted.

She wiped the tears from her cheeks, drew herself up, and pulled the worn bell rope hanging beside the door. From far inside she heard a tinny clang.

The doors creaked open. A gnomelike woman stood in the entranceway to an ill-lit, dingy foyer. Short and plump, the woman peered at Tria with eyes like raisins in a doughy gingerbread face. Her gray hair was pulled back into a bun from which it struggled to escape, loose strands poking out in all directions.

"You'll be Tria Tesserell," the woman announced as if Tria needed convincing of her own identity. "Come in. You're expected. The bus was late, but then it always is."

"I have a trunk." Tria pointed to the leather and brass repository of her meager possessions. "I'll need help bringing it in."

"I'll send two of the boys to fetch it and put it in your room," the maid said, beckoning Tria inside. "I'm Veronica, the house maid. Come along, now. You're to be taken directly to meet Headmistress. You'd best not keep her waiting."

Tria was taken aback. She had expected to wash off the dust of the journey and change into fresh clothes before meeting anyone. But Veronica gave her no chance to object. She bustled along, strands of hair wriggling like worms in a bait box. *After all*, Tria thought as she marched after her, *why should I care if I make a poor impression? The Headmistress can't possibly be as disappointed in me as I am in the school.*

They passed through a narrow, dim hall into a parlor filled with furniture dingier than what they'd had on the farm. The velour cushion covers might have been elegant once, but were now so badly worn that the outline of the springs was clearly visible through the cloth. One wing chair matched the davenport, but the rocker and straight chairs were a mismatched lot. What was worse than the age and poor condition of the furniture was the dust that coated the end tables and the art-glass lampshades. At least she and her mother had kept the farmhouse clean. *What does the maid do all day?* she wondered, gazing at windows too dirty to let in the bright fall sunshine.

Over the mantel above a soot-caked fireplace hung a badly done portrait of a young man, its dark colors adding to the general gloom. Veronica waved a hand in the direction of the painting. "That's Lesley Simonton," she said. "The school's named for him."

With no further explanation, the maid led her into the hall beyond the parlor, where rough wood creaked beneath her feet, paint peeled from the walls, bare bulbs hung from high ceilings. Tria thought it the most depressing place she'd ever seen.

The odor of overcooked cabbage rolled out of one long intersecting hallway. Surely that stench could not be a portent of the evening meal. Hungry as she was, her stomach would rebel if she sent it anything that smelled that bad.

They reached and ascended a stairway whose boards protested every step. As she climbed, Tria fought the temptation to bolt and run from the school. She hadn't yet paid the balance of her tuition; she could leave and give the money back to her father. But she'd promised to make her mother proud.

She pictured her father receiving her, face taut, angry. She could hear his caustic greeting. "So, you've returned a failure as I predicted. You'll be nothing but a drudge for the rest of your life. School for the Magically Gifted! Didn't I tell you it had to be a hoax to swindle fools with delusions of godhood?"

And her mother would look more defeated than ever, more hunched, her blue eyes more faded, though she'd welcome Tria home and try to hide her despair.

*No, Momma, I won't do that to you. I made you a promise, and somehow I'll keep it.*

On the second floor Veronica stopped before the door opposite the landing. Beyond it a long hall stretched away from the stairs. A call from within answered the maid's knock. Veronica opened the door and stood aside, allowing Tria to enter alone. She heard the door close behind her.

She stood in an office lined with bookshelves. The books, their bindings old and tattered, leaned this way and that, rested on their spines, or were stacked in haphazard piles. A green-shaded lamp illuminated the cluttered desk, but left in shadow the figure behind it. Tria could see the woman's rigid posture but not her features.

"Welcome to Simonton School, Miss Tesserell. Please take a seat." A gaunt hand waved through the zone of light at a straight-backed wooden chair in the corner of the office. Tria moved it forward and sat facing the desk.

A second long-fingered hand moved into the light, this one wearing a ring with a large orange gem that sent reflected sparkles dancing over the papers and books piled on the desk. "I always acquaint myself with my students immediately upon their arrival," the Headmistress said. Together the two hands plucked apart a stack of papers and drew out a single sheet. Tria recognized her application form. "I personally craft the course of study suited to each individual's needs and talents. Your instruction begins the moment I sign you in."

As if to emphasize her words, the Headmistress picked up a pen and scrawled something across the bottom of Tria's application. With a sickening jolt, Tria realized that she had just been officially enrolled. A sense of foreboding caused her stomach to cramp, and it was a moment before she realized the Headmistress had asked her a question.

"I—I beg your pardon," she stammered.

"Conceded," the woman said. "I asked you when and how you realized you had supernormal powers."

"Why, I . . . I always knew I was different."

"Nonsense!"

Tria jerked at the sharp rebuke.

"You have not 'always' lived. You must learn to speak with precision. Try again."

"Well, of course, I meant for as far back as I can remember," Tria said with ill-concealed indignation.

"And how long is that?" the Headmistress persisted.

"I don't know . . . I think . . . I remember things that happened when I was a baby."

"Too vague." The Headmistress tapped her blunt nails on

the application. The sound grated on Tria's already raw nerves.

The woman persevered. "A young child is not aware of its uniqueness. One learns gradually that one has abilities others do not possess, a process that requires several years. Try to recall what first brought you that knowledge."

Tria frowned, thinking back. A picture formed in her mind. She stood in her crib. A shaft of bright moonbeams streamed through the window. Gleefully she captured handfuls of moonlight, fashioned it into balls, and tossed the glowing spheres into the air above the crib. Her mother dashed in, snatched her up, and shook her. "You must not do that. Never, never, never," her mother's frantic voice scolded. "It is bad, bad, bad to play with light that way. If Poppa sees you, he'll spank you hard." With that warning, her mother set her down in the crib and drew the curtains, banishing the silver light and leaving Tria to cry herself to sleep.

How old had she been? At the age of three she'd been moved from the crib to bed with her sister, Kate. The crib was needed for Timmy, the new little brother who'd lived only a few months. There were no more babies after that, but Tria had grown too big to go back to the crib, and she and Kate shared a bed until Kate left home at seventeen to wed the son of a wheat farmer, and everyone said what a fine match it was.

"Well?" The impatient query cut through the memories.

"I couldn't have been more than two when I was scolded for making balls of moonlight. That's when I knew I had a power I wasn't allowed to use."

"But how did you know everyone else did not have the same power but kept it hidden as you did?"

Tria stared. The concept was ridiculous. "I knew," she insisted. "If everyone could do it, there'd be no need to keep it hidden."

"You reasoned that out at two years of age, did you? Hmmm."

A SCHOOL FOR SORCERY

The Headmistress made a notation on the form. "I can see I'll have to start you off with a class in elementary logic. And you failed to list the shaping of light as one of your talents on this form."

"I forgot," Tria said apologetically.

"Does that mean you regarded it of no importance?" Giving Tria no chance to answer, she lifted the paper and read, " 'Making flowers bloom out of season, calling fish to the surface of a lake.' Can you call birds and animals to you as well?"

"I . . . I don't know. Maybe. I've never really tried."

"Hmmph. You know pitifully little about yourself. 'Causing stones to fly through the air.' Quite vague. It's not clear from this whether your talent amounts to anything. Well, we'll know eventually. In the meantime I'll put down 'Has not yet attained the first level.' " She wrote the words across the top of Tria's application.

Gathering courage, Tria asked, "What does that mean?"

"Woefully uneducated," the Headmistress said, shaking her head. "There are seven levels of giftedness, Miss Tesserell. To graduate from this school you must reach the third. Most students need at least three years to attain that level; a few reach it after only two. A *very* few students have ascended to level four before completing their studies with us. One amazing student attained level five." Headmistress paused and leaned back, as if silently contemplating that prodigy. "Actually, few of the gifted reach that level in their lifetime. However, I am proud to say that the entire faculty of Simonton School are masters, having achieved either the fifth or sixth level."

"What about the seventh level?" Tria dared ask.

"The seventh level is limited to those rare and revered beings, the Adepts."

"Like the one who confirmed that I was gifted and should

come here to school?" Tria did not attempt to hide her bitterness.

"We are fortunate to receive the assistance of that person from time to time. You will find information on the seven levels and other more practical matters in your student manual. Read it carefully. I'll have you shown to your room." She extracted a small bell from under a pile of notebooks. A vigorous shake produced an unmelodic jingle. "You have two hours before supper. I suggest you use them to sharpen your recollections and arrive at more precise descriptions of your supposed abilities."

With that, the woman stood, startling Tria by her towering height. Awed, Tria scrambled to her feet and backed to the door. Her guide waited outside.

"You've passed your first ordeal, missy," Veronica said with a mirthless chuckle. "We'll see how you do with your next." She turned toward the stairs.

But Tria's attention was drawn to the hall beyond Headmistress's office. A shadow solidified into human form. A young man dressed entirely in black stood in the middle of the corridor and stared at Tria, his eyes deep and intense. She thought he would offer a greeting, but he said nothing. Embarrassed, Tria turned away.

"That's Oryon Brew," the maid told her with a sniff of disapproval and without bothering to lower her voice. "This is his second year with us. Highly talented, but a bit too ambitious. The gentlemen's rooms are down that way. The ladies all live on the third floor. The stairs are warded at night." She gathered up her dowdy skirt and led Tria up another creaky stairway.

# 3

## RIGHTS AND RESPONSIBILITIES

At the top of the stairs, preceded by her rotund guide, Tria started down a long, narrow corridor. A bare bulb hung above the landing; another shed its dim light at the corridor's far end. Between them, shadows filled the hall.

Muffled voices came from behind two or three of the closed doors, and through one open door Tria caught a glimpse of someone moving around a small room. Her guide hurried her past so quickly she had no chance to satisfy her curiosity about her fellow students. At least she knew there *were* other students.

"How many are enrolled in the school?" she asked when the maid stopped at a door midway down the hall, where the shadows were thickest.

"When they all arrive, there'll be thirty-six," the woman said.

Thirty-six! Tria's sick feeling grew. So few students in a school that boasted of being the finest school for the gifted in all Arucadi! True, the gifted comprised a small minority of Arucadi's total population, but that population exceeded one hundred million, and a legitimate school should have been able to attract far more than thirty-six students. Her father was right: she'd fallen victim to a cruel hoax.

Veronica must have sensed her dismay. "The emphasis here's on quality, not quantity," she said.

Tria fought down the urge to burst into hysterical laughter.

The little woman unlocked the door and pushed it open. "This is your room. Your roommate won't be in until tomorrow, so you'll have it to yourself tonight. If you need me for anything, call."

"My trunk—"

"Right there." Veronica pointed to the spot beneath the window between the two cots.

Tria blinked. The trunk *was* there. She hadn't seen it when they entered, but the light was poor and her mind had been preoccupied.

How were two people going to fit into this tiny cell of a room? Although the narrow cots were pushed against the side walls, the space between them was no greater than the width of her trunk, which was, coincidentally, the same width as the window. At the end of each cot, a small desk took up most of the remaining floor space. No dresser; she'd have to keep most of her things in her trunk. No closets, just a wooden rod set into metal supports that held it out from the front wall to one side of the door. Three wire clothes hangers hung on it, hardly enough for both Tria and her roommate to hang their clothes there. And where was her roommate to put *her* luggage?

"Who will my roommate be?" she asked as Veronica withdrew.

"Young woman by the name of Lina Mueller," Veronica said. "From Stansbury. Bath's at the end of the hall on your right. Dinner's in two hours. Come quickly when you hear the bell.

You'll be punished if you're late." Veronica shut the door, preventing any more questions.

Tria's head whirled. So much to absorb, so much to worry about.

Punishment for being late to a meal? What punishment? Tria's distressed imagination conjured up a host of diabolical tortures.

And a roommate from Stansbury! That she had been paired with a roommate from the east coast was bad enough, but Stansbury was the largest city of Arucadi, and Tria had never even been in a town larger than Harnor, the Inland Province river port that served Carey, her home town. They weren't likely to have anything in common.

A round mirror hung on the back of the door. Tria peered at her reflection in the dirty glass. Her hair was a dusty jumble of long, unruly curls; that smudge really was on her face and not on the mirror, and her middy blouse was soiled from the long bus ride. What a peasant she must have seemed to the Headmistress!

Although apparently the woman took little notice of dirt. Tria cast a disapproving eye at the dusty windowsill; the sagging, stained mattresses; the rusted metal frames of the cots. She set her valise on a desk and fought back tears.

"No time to waste crying," she lectured herself. "I've got to clean this rat cage."

In the bathroom she found a pail under a chipped washbasin; a mop leaned in the corner of a shower stall. A can of scouring powder sat on a toilet tank.

Carrying the pail of water in one hand, the mop resting on her shoulder like a rifle, Tria marched back to her room to do battle. A door opened as she approached and a moon face with small round eyes peered out briefly, then ducked back in as though frightened off by the sight of Tria. The incident made her wonder whether other newly arrived students were as upset and disillusioned as she. When she met them at supper, she'd have a chance to find out. But she'd have to rush to get the room and herself clean and presentable in only two hours.

She dug out the clock packed in her trunk, wound it, and set it on a desk.

After opening the window, she grabbed the thin pallet from one cot and, kneeling on her trunk, dangled it outside the window and shook it against the outside wall. Dust flew out in a great cloud that gradually dispersed and settled onto the rows of vegetables in the field below her window. She wasted precious minutes watching the dust motes circle one another in the sunlight, forming tiny planetary systems. She imagined glowing suns, each with its coterie of planets, each planet orbited in turn by a collection of infinitesimal moons. Like a great goddess she reached out her hand, waved it around, disrupting the orderly motions, sending the motes into frenzied dance, watching them settle into new constellations.

*What am I doing, dawdling like this?* she scolded herself. *I've got no time for idle dreaming.* She ducked back inside and applied herself with renewed diligence to her scrubbing and scraping, dusting and derusting, polishing and prettying. At last she stood back and surveyed the results.

The glass of mirror and window gleamed. The floor and walls were spotless. No more cobwebs festooned the ceiling. One bed was made up with crisp white sheets and a soft pink blanket. The ceiling light, properly cleaned, sent out a warmer, more even glow. Her room was cramped—she could do nothing about that—but it had been made livable.

As she stood, hands on hips, admiring the results of her

E. ROSE SABIN

labor, a bell clanged. Up and down the hall doors opened, footsteps pounded past her door.

Dinnertime! And she was filthy, the room's grime transferred to her clothes and skin. She could not go to dinner in such a condition, could not meet her fellow students looking like a chambermaid or a chimney sweep.

She glared at the clock as though it was to blame for her dilemma. Beneath her fixed stare the clock face blurred, wavered. It swam before her, large as a sun, its hands indistinct shadows across its bright surface, its numerals vague blurs swimming around its gleaming edge.

Thunder crashed. The building shook. A wave of intense vertigo rocked Tria. She clutched the back of the desk chair to keep from falling.

The room righted itself. The clock snapped back to its normal size. Tria's nausea subsided.

The hands of the clock showed one hour earlier than they had a moment ago.

She stared, not able to believe what she saw. What had she done? Merely moved the hands of the clock? Or? . . .

She whirled around, opened the door, and peered into the hall. No students hurrying from their rooms, no sound of steps clattering down the stairs. The corridor was empty, as it had been all afternoon until the dinner bell had sounded. She must have, somehow, incredibly, set time back an hour.

No time to marvel. She mustn't waste the unexpected gift. Tria snatched clean clothes from her trunk and hurried to the bathroom.

She emerged thirty minutes later thoroughly scrubbed, neatly dressed in a blue-and-white striped overblouse and a dark blue, box-pleated skirt, damp hair tied back into a ponytail secured with a bright blue ribbon.

Veronica waited at the door to Tria's room. "Headmistress sent me to fetch you," she announced. "You're to come immediately."

The confidence inspired by her improved appearance drained away. Stomach churning, she followed the little maid back to the Headmistress's cluttered office.

This time the woman was standing, leaning toward her, tall and menacing, her sharp-featured face reminding Tria of a vulture.

"Young lady," she began, "you have been at Simonton School only a few hours, and already you have violated two of its most sacred principles."

She paused, glaring down until Tria felt that the weight of that stare would hammer her through the floor. Tria's knees trembled; she did not trust herself to speak.

The implacable voice continued. "You have used your power without permission and in an irresponsible manner. No student may use his or her power on these premises except in the presence of and with the permission of an instructor. Failure to comply with this regulation will bring a severe penalty. Repeated infractions will result in expulsion."

"I'm sorry," Tria stammered. "I . . . I didn't know."

"Your ignorance only adds to your offense," the Headmistress snapped. "Your dormitory room holds a copy of the *Student Rights and Responsibilities Manual*. I spoke of it in our interview. Your proper course of action should have been to use the afternoon to study it."

A manual. Could that have been the tattered spiral-bound book she'd found in a desk drawer under a mound of pencil shavings and a dead beetle? The title on the faded cover had been illegible, and she had supposed it to be an old notebook left by a previous resident. She tried to remember what she had done with it. Probably threw it into the trash.

Yes, she remembered dumping the contents of the drawer into the trash bin by the head of the stairs. Maybe she could retrieve it later, though the thought of having to root through the filth in the bin sickened her.

The Headmistress straightened to her full, incredible height and said, "Now the second offense, Miss Tesserell. The second is the most serious offense a student can commit." Again she paused while Tria writhed beneath the vulturine glare.

"For a student to engage in the capricious manipulation of time is a repudiation of every ethical standard upheld by this institution, its faculty, and its student body. It reveals a blatant disregard for the safety and well-being of our entire society. What have you to offer as a reason for such criminal behavior?"

*Criminal behavior!* Tria felt faint. She grabbed at the edge of the Headmistress's desk.

Her only defense was to tell the truth. "I'm sorry, ma'am. I didn't know what would happen. I'd been cleaning my room, I looked a mess, the dinner bell rang, and I just stared at the clock. And . . . everything went blurry, and when it cleared, the clock had gone back an hour. I hadn't meant to do it. I didn't know I could."

"Hmmm. I ought to dismiss you immediately, but you are too dangerous to be set loose in society. You will be allowed to remain here, but you will be kept under close supervision. Under no circumstances are you to use the least bit of your special talent until I myself permit you to do so. I will notify your instructors that you are required to master the theoretical aspects of the classes but are forbidden to participate in the practical aspects. That policy may affect your grades, but you've brought that consequence upon yourself."

Tria blinked, holding back tears. She would not give this stern, heartless woman the satisfaction of seeing her cry. She

A SCHOOL FOR SORCERY

would accept her punishment with dignity. She only wanted the interview to end.

But the Headmistress had not finished. "The hour you stole has reached an end." As she said the words, the dinner bell rang. "You have disturbed an equilibrium which one day must be restored. You will be required to return the hour you took. When or under what circumstances I cannot say."

The Headmistress moved out from behind the desk and glided around it to stand beside Tria. A bony hand grasped Tria's shoulder. "You will accompany me to the dining hall. I will present you to your classmates, and you will confess your wrongdoing and ask their forgiveness."

Tria gasped. She couldn't! She'd ask the woman to dismiss her instead. If her father wouldn't take her back, maybe Kate would take her in. Nothing she would endure at home could be any worse than what she was enduring here.

But the fingers dug into her flesh and pushed her backward from the office, giving her no chance to speak. In the corridor she was turned around and marched like a naughty child down the steps and through a hall to a large dining room reeking of cabbage. She was paraded past tables surrounded by gaping faces and conducted to the only table graced with a white linen cloth and set with fine china. The Headmistress stood behind the center seat at the table, facing the other diners. She motioned to Tria to stand at the place next to hers. Although other places were set at the table, no one claimed them. Tria felt horribly conspicuous and wished she could become invisible or bid the floor open and swallow her up.

The Headmistress tapped her ring against a water glass. Throughout the room everyone stood at attention behind his or her chair, and all eyes focused on the Headmistress. Few though the students were, the gathering seemed unbearably large to Tria.

E. ROSE SABIN

38

The tall woman began to speak. "Students of Simonton School, as we enter a new scholastic year I extend greetings and a warm welcome to you all. Tomorrow the term will officially open with a solemn convocation in the assembly hall at ten. Everyone is required to attend. At that time, the members of the faculty will be formally presented to our beginning students. Following that assembly, students will receive their individual fall class schedules at tables set up for that purpose in the quadrangle. Classes will begin at eight the following morning."

The length of these opening remarks gave Tria an opportunity to look over the assembled diners. Most were her age; a few were two or three years older. The group was about half male and half female. She spotted the boy she had seen earlier; his black garb made him easily recognizable. He met her gaze with an insolent smirk; she turned quickly away and scanned the other faces, hoping for evidence of friendliness and sympathy. The faces registered polite attention but little animation; they could have been wearing identical wooden masks for all Tria could read in their expressions. She saw little hope of finding friends among them.

"Now, students, I am sorry to delay your meal, and I deeply regret the reason for the delay."

*Here it comes*, Tria thought. Her head pounded with a tension headache. Her stomach felt full of rocks.

"You must be aware that we experienced an unusual event this afternoon. The anomaly was the result of a serious violation not only of school rules but of the ethics of power use. The student responsible for the deed stands here before you. You will hear her confession."

All eyes turned to Tria. Her head swam; tears blurred her vision.

*I can't disgrace myself by crying*, she thought. *I won't provide a spectacle for them.*

She took a deep breath, dug her nails into her palms, and spoke slowly. "My name is Tria Tesserell. This afternoon I used my talent to turn the time back one hour. It was not deliberate. I didn't know until it happened that I had that gift. I am sorry to have acted irresponsibly and caused so much trouble. I ask your pardon."

*There! I hope that satisfies her. I don't see that I really caused any trouble except for myself, and I certainly am sorry about that!*

At a nearby table someone giggled. At a glare from Headmistress, the sound transformed into a cough.

"I have made it clear to Miss Tesserell that such behavior will not be tolerated here at Simonton," Headmistress said. "You may all be seated, and the meal may be served."

Tria sank into her chair and fixed her gaze on her empty plate. Bowls of food were placed on the table. Tria did not look up to see who served them, though later she caught a glimpse of Veronica moving among the tables carrying a serving tray.

The rank smell of overcooked cabbage made her gag. Small potatoes, hard and unseasoned, and charred slices of a stringy meat that could have been cut from an old shoe complemented the cabbage. She placed small portions from each bowl onto her plate but could not choke down a single bite. After stirring the food around to make it look as though she had eaten, she sat in shamed silence until Headmistress folded her napkin beside her empty plate and rose, signaling the end of the dinner hour. Chairs scraped against the floor, feet shuffled, plates clattered.

Tria also rose. Head held high, she ignored the curious stares and muffled snickers. Wearing a look that defied anyone

E. ROSE SABIN

to speak to her, she strode through the corridors and up the stairs to her room.

She closed the door behind her and fell sobbing onto her cot. She *could not* stay in this terrible place.

# 4

## MEETINGS

Breakfast was weak tea and a watery porridge made more unpalatable by the curious stares of her fellow students. The hard brown bread that accompanied the porridge could be rendered edible only by soaking it in the tea. A nagging headache warned her that she had to get something into her stomach; she'd eaten almost nothing the day before. Somehow she forced the awful stuff down.

At least the meal was free of the daunting presence of the Headmistress. A bearded old man in a wrinkled black robe presided at the head table. He nodded and beamed at the students through thick, gold-rimmed spectacles.

Conversations buzzed all around, but no one spoke to her. She ate as fast as her tortured stomach permitted, excused herself, and returned to her room.

On the way, she paused and dug through the dustbin to retrieve the discarded manual. She had been too upset last night. She found the book, dirty, damp, and smelling of cleaning solutions, and carried it back to her room, holding it at arm's length between thumb and forefinger. After wiping it off as well as she could, she spread it open on her desk.

Gingerly she turned the damp pages. The first page must have extended a welcome to the student: she made out the letters W E L    O M in the title. The rest of the page was completely illegible—appropriate in view of the reception she had thus far encountered.

The next couple of pages held a history of the school, also largely illegible, to Tria's disappointment. She had wanted to discover the age of the building and learn whether the school could claim any recent honors. The brochure that had lured her here boasted of the school's many distinctions, and she suspected that it claimed achievements decades in the past. But the stained pages kept their secrets. The only decipherable portion revealed that the school was named for Lesley Simonton, a man of great power, though the specific deed for which he was memorialized was obliterated by grime.

The pages containing the long list of school rules had suffered less damage. She could read them before the morning convocation.

She discovered that students were not only responsible for cleaning their own rooms but were also assigned on a rotating basis kitchen duties, gardening, laundry, and other housecleaning and maintenance chores. "The school has only a small support staff of cooks, custodians, and maintenance personnel," the manual explained, "so student assistance is essential to the school's smooth operation."

*Support staff!* Tria sniffed. *I don't believe they really have one. I've only seen Veronica. And when do they expect us to study?*

She found the answer to that when she read that, although the school day was divided into five class periods, each student took only four classes per term, leaving one class period free for study, work, or supervised practice of the magical arts.

*Four classes—that's so few. We had twice that many all through*

*Basic School. They really don't expect us to learn much here. I know they just want to collect our tuition.*

She reached the section setting forth restrictions on use of power and was dismayed at its length. It opened with the general rule that students were to use their gifts only with the permission of and under the supervision of an instructor.

A long list of specific prohibitions followed. Tria ran her finger down the side until she spotted the one that read, "No student may ever, under any circumstances, adjust the flow of time in any manner."

That was plain enough. Now that she knew she could do it, she'd take care not to allow it to happen again. Since her father had forbidden her to perform what he called "tricks of magic," she'd always exercised power more by accident than with deliberate intent.

She continued to study the list to learn what other abilities she might have that she did not know about and might stumble on in embarrassing circumstances. Grudgingly she admitted Headmistress was not wrong in declaring that she needed to learn control. Perhaps the school, despite its inadequacies, could teach her that much.

She read other items in the list:

"Use of magic as a weapon against another is strictly prohibited.

"Except under carefully controlled conditions, with the consent of those involved, no spell may be placed on any member of the faculty, staff, or student body." Tria disliked the idea of placing spells. She knew little about them, but her understanding was that they required the gathering of specified materials and the chanting or singing of mystical phrases to accomplish their purpose. She wanted only to learn to use her own natural gifts; she was not interested in feats done with mirrors and shadows and such. But the book contained several rules governing spells.

"Candles used in spells must be carefully extinguished when the spell is complete. Never leave a burning candle unattended.

"Animals used in spells must be treated humanely.

"The Dire Realms shall not be subject to exploration by any means. Their denizens shall not be invoked. NO EXCEPTIONS TO THIS RULE."

Exploring the Dire Realms! Tria shivered. The Dire Realms were the abode of the Dire Lords, male and female guardians of other planes of existence, alternate universes, and spirit realms, including the realms to which the human soul travels after death. She knew that there were believed to be evil Dire Lords, good Dire Lords, and indifferent or amoral Dire Lords. Her mother had worn an amulet to protect against the evil Dire Lords, though her father scoffed at such superstition.

Her mother had taught her that, while normally none of the Dire Lords takes interest in the affairs of living humans, the use of magic power attracts their attention, since those powers originate in and are drawn from the Dire Realms. For that reason, those who practice magic must take special care not to anger the Lords and Ladies of the Dire Realms.

The thought of invoking any denizen of the Dire Realms, be it a creature of the Dire Lords or a Dire Lord himself, gave her chills. She couldn't imagine wanting to do anything so terrifying. That rule was one she would never have to worry about breaking.

She read the next rule on the list: "Shapeshifting is permitted only on field trips designed for the purpose. Students with that talent are prohibited from exercising it on the school premises."

Shapeshifting was a talent Tria had never thought about.

She probably didn't have it, but she certainly dare not explore the possibility.

Despite her depression, the next rule made her smile. "No student may create life in any form."

Surely no student could accomplish any such thing. The rest of the statement only added to the absurdity. "Students are not ready to accept the grave responsibility attendant upon any creative act." She giggled. *They don't need to worry. I won't create any stray universes in my spare time.*

In a lighter mood she read on. "Thought-reading and mind-speaking are to be engaged in only with the knowledge and consent of the targeted person.

"Do not attempt interdimensional travel without an experienced guide." Whatever that meant!

The possibilities inherent in these various prohibitions fascinated Tria, and she was annoyed when a tapping at her door interrupted her reading. She rose and opened the door.

A heavy-set girl with a round face and a frightened look peered at her with pale blue eyes. "Hi," she said in a voice scarcely more than a whisper. "I live just down the hall from you." She pointed vaguely in the direction of the washroom. "I'm Nubba Balder. I'm a second-year student. May I come in?"

Tria saw no need to introduce herself; the girl obviously knew who she was. By way of reply she pulled the door open wide and allowed her visitor to enter.

Nubba wedged herself into the narrow space between the cots and did a graceless pirouette, taking in every detail of the tiny room. "Ooh! You've fixed this up so pretty! But don't you have a roommate?"

Tria's headache hadn't gone away, and she was in no mood to entertain a guest, but this was the first student who'd been friendly to her. She had to be polite. "I have one, but she hasn't come yet. Veronica said she'd arrive today, but she didn't say at what time."

"Time." Nubba latched onto the word and echoed it like a mantra. "Time. Is it true—" her voice dropped to an awed whisper, "—did you *really* fold time?"

Tria felt her cheeks flush. "I didn't mean to. I—I really *am* sorry about it."

Nubba ignored the apology. "That's so awesome," she gushed. "I've never known anyone with that much power."

Tria stared at her. It had not occurred to her that some students might admire what she had done. "It didn't seem to take much," she confessed. "It just happened."

"How?" The girl's face resembled a fat frog ready to snap up a fly.

Tria shrugged. "I looked at the clock, and things went all blurry, and—and it happened, that's all."

"Oooh! You make it sound so easy."

Nubba's worshipful gaze was embarrassing. Surely the ability to adjust time could not be as rare as she claimed. If that were the case, why would the student manual take such pains to warn against it?

"Unless you can change the time again, we have to go to the convocation." Nubba pointed hopefully at Tria's clock.

Tria rubbed her aching temples. "I don't dare do it again. As it is, Headmistress said I'd have to pay back that hour someday." She headed for the door.

Nubba dogged her footsteps. "Are you walking over with friends?"

"I haven't had a chance to get to know anyone yet."

Nubba's face beamed. "Then you can go with me. We'd better hurry. We get extra work details if we're late."

They entered the flow of students passing in groups of twos, threes, and fours through the halls and down the stairs. One

E. ROSE SABIN

or two nodded at Tria and Nubba as they approached, but none joined them.

"I think they're all a little afraid of you," Nubba whispered.

"Afraid of *me*?" The idea was ludicrous. Tria did not consider herself powerful, despite Nubba's enthused adulation. "I told you what happened—that time-changing thing—was an accident. I probably couldn't do it again if I tried, which I won't."

"Still, it shows you have a lot more power than most of us," Nubba insisted.

Tria could think of nothing to say, and they walked in silence through a long corridor and out a door opening onto a quadrangle bounded on their right by a stone wall, on their left by a long, narrow two-story building which Nubba identified as the faculty residence hall, and on the far side by a one-story building that was clearly the assembly hall. These buildings, not visible from the road, were of the same faded yellow brick as the main building and were in the same state of disrepair. Flagstone walkways crisscrossed the courtyard and water sprayed from a fountain in its center. Scraggly rosebushes and flower beds in need of weeding filled the spaces between the walkways, making it necessary to follow a zigzag path instead of crossing directly to the assembly hall, which boasted seven marble steps rising to a wide front entrance. The white marble could have used a good scrubbing.

Here the students converged to pour up the steps and into the building.

As a tall blond boy passed them, he called out, "Hey, Nubba, you bring the Shalreg back with you?"

Nearby students snickered. Nubba's face turned fiery red, warning Tria not to ask what he meant.

"That Kress Klemmer thinks he's so smart!" Nubba muttered. Grabbing Tria's elbow, she held her back until the boy was well past them. They were among the last students to climb the steps and enter the hall.

The auditorium had been built for a much larger student body. The two side sections had been roped off, forcing the students to occupy the center, and plenty of empty seats remained in it. Tria counted only thirty-four students after all had found places and the rear doors were shut. No one else sat in the row she and Nubba selected.

Six faculty members sat on metal folding chairs arranged in a semicircle behind the lectern on the stage—three men and three women, besides the Headmistress. The Headmistress opened the program by droning a long invocation to the Power-Giver. Tria nearly fell asleep before it ended.

Introductions followed. Headmistress identified each faculty member, beginning at the end of the semicircle to her right with the doddering whitebeard who had presided over breakfast—Master Tumberlis, Professor of the History and Philosophy of Metaphysics. Next in line a pinch-faced, thin-lipped woman well past her prime was introduced as Mistress Dova, Instructor of Arcane Rites and Esoterica. Third, a much younger woman, a pale wraith with long white hair that hung round her like a shroud, was presented only as Aletheia, Specialist in Interdimensional Concourse. Tria thought she looked lost in another dimension. Odd that she was not accorded the title of Mistress.

Next was Master Hawke, Professor of Alchemy, the Mandala, and the Healing Arts. Shoulders broad but stooped, he leaned on an intricately carved cane.

Master San Marté was a foppish little man, with a waxed mustache and a toupee a shade or two darker than his fringe of graying hair. Hearing that his specialty was ethics, Tria groaned, sure that Headmistress would assign her to all the ethics classes the school offered.

E. Rose Sabin

Last was Mistress Blake, a pretty woman whose youth and ready smile seemed out of place among her colleagues. Scarcely more than a girl, she could have gone unnoticed among the students. Tria was surprised to hear her called the Gifting Mistress and presented as an expert in the development of all supernormal gifts.

Following the introductions, each instructor came forward and made a welcoming speech consisting mostly of boring repetitions of Headmistress's opening remarks. Tria let her mind wander. She glanced at the other students, found many of them gazing around as she was. One student nudged another and pointed a finger at a third who'd fallen fast asleep. A sour-faced young woman was cleaning her fingernails with the point of a wicked-looking dagger.

"Taner better be careful," Nubba whispered, having evidently followed Tria's gaze. "She'll get in trouble if she's caught with that out. She's supposed to keep it sheathed."

A girl slipped a note to a friend. A young man stared fixedly at the ceiling as if studying the pattern of the acoustical tiles. Next to him a tall, fair-haired youth fidgeted, turned, and met Tria's eyes. Before she could look away, he grinned and winked. Her face flamed, and she was relieved when he returned his attention to the speaker.

"That's Wilce Riverman," Nubba informed her in a loud whisper. "He's a second-year student, one of the nicest. He's a peace-bringer and a truth-reader."

It seemed that Nubba missed nothing that went on. At least through her Tria was becoming acquainted with her fellow students. This Wilce would be a good person to get to know, though Tria was painfully shy around boys. But she could find out from Wilce about the school's validity. A truth-reader couldn't be taken in by fraudulent claims, not ones made in direct conversation. He could have been fooled as she had

A School for Sorcery

been by the deceptive brochure, but if the school was no more than a swindle, he would certainly not have come back for a second year. If he really was what Nubba claimed, his presence offered hope.

The professorial greetings ended, and Headmistress spoke again, issuing a challenge to the students to apply themselves and strive for excellence. Tria tuned out the harangue and sent her thoughts homeward, imagining her parents going about their daily chores; her mother taking on the additional tasks of feeding the chickens, milking the cows, and slopping the pigs, all things Tria had done; her father and the Cromley boys harvesting wheat and gathering it into the storage barns.

Her mother would miss her. Her father might miss her help, but she was certain he'd never admit that a daughter of his had gone to a school for the magically gifted. She imagined him explaining her absence. "Tria's gone to apprentice herself to a dress designer in Tirbat," he'd tell a nosy neighbor. Or perhaps he'd boast to a friend, "Our Tria's gone to the west coast to wed a wealthy widower in Port-of-Lords."

She began again to picture his disgust if she returned home, when the convocation ended. Headmistress and her staff filed out, and the student body rose and followed.

In the courtyard, a long table had been set up and Mistress Dova, Master Hawke, and Mistress Blake sat behind it distributing the schedules for the new term. Tria would have liked to claim hers from Mistress Blake, but they were distributed alphabetically, with Master Hawke handling Tria's portion.

"Tesserell," he repeated when she gave him her name. "Ah, yes." With that enigmatic if meaningless comment, he pulled a folded paper from a metal file box, handed it to her, and turned to the next student.

Tria unfolded the paper and glanced at the top where her name was neatly printed: TESSERELL, TRIA FAY. Next to the

E. ROSE SABIN

name, in the blank following *Level*, was printed the word "One."

So she was no longer considered below first level.

She was staring at that apparent advancement when Nubba came up and leaned on her shoulder. "Whose classes are you in?" She peered at the schedule.

Tria shared the paper with her, saying apologetically, "Headmistress told me I'd only be allowed to learn theory, so that's what all my courses seem to be."

"She's just trying to scare you," Nubba said with a chuckle. "All first-year students just learn theory and history and stuff. It isn't until second year that you start getting practical courses. And even most third-years don't have all practice."

Nubba pointed to the schedule. "See, your first class is Metaphysical Theory. I'm in that too, so we'll suffer together. Master Tumberlis is so old his bones rattle." She scanned the rest of the schedule. "Oh, you poor thing! You have Elementary Logic with Old Tumbles, too. He'll bore you to death. Ugh! Beginning Ethics with Master San Marté won't be any better. Well, at least you have Survey of Ancient Rites with Mistress Dova. She's tough but interesting. Three morning classes and one in late afternoon. Too bad. Doesn't leave a long-enough stretch of free time to go into Millville or anything. Well, better luck next term."

Nubba's pessimistic assessment depressed Tria. She had to force herself to summon the courtesy to ask Nubba about *her* schedule. Nubba seemed pleased with it, but Tria didn't bother to listen or remember more of it than the single class they would, as Nubba said, suffer through together.

"Speaking of suffering, Nubba, please excuse me, won't you? I have a headache and need to lie down."

"But it's almost lunchtime," Nubba objected, following Tria toward the building.

A SCHOOL FOR SORCERY

"I know." Tria walked faster. "I'll only have a few minutes to rest after I take a headache powder. That's why I have to hurry."

Clutching her schedule, she broke away from Nubba and dashed into the building and up the stairs. Not daring to look behind to see if Nubba was following, she rushed to her room and stepped inside.

And stopped, halted by an array of suitcases, a leaning stack of hatboxes, a large trunk, and several crates, piled on every available inch of floor space, on both desks, on Tria's trunk, and on her neatly made bed.

The only free space in the room was the second bed, newly adorned with a green silk coverlet and several splendidly embroidered throw pillows. Seated cross-legged on that bed was a beautiful girl, her black hair cut short in a stylish bob, her catlike green eyes gazing at Tria from beneath long, curling lashes.

"I gather you're my roommate," the girl said in the tone one might use to comment on the presence of a cockroach.

"I'm Tria Tesserell." Tria tried to be polite. "You must be Lina Mueller."

"My fame precedes me." Her voice became a saccharine purr.

"The maid told me your name," Tria snapped, losing patience. "And what are you planning to do with all this stuff?" She flung out a hand, striking and toppling the stack of hatboxes.

"Careful of those." Lina pointed a perfectly manicured finger at the fallen boxes. Slowly they righted themselves and floated upward to reform the tall stack.

Tria snorted. "Look, I could do that, too. But we're forbidden to use our power without permission and without supervision."

"Oh, are we?" Lina arched beautifully shaped eyebrows. "And who is to know what we do in the privacy of our own room? Unless we have a tale-bearer."

"I'm no tattler, but I would like to get to my bed and sit down on it." Tria glared at the girl.

"You'll be able to do that eventually. The maid promised to help me find room for all this later this afternoon."

"Do you expect her to work a miracle? You can see for yourself there's no possible place to put all this. Let's move it out into the hall until you can send most of it back home." Tria stooped to pick up a heavy crate.

A snarl stopped her. She looked up. A sleek black panther stood on the bed, its tail twitching, its lips pulled back to expose its fangs.

Tria screamed.

The panther hissed and settled back on its haunches.

The door popped open, and Tria looked around to see Nubba stick her head in, panting for breath. "What's wrong, Tria?"

Tria jerked her head toward the bed.

It held only Lina, who said with a demure smile, "My roommate was startled by a little spider that climbed out from between the boxes."

Tria repressed the denial that rose to her tongue. "It's nothing, Nubba. Thanks for checking, but there's no problem."

"And don't you know it's rude to enter without knocking?" Lina added coldly.

"I—I'm sorry. I hope your headache is better, Tria." Nubba backed from the room, closing the door behind her.

"Did you have to be unkind to her?" Tria asked sharply.

"She needed to be put in her place. Nosy pig."

The loud ring of the lunch bell cut off Tria's angry retort. She reached for the door handle. "We have to go to lunch."

A SCHOOL FOR SORCERY

Eyeing the barrier of luggage and crates, she added maliciously, "If you can get to the door."

A panther leaped from the silk-covered bed to the top of the trunk, vaulted effortlessly over the stack of hatboxes, and landed in the space Tria vacated by jerking the door open and jumping outside.

Laughing, Lina stepped into the hall beside her.

Tria looked to see whether anyone was near enough to hear, and assuring herself that no one was, she said in a furious whisper, "Shapechanging is strictly forbidden. You'd better read the rule book."

Lina laughed again. "I make my own rules," she said.

# 5

## LINA

Lina claimed an empty table near the door and occupied it with a queenly air. Tria spotted Nubba near the front and hurried to the last place at that table, preferring Nubba's company to Lina's. She slipped into the chair beside Nubba and nodded at the other three girls at the table.

With an air of self-importance, Nubba performed introductions. "This is my roommate, Irel Lane. She's a first-year student."

Irel, thin and pale with a haunted face and downcast eyes, acknowledged the introduction in a soft murmur spoken to her plate.

"Sometimes Headmistress assigns a second-year student to room with a first-year to act as a mentor," Nubba said. "She thought Irel needed special help."

That explanation must have been embarrassing to Irel, but the girl said nothing and kept her gaze averted.

A plain girl with strikingly beautiful eyes—deep, wide-set, and of an unusual turquoise hue—said, "I'm Rehanne Zalos. I'm a first-year student, too. I'm sure all of us first-year students are finding a lot to adjust to. I know we all appreciate the help of second-years like Nubba and Verin."

Tria decided she liked Rehanne and resolved to get to know her better.

Nubba plowed on, apparently oblivious to the discomfort she must have caused Irel as well as to Rehanne's haste to ease that discomfort. Indicating the remaining girl, she said, "This is Verin Savrile, a healer."

"Welcome to Simonton School," Verin said. Her dark skin, dark eyes, and long, dark braids complemented her serious manner.

Tria acknowledged the introductions, delighted that her table companions neither acted awed by her as Nubba had been nor contemptuous of her as some seemed to be. They accepted her. Tria looked forward to getting better acquainted. She was sorry that Nubba had only identified Verin's talent and not that of the others. Although curious about what talents other students might possess, Tria thought it was probably impolite to ask.

Mistress Dova, who sat alone at the head table, asked the Power-Giver's blessing on the food. It occurred to Tria that all prayers she had heard here had been addressed to the Power-Giver, and she had not seen altars to any gods, not even to Liadra, Patroness of Castlemount Province. In her home her father had maintained an altar to Harin, Patron of Inland Province, and the family had held a brief worship service there daily at her father's insistence. The ritual had meant little to Tria, and she was relieved that the school required no such custom.

The lunch Veronica set before her was a single dry fish cake on a mound of sticky rice garnished with a sprig of wilted watercress. Tria shuddered but picked up her fork.

"Look at that little minx!" Nubba's exclamation drew her tablemates' attention from their food.

A glance over her shoulder confirmed Tria's guess. Nubba was pointing at Lina. All Lina's table companions were male, and every one of them stared at her as though no one else were present.

One stirred his food with his fork but never lifted a bite to his mouth. Another pushed his plate away, rested his elbows on the table, chin on his hands, and gazed at Lina in total disregard for good manners. Oryon, in his usual black, chatted and gestured, vying for her attention with the tall, blond youth seated opposite him. Tria recognized that one as the one who had taunted Nubba earlier. What had Nubba called him? Kress, that was it.

Lina smiled and teased, bestowing her favors on all four, though without neglecting her lunch. She ate with great enthusiasm. *Like a hungry cat,* Tria thought. *It's a wonder she hasn't complained about the terrible food.*

Verin frowned. "I'm not surprised at Fenton. He chases all the girls. And I hardly know Jerrol. But I've never seen Oryon with any girl but Taner, and as for Kress, I thought he had more sense."

"So did Kathyn. See how she's glaring at him?" Rehanne pointed to a pretty blonde at a nearby table.

"Kathyn is Kress's twin," Nubba explained the girl's resemblance to Oryon's blond rival.

Tria didn't care. She wished the others would forget about Lina and her entourage. It was hard enough knowing she was somehow going to have to endure rooming with the catgirl. But Nubba, Verin, and Rehanne refused to talk of anything else. Only Irel seemed uninterested, and Tria's efforts to engage her in conversation were useless. Irel replied with whispered monosyllables and kept her eyes lowered. Her hands shook as though she suffered from a mild palsy. Tria gave up trying to

A SCHOOL FOR SORCERY

talk to her and concentrated on choking down the unappetizing meal.

At the conclusion of the lunch hour, Mistress Dova announced that the duty rosters for the week were posted on the corkboard by the dining-hall door and told everyone to check them before leaving.

Tria located her name among those assigned to tend the garden. So she hadn't gotten away from farm work, but the job would keep her away from Lina. It also freed her from Nubba, who was assigned kitchen cleanup and had to report immediately. The others continued to study the roster.

"I don't see your new roommate's name on any of these lists," Rehanne said. "If she's been excused from work detail, we ought to file a complaint."

Tria was searching the lists to verify Rehanne's discovery when ear-splitting screams spun her around. She dashed toward the sound, pelted into the kitchen, and found Nubba cowering against the wall just inside the door, her broad features contorted into a grimace of terror. Most of the cleanup crew stared at her with bewildered expressions.

"What is it?" Tria asked.

Nubba pointed to the center of the kitchen, an area that held nothing but empty space.

"I don't see anything. What's wrong?" Tria walked toward the spot, saw only a floor covered with old, cracked linoleum long since bleached of whatever colors it once had. Disgusting, but nothing to scream about.

"Does anyone here know what she sees?" Tria asked.

The first-year students shook their heads. A second-year student pointed to his temple and drew a circle with his index finger, while another said in disgust, "It's her way of getting out of work."

Nubba crept crabwise along the wall to the doorway and

stepped outside the room. "Be careful!" she shouted to Tria. "It's the Shalreg."

Tria went to Nubba. "What are you talking about? What's a Shalreg?"

"That . . . that thing. Can't you see it?" Nubba pointed a trembling finger.

"There's nothing to see," Tria repeated.

"Ohhhh!" Nubba sobbed so that she could barely speak. "Nobody else can ever see it. Why does it only show itself to me?" The question ended in a loud wail

Mistress Dova stepped up behind Nubba. "Again, Miss Balder?" she said.

Nubba was too distraught to answer. Tria said, "Something frightened her. She called it a Shalreg."

"We know it well. Her private ogre." Mistress Dova grasped Nubba's shoulder. "Miss Balder, cease that caterwauling at once and listen to me."

Nubba's wailing tapered off to soft sniffles. Her face, red from weeping, took on a sullen expression. "It is there," she said defiantly.

"No one has contested that. But it hasn't harmed you."

"It wants to. It clicks its awful pincers at me and shows me its fangs. They're that long." Nubba stretched her thumb and forefinger apart as far as they would go.

"I'm sure its appearance is quite fearsome, but the fact remains that in all the years it has haunted you, it has never done you any physical harm."

"That's because I always run from it."

"If it were as fearsome and as powerful as you claim, you would not be able to escape it no matter how far or how fast you ran. I assume you are on kitchen detail. I suggest you get to work."

She clapped her hands. "All of you. To work. No more gawking and no shirking."

Mistress Dova turned and marched away.

But Nubba broke into fresh sobs. "I can't go in. That thing is waiting for me. I *can't* go."

"All right, Nubba," Tria said. "Go on upstairs. I'll serve your kitchen duty for you. I don't have to report to the garden for over an hour."

"You will? You'll do that for me?" Nubba's fat face beamed through her tears.

"This time I will. Go on, now."

Nubba needed no more urging. She fled through the dining hall and vanished from Tria's sight.

Now Tria knew why Kress had taunted Nubba about a Shal-reg, though she still wasn't certain what it was.

"You shouldn't have let her off," said the youth whose gesture had indicated his opinion of Nubba's sanity. "That Shal-whatever is a convenient invention for avoiding work." But his broad, freckled face held a grin that took the sting out of his rebuke, and when Tria smiled back, he added, "I'm Gray Becq," and held out his hand.

Tria shook hands, suddenly conscious of her callused palms. "I don't mind, really," she said. "I'm used to working hard all day on a farm."

"All that screaming was just an act?" Soapy hands on hips, a big-boned, square-faced girl left off filling the sink to turn and scowl at Gray.

"Now, Petra," Gray said soothingly, "I didn't say that. Wilce claims she's telling the truth about seeing *something*, but it does appear at convenient times."

"Wilce?" Tria remembered the friendly fellow who'd winked at her in the assembly hall.

"Wilce Riverman, my roommate. He's a truth-speaker." As

he explained, Gray scooped a handful of soapsuds from the sink and with a single deft motion sculpted them into a close likeness of Wilce's face. The frothy portrait hung in the air a few seconds before the bubbles popped.

Tria clapped her hands. "What a marvelous talent!"

"It's not much use, and it's the only one I seem to have," he said. "I don't know what good it will ever do me. I'll probably wind up back home working in my parents' hardware store." Gray's freckled face turned bright red, and he added as if to cover his embarrassment, "Come on, gang, let's get to work before the dragon catches us."

He waved a hand over the dirty silverware spread over a steel table. It sprang about, rearranging itself into a coiled dragon with Headmistress's face, serving spoons forming puffs of smoke issuing from the open mouth. Everyone applauded as the dragon leaped from the table and splashed into the sink full of soapy water.

Laughing, Tria walked to a counter stacked with dirty dishes, picked up a rubber spatula, and scraped uneaten food into the garbage can. Petra, also laughing, plunged her hands into the dishwater and began to scrub the disassembled dragon.

The kitchen crew sped through its tasks, and Tria, her headache gone, rushed outside to her own work detail. Her newfound sense of well-being expanded when she discovered that Wilce headed the garden crew.

He hurried toward her. "I heard what you did for Nubba," he said. "That was generous. You shouldn't have to serve double duty."

"It's all right. I like gardening." Tria smiled up at him, touched by the friendly concern in his warm brown eyes. She gathered her nerve to ask about his truth-reading and whether he had ever used it on Headmistress.

A School for Sorcery

She didn't get the chance. A loud argument broke out between two students picking beans several rows away. Wilce excused himself and hurried to the two. In his presence they calmed and were soon laughing and joking like the best of friends. To Tria's disappointment, Wilce stayed to help harvest beans.

Tria busied herself showing inexperienced students how to judge when a turnip or carrot was ready for pulling, how to search for cutworms and caterpillars, and how to remove them without damaging the tender leaves of cabbage and lettuce. She had no more chance to talk to Wilce.

The garden covered two or three acres and was filled with a variety of vegetables, healthy and ready for harvesting. This abundance of good, fresh vegetables ought to result in better meals. It might be poor management or incompetent cooks, but Tria couldn't help suspecting that the harvest was sold for a profit and inferior products purchased for student consumption. Or perhaps most of it went to the faculty residence hall. They must have their own dining hall because, except for the faculty member assigned to preside at each meal, the staff did not eat with the students. Not for them the disgusting stuff they foisted off on the poor students.

She was sorry to see the duty time end. It meant she could postpone no longer the return to her room. After washing off at an outside spigot, she climbed the stairs, stood outside the closed door a few moments, took a deep breath, and swung the door open.

And stared in amazed bewilderment at the changes.

The stacks of boxes and suitcases were gone. A soft velvet rug with a geometric design of green and beige covered the floor between the beds and desks. An ornate gold lamp graced the desk at the end of Lina's bed. Bookends of carved ivory held a row of expensive-looking books. In front of them a gold pen rested in a heavy gold stand. The desk itself was different—larger, finer, with carved, shaped legs, and the sheen of fine mahogany.

Tria's desk was unchanged, though it now held only her own things, nothing of Lina's.

In the space between Lina's desk and the front wall stood a large chifforobe of matching mahogany. It was wide and deep and had a tall wardrobe section with a full-length door and a section of drawers over which a lovely oval mirror was suspended in a frame that could be tilted back and forth. The clothes rod that held a dress and a skirt and blouse of Tria's looked more tawdry than ever by comparison.

Tria felt her face flush in fury when she saw on her side of the room a vanity table with another mirror. The perfume bottles, cosmetic jars, jewelry boxes, and silver dresser set scattered over it assured her it was not intended for her use.

"How long are you going to stand there gaping? Come inside and close the door."

Lina lounged on her bed in a white satin dressing gown. Behind her, green silk curtains that matched her bedspread billowed in the breeze. A fringed green scarf draped over the trunk beneath the window made Tria slow to notice that the trunk was not hers but Lina's.

"How did you get that furniture?" She waved her hand toward the chifforobe and desk.

"I asked for it. You didn't think I intended to live out of boxes, did you?"

"*Asked* for it?" Tria couldn't believe her ears. "Who did you ask?"

"The maid. I told you she offered to help me. She was of great assistance."

So Veronica played favorites. She hadn't offered to do anything to help Tria. "What have you done with my trunk?"

"Stored it under your bed. It was too ugly to leave sitting out in the open."

"Too ugly . . . Under the bed . . . ," Tria sputtered. "It couldn't possibly fit under the bed."

"I adjusted its size a bit. I don't think I caused any permanent damage."

Tria bent down and peered beneath the low cot. In the dark space lay a flatter, longer version of what had been her trunk.

"This is outrageous! You had no right. What about the things inside?"

Lina yawned. "Must you raise such a fuss? Everything is in it. I have no interest in your shabby peasant outfits. And speaking of shabby, you must do something about that ugly pink blanket. It clashes terribly with my bedspread."

Tria could scarcely contain her rage. "The blanket stays," she snapped. "And my trunk goes back where it was." She pulled the misshapen trunk from under the cot. "It may not be as fancy as yours, but it was there first. You can squash *yours* and put it under your bed."

"Ah, but I won't. If you have the power, you put it where you want it."

The scornful curl of Lina's lip fueled Tria's anger. Hands doubled into fists, she stared at Lina's trunk. Her vision blurred. The trunk seemed to recede, to shrink. She kept her bleary gaze fixed on it until she blinked. Her sight cleared. The silk scarf lay on the floor beneath the window. She picked it up, exposing a miniature trunk suitable for a dollhouse.

"There," she announced. "I doubt that I did any permanent damage to all the fancy things you have in it." With great satisfaction, she kicked it under Lina's bed and turned her attention to her own trunk. A brief period of intense concentration restored it to its normal size and shape.

She took hold of its handles to move it into its place beneath the window. With a snarl, a panther sprang onto the trunk. Tria jumped back barely in time to avoid being raked by its extended claws.

Hissing, back arched, tail lashing, it prevented Tria from coming nearer and dared her to touch the trunk.

She backed to the door, but her anger overcame her fear. "We'll compromise," she said. She grabbed her desk chair and held it out in front of her in animal-trainer fashion. With that shield, she dared to look away from the panther. Her power found Lina's tiny trunk, drew it out from under the bed, and set it under the window, where she increased it to normal height but half its former width.

The panther hurtled toward her. She held the chair to meet it. The panther struck the legs of the chair, clung to them, and hauled itself up toward Tria.

Tria was only subliminally conscious of using her power. She knew that on her own she did not have the strength to hold the chair up with the heavy cat on it. Yet she not only did so, she hurled the panther and chair from her and grabbed the other chair as the black cat, spitting and howling, leaped toward her again.

"I *said* we'd compromise." Tria spoke through clenched teeth as she swung the chair to fend off the panther. "You aren't going to have it all your way."

The cat opened its mouth for yet another snarl. Tria jammed the chair leg into its mouth. The enraged animal bit down, sinking its fangs into the wood. Tria slung chair and cat against the side of Lina's desk. With a yowl of pain, the animal released its hold and dropped to the floor. It stood up on its rear legs and reverted to human form.

Pouting, rubbing her jaw, Lina retreated to her bed. "Very well, have it your way." She gave Tria a sulky look.

"I don't want it all *my* way." Standing where she was, between the two desks, Tria used her power to arrange the two trunks side by side in the space under the window, pick up the green silk scarf, and spread it over both trunks.

Lina shrugged. "If that's all you want, I suppose I don't object."

"It's not all I want," Tria said, moving to the dressing table with its collection of Lina's things. "Since this vanity is on my side of the room, I expect to use it. I'll share it with you; I know you have to have a place to put all this junk."

She gathered the bottles, jars, and boxes together and confined them to one side of the table. "That's half for each of us. And the chifforobe is all yours. I can use the clothes rod. That's more than fair. You'll have to live with it."

Lina stretched languidly as though bored with the discussion. "For now," she said with a yawn. "Only for now."

Tria could not conceal a grin of triumph. She realized though, that Lina would not easily forgive. She'd look for a chance to get her revenge. Tria would have to be on guard. Especially at night.

# 6

## LECTURES AND LESSONS

Tria slept only fitfully all night, never losing her awareness of Lina's presence. Nevertheless, the excitement of embarking on her first day of classes drove away her tiredness. She entered the classroom wing on the first floor of the main building and found the corridor crowded with students streaming to their first class of the new term. With only six classrooms plus a small seminar room, it took only a few moments for her to find her Metaphysical Theory class, a corner room with four rows of three desks each.

She selected a desk in the front row and dusted it off with her handkerchief before she sat. Her nose wrinkled at the odors of ink, chalk dust, and old books. With two walls of windows, the room should have been bright, but the sunlight had to strain through layers of dirt; dead flies littered the sills.

Nubba came in and headed for the third row. "Psst, Tria, come back here," she whispered. "Old Tumbles is nearsighted; he only calls on the people in the first row."

Not wanting to be rude, Tria slipped back quickly just as Master Tumberlis tottered in. The two back rows filled, leaving the front rows for late arrivers.

Master Tumberlis leaned on the lectern, cleared his throat, and peered through his thick spectacles. He greeted his pupils in a quavery voice and launched into the opening lecture.

"The worlds are born of dust and the tears of the gods," he said. "How many worlds we cannot comprehend. The dimensions of existence are infinite, yet even most of the gifted experience no more than three or four. What mankind calls magic is the touch of another dimension. To the ignorant, those who move in dimensions closed to most are magicians, mages, sorcerers—even gods."

To Tria's surprise, she found it fascinating despite the old man's dry delivery. She scribbled furiously in her notebook, trying to record every word. But his next words so startled her that she forgot to write.

"The School for the Magically Gifted is a microcosm of the multidimensional universe. The uninitiated see only this modest building." He waved his hand in a vague motion evidently intended to encompass their present location. "Its apparent limits are deceptive. Some believe it haunted because they catch fleeting glimpses of resplendent chambers they cannot enter. You may find open doors in unexpected places. Explore all such passages. See more than you can; strive to expand your senses. You will never know the whole, but go through those doors that open to you."

She recalled her mother's counsel to go through a door when it opens, but whatever her mother had meant by the advice, Master Tumberlis seemed to mean much more.

"Master Tumberlis," red-haired Fenton Rhoze interrupted brazenly, "do you mean I can go up to third floor and visit any girl whose door is open?"

The class snickered. Master Tumberlis squinted in a pathetic effort to locate the offender. "Those who make light of serious matters will never ascend beyond the lowest levels," he said.

The class quieted, but the serious mood was broken, and the rest of the lecture was uninspired.

*But can it be true?* Tria wondered. *Could there be more to the school than I can see, or is this just another fraudulent claim? I wish I could talk to Wilce about it.*

After class ended, she asked Nubba, "Have you ever seen anything like what Master Tumberlis was talking about? Secret passages, hidden rooms, that sort of thing?"

Nubba shifted her gaze away from Tria. "I don't think secret passages and hidden rooms were exactly what he meant." She sounded evasive. "There's things . . . I've seen . . . well, glimpses, like he said. Out of the corner of my eye. Nothing clear. No door I could go through."

Tria pondered that unsatisfactory reply on the way to her next class and concluded that Nubba had seen nothing but was ashamed to admit it.

The opening lecture in Beginning Ethics seemed dull and pointless, but Master San Marté proved amusing in another way: the prissy little man wore an ill-fitting toupee that crawled from one side of his head to the other like a flat ferret as he paced and gestured. It became a game for his students to guess in which direction the toupee was going to slide next.

After a break that Tria, along with most of the students and instructors, spent on the quadrangle imbibing fresh air, she went to Survey of Arcane Rituals.

Oryon was also in the class, and his presence made her a bit uncomfortable at first, though she wasn't sure why. Perhaps it had to do with his habit of dressing entirely in black, or perhaps it was the sardonic expression in his dark eyes. Only two other girls were in the class, along with six boys, but none of the other boys affected her the way Oryon did. Davy, Britnor, Fenton, Jerrol, and Emory seemed no different than the boys she'd had classes with in Basic School back home. She told herself that it was silly to let Oryon bother her; he had not done or said anything to her to merit that reaction. The interest he showed in Lina should certainly not disturb her.

Fortunately, Mistress Dova's vivid descriptions of ancient ceremonies captured her interest and let her forget Oryon. A description of a rite for calling the wind and interpreting its speech reminded Tria of her mother's tales of windriders. Mistress Dova said that the rite went back to Lady Kyla, who had restored magic to the land more than a hundred years ago. Mistress Dova warned that the old rites could not or should not be used today, but Tria couldn't help speculating on how they might be used and what the effects might be.

Tria had no class the first session after lunch, but weeded the garden that hour. She hoped for a chance to chat with Wilce, but his duties as detail leader kept him busy. She managed no more than an exchange of greetings.

Her last class of the day was Logic. The hot and muggy afternoon urged sleep, and she nodded through Master Tumberlis's long, droning lecture.

Still fearing that Lina would make good on her threat, Tria slept only fitfully again that night and each night thereafter, always afraid that if she fell into a deep sleep, she might awaken to find a panther clawing at her throat. She had no classes with Lina, so the classrooms were the one place she could let down her guard. Staying awake in class grew harder with each passing day, not only in Logic but in the other courses as well. Midday of the second week Tria lost her battle and slept through Metaphysical Theory.

She probably would have slept through Beginning Ethics, as well; Master San Marté's sliding toupee no longer entertained her. But he fixed his gaze directly on her and launched into a discourse on the peril of allowing oneself to be drawn into a contest of power.

E. ROSE SABIN

*He knows about my clash with Lina,* Tria thought.

She had not used her power since the day of Lina's arrival and their contention over the trunks, but she had lived in dread of being hauled before Headmistress and accused of violating not only the school rules but also the restrictions placed specifically on her. It had seemed to her that the clash of powers could not have gone undetected. But as days passed with no repercussions, she had decided that the transgression had remained a secret.

Master San Marté's lecture revived her fears.

"When one Power-Bearer pits his or her strength against another, he or she must first be fully cognizant of the limits of his or her own power and that of his or her opponent." His careful inclusion of the feminine pronoun only annoyed Tria; she saw it as an unnecessary affectation.

"Furthermore, he or she must be able to calculate the energy that will be generated from the conflict between opposing forces." He paused to adjust his toupee, which had slid over his left ear, and went on without shifting his gaze from Tria's face.

"Ethicists differ," he said, "on whether a prearranged duel between two disputing sorcerers is acceptable if the two contestants can prove that they have considered these factors, are evenly matched, and have agreed to restrict the conflict to the safe limits determined by their calculations." He reached up again to adjust the recalcitrant toupee. "Zoander held that where both contestants are known to be honorable and sufficiently skilled to arrive at a precise calculation of the expenditure of power, such a duel is permissible. On the other hand, Devis Saxon insists that the ideal conditions stipulated by Zoander cannot exist, and that if they could, the two sorcerers would then be wise enough to work out their differences without recourse to a power duel."

A SCHOOL FOR SORCERY

He cleared his throat, rose on tiptoe, and swayed back and forth as if to emphasize the next point. "Zoander himself would agree that duels fought in the heat of anger or by contestants too young or ill-trained to perform the necessary calculations are totally unethical and must be soundly condemned by the Community of the Gifted."

Tria squirmed beneath the little man's constant stare.

"You may well ask why the conduct I've described is so completely unethical." He paused, and Tria nodded. Master San Marté frowned and pursed his lips. "Think back, please, to last Fiveday's lecture. What did I declare to be the foundation of ethical use of magical power?"

Sure the question was directed to her, Tria delved into her memory, trying to recall and remembering only that she had dozed through most of that lecture. She opened her mouth to confess her ignorance, but Coral Snow spoke up.

"It's to avoid harm to innocent bystanders."

To Tria's immense relief, Master San Marté transferred his gaze to Coral. "Quite true, Miss Snow. Expressed another way, it is the avoidance of all unintentional harm. I trust you all recall my explanation of why our ethics are founded on the negative principle of 'do no harm.'" This time he went on without waiting for an answer. "It is because the peripheral damage that accompanied irresponsible acts of magic provided just cause for those jealous of our abilities and wary of our powers to mount a campaign of persecution. If two gifted clash, though with good cause, and that clash results in injury or death of an uninvolved spectator, we have no defense against the charges hurled against us, and the safety of our Community is at risk."

*But no one was hurt when Lina and I fought.*

Tria answered her own mental objection. *They could have*

*been. We weren't taking any precautions. I don't know the limits of my power, and I doubt that Lina knows hers.*

She had been guilty of a serious breach of ethics. Never mind that Lina had been equally or more so. What should she do about it? Confess to Headmistress? Tria shuddered at the thought.

Perhaps she should speak to Master San Marté. If he already knew of her transgression, she could make matters no worse. But would the funny little man understand and absolve her of her guilt? He was more likely to condemn and punish.

The bell rang and the class filed out. Tria headed for the quadrangle, and Coral Snow kept pace with her.

"Marty-boy can really make you feel guilty when he aims his lecture at you, can't he?" Coral said. "I saw you squirming. I was the chosen one yesterday, so I know how it feels. But don't take it personally. Taner, my roommate, tells me that he picks on a different student every day, and every so often somebody feels so guilty he blurts out a confession. Does Marty-boy ever love that!"

Tria felt herself blush. Coral must have guessed her thoughts. She'd been saved from making a terrible mistake.

But she *was* guilty of breaking the school rules and of violating the ethics of magic.

She spotted Lina standing by the fountain, surrounded by a coterie of male admirers. *She* certainly wasn't bothered by a guilty conscience. Tria gritted her teeth at the sight of her roommate laughing at tall, good-looking Kress, reaching up to touch his cheek, turning away to cast a teasing glance at Oryon, dark and intense as ever.

Kress doubled his fists and glared at Oryon. His rival sneered. Lina turned back to Kress, and with a rapid motion Oryon drew a sign in the air. Kress slapped at his neck as though stung by an insect, slapped again at his cheek. Oryon grinned. Kress scowled and leaned toward the fountain, scooped up a handful of water and splashed it on his neck and cheek. The water in the fountain surged; as if caught by a sudden gust of wind, the spray blew over Oryon, drenching his black shirt.

Lina laughed, caught both boys by the arm, and moved them away from the fountain.

Coral grasped Tria's elbow in a sudden painful grip. "She's keeping them from fighting," she said, nodding toward Lina. "But the friction. So strong. I can't shield." The girl seemed to be having trouble breathing. An empath. Tria hadn't realized.

She pried Coral's fingers from their bruising hold and, supporting her, led her back inside. As they distanced themselves from the quadrangle, Coral's breathing returned to normal. Tria guided her into an empty classroom, and they both sat down.

"I'm sorry. It came over me so quickly. She's doing it on purpose—toying with them, making them jealous of each other." She paused, shuddered. "I think she feeds off discord. Did you see her, deliberately playing Kress against Oryon? I felt the burning darts fly between them . . . burning . . . burning . . ."

"Coral, snap out of it." Tria squeezed the girl's hand, alarmed by her unfocused gaze and trembling voice.

Coral shook her head. "It's so strong. Even in here I can feel it. But, there, I've shielded. I'm all right." She sat up straight. "But *they* aren't. She's goading them toward an explosion."

"You think they'll use their power?"

Coral nodded. "A duel—like Master San Marté was talking about. Too bad neither Kress nor Oryon is in that class. Or

Lina. Why didn't Headmistress put *her* into the Ethics class? She needs it more than anybody."

Tria wondered the same. "And why doesn't Headmistress or someone on the staff do something about Lina?" She voiced the question that had been haunting her. "Why do they let her break so many rules?"

Coral slapped her palm against the desk. "That's what we all want to know. She doesn't get assigned to any of the duty crews. She's only a first-year student, but she's taking advanced classes. And she's using her power to attract the boys. Why don't they stop her?"

"Maybe they can't stop her," Tria blurted her suspicion. "Maybe she's too strong."

Coral shook her head. "I can't believe that." She studied Tria as though weighing in her mind how much to confide in her. Slowly she said, "When Master San Marté was lecturing, I felt you struggling with guilt. It can't be easy, rooming with Lina. You've had to use your power against her, haven't you?"

So. She couldn't keep it hidden. She'd wanted to confess, but not to a fellow student. But Coral could sense the truth. Quickly, briefly, Tria told her of her contest with Lina.

When she finished, Coral sat silent. Then she let out a low whistle. "Shapechanger! Wow! I wonder if she put that on her application. Do you suppose Headmistress doesn't know?"

"If she knew, she'd stop it, wouldn't she? Or expel her?"

"You'd think so. But who can know why Headmistress does what she does? I'm glad you're the one who has to room with her. I don't know of any other first-year student who'd be able to stand up to her. And I'm not sure about the second- and third-years."

A bell signaled the end of break. They rose to go to their next classes. As she left, Coral clasped Tria's hand. "I'm glad

A SCHOOL FOR SORCERY

we had the chance to talk," she said. "You may be the only one who can stop Lina before she goads Kress and Oryon into a fight that could have tragic consequences. If they use their powers, it could even turn into a bloodbath."

That parting word revolved round and round in Tria's brain as she tried to listen to Mistress Dova's lecture. She found herself casting covert glances at Oryon, wondering whether he'd really let Lina draw him into a duel of power with Kress. Coral had to be wrong; Tria couldn't be the only one who could stop such a contest. Her use of power against Lina had made the girl wary of her, but someone else—Headmistress, a faculty member, a higher-level student—would have to control Lina.

Although Oryon made her uncomfortable, she scarcely knew him and knew even less about Kress. The only male students she'd become friends with were Wilce and Gray. She had never seen either of them with Lina, never noticed them stealing a glance at the catgirl. It pleased her to believe that Wilce, especially, had too much common sense to be fooled by Lina.

She should be listening to the lecture, not thinking of Oryon or of Wilce. She yawned, rested her elbow on her desk, propped her chin on her hand, and tried to concentrate.

"The ancient rites often required the use of a special language known only to initiates and never spoken in the presence of an outsider. More than one such language is known to have existed before magic was lost to the land, and some were more widely used than others. Some Adepts used these languages for recording the mysteries. Others inscribed spells and conjurations. Unfortunately, only a few of these books have come down to us, and some of those defy all attempts at translation. For example, the Mage Alair left us a book called the *Breyadon*, believed to contain both his cosmological observations, the spells he used, and the records of his greatest discoveries."

She opened a large, flat box on her desk and reverently lifted out a leather-bound book that resembled a ledger. "This is an exact replica of the *Breyadon*," she said, holding it up for the class to see. "The original is, of course, kept in a secret and well-warded place. It was preserved by the Lady Kyla, but unfortunately she did not provide a translation, though it is said that she could read it.

Too sleepy to be impressed, Tria peered at the book through heavy-lidded eyes.

"Many of our scholars have devoted their lives to the study of this book, but none has succeeded in deciphering it. Alair, writing about the book in the common speech, gave us the meaning of its title. *Breyadon* means 'Doors.' That is all we know. We are sure that the book is the door to a vast store of lost knowledge, if only we could find the key."

She laid the book on her desk and opened it. Since Tria could not see the pages from where she sat, she let her eyes drift shut while Mistress Dova continued her lecture.

"It has long been maintained that the persona of the mage is so closely bound to the words he inscribed in the *Breyadon* that anyone who succeeds in translating the secret language and using its wisdom may reach the spirit of the great mage Alair himself. I do not know whether the tradition is true, but if it is, the book offers both power and peril. The user would have access not only to the wisdom contained within the book but to the mage's own power. But the power of the mage could be used only in accordance with his principles. An attempt to wield the power in opposition to those principles would destroy the user.

"Unfortunately, little is known of the mage Alair, and the

convictions he held are a matter of scholarly controversy. My fondest desire is to achieve a breakthrough in the translation, but if I were to succeed beyond my wildest hopes, I would not dare to put its knowledge into practice." She paused and cleared her throat.

"That just proves what a fool she is." Oryon's whispered comment was directed to Davy, but Tria heard it. So did Taner, judging by her sudden scowl.

Apparently Mistress Dova did not hear; she continued her lecture. "I will read a brief poetic passage from the *Breyadon* so that you may hear the sound. Of course, I can't be certain of the pronunciation; I can only reproduce the best guess of the scholars. Let me assure you that this particular passage has been recited by careful experimenters in many places, under many conditions, without producing any effect whatever. It is safe, therefore, for me to repeat it, but I adjure you not to try it. Material from the ancient sages is never suitable for student experimentation."

To stay awake, Tria attempted to anchor her consciousness to Mistress Dova's words, repeating them softly under her breath.

In a high-pitched tone unlike her normal speaking voice, the instructor intoned the chant:

*"Bororave Anthrillosor*
*Laysa Grilden Madramor*
*Vernee Shushar Okravor*
*Reven Simi Ith Shathor."*

Tria drowsily whispered the final line. In her state of near sleep, her tongue tripped, transposing syllables and sounds: *"Renev Misi Ish Thathor."*

With the suddenness of summer lightning, her mind became alert and her eyes popped open.

Walls, chalkboard, desks, students, teacher—all had vanished. She stood inside what seemed to be an immense crystal. A bright light shone through its faceted walls, sending a myriad of rainbows shimmering around her. It was a place of delicacy and utter silence where the dancing spectra offered a substitute for sound.

Unaccountably, she felt no fear. She lifted her arms in a gesture of delight, smiled to see her rainbow-hued skin. She twirled around, disrupting the patterns of light and watching them reform as in a kaleidoscope.

A voice spoke in her mind. *Well come, daughter. Not for many eons has this lonely man had a visitor.*

Tria opened her mouth to speak, closed it again, sensing that it would be sacrilege to utter a sound in this place. Instead, carefully she formed words in her mind. *How did I come to this place of wonder?*

It seemed to Tria that the dancing lights slowed, the rainbow colors dimmed. *Do you not know, my daughter? Did you but tread a path forged by another?*

*I—I repeated a chant from a very old book. But I got one or two words wrong, I think.*

The voice in her mind seemed to chuckle. *Got them wrong? I should say that you got them right. Open your mind fully to me, daughter. Let me see from whence you come and how and why. Let me taste your power.*

It felt so profoundly right to Tria to be here and to be conversing with the unseen resident of this crystal place, she assented without fear.

The rainbows glowed and spun, bathing her in tangible color. A burning spread outward from the center of her being, exploded through her limbs, spread beyond her in a blinding burst of white light that swallowed up the color.

*I see, daughter. You have much power, but it is scattered, unfocused, diffuse. You are in a place of learning, where you may*

A SCHOOL FOR SORCERY

find the wisdom you need. You may also find false guides who would direct you to paths of darkness. Be not led astray. Gather your strands of power slowly and carefully, and send that power where you will, not where others will. The light receded and the rainbows returned.

*Can you not guide me, father?* Tria cried in her mind.

*In the world of men I have no voice.*

*But I can come here,* she insisted.

*This place will open to you again only in a time of direst peril, but if you choose to come, you may not be able to leave. You must find other places of power, other means of growth. Seek paths that create rather than destroy; pass through doors that lead to life, not death, to greater knowledge through responsibility, not to greater power through knowledge.*

*Return, daughter, and speak of this meeting to none but those who know my name.*

*But I don't know your name!* As Tria shaped the words, the rainbows winked out and the crystal dissolved.

Someone was shaking her, calling her name. "Miss Tesserell. Miss Tesserell. What happened to you?"

Tria got her eyes open and saw the worried face of Mistress Dova.

"The bell rang, the other students left, and you sat as if in a trance. What happened? Are you ill?"

"No." Tria shook her head. "I'm so sorry. I—I fell asleep. I haven't been sleeping well at night. I apologize. I'll get the class notes from another student. And I won't let it happen again."

The crease deepened in Mistress Dova's brow. "Your face—you seemed . . . transported. Are you sure it was nothing more than sleep?"

"I was dreaming." Tria closed her notebook and gathered

her books. "A vivid dream, nothing more." She rose so that Mistress Dova was forced to stand aside.

She left the room and saw Oryon leaning against the wall, lingering as though he'd waited for her. She was sure he wanted to ask what had happened to her, but she wanted no more questions. Staring straight ahead, pretending not to see him, she hurried past him and escaped into the dining hall.

She had said she'd had a dream, but she was sure the experience was no dream. And if her visit to the crystal place had been real, she must have found her way into one of those other dimensions Master Tumberlis had spoken of.

She would not need to ask Wilce about the school's authenticity. She was satisfied.

# 7

## TRIAL BY FIRE

Tria sat at her desk supposedly studying Logic but mostly trying not to fall asleep.

For what must have been the tenth time, she read the statement she was expected to defend: *The responsible use of power will produce great good. The irresponsible use of power will produce great evil. Power will be used either responsibly or irresponsibly. Therefore, any use of power will produce either great good or great evil.*

The statement did not seem true to her, and though she could offer nothing to refute it, neither could she defend it. Old Tumbles's lecture on the subject, the part she hadn't slept through, had made no sense. She'd thought logic was nothing more than common sense, but now she concluded that the two were totally unrelated.

Lina sat on her bed painting her fingernails and reading a magazine with a lurid cover. She jumped up at the sound of a light tap, checked the clock, and hurried to the door. Tria heard her say disgustedly, "Oh, it's only you," and turned to see Nubba standing in the doorway.

Whom had Lina been expecting?

"Come on in."

Instead of responding to Tria's invitation, Nubba cast a nervous glance at Lina and spoke past her. "Could you come to my room for a few minutes? I need some help with Metaphysical Theory. Something in the notes I can't understand."

"Well, come in," Tria urged again. "I can show you my notes, though I don't know how much help they'll be."

Lina returned to her bed and picked up her magazine, but Nubba didn't move.

"I didn't bring my notes, and I have to refer to them."

Knowing how stubborn Nubba could be, Tria yielded and got up from her desk, not truly sorry to have an excuse to set aside the Logic. She followed Nubba down the hall and into the room shared by Nubba and Irel.

She was startled to see several other girls crowded into the tiny room: Coral, Verin, Kathyn, and Taner. Nubba pushed her inside and closed the door.

"I used the theory notes as an excuse to get you here," Nubba explained. "I couldn't let Lina know."

Feeling trapped, Tria walked in and squeezed herself into a corner of the bed beside Coral and Kathyn. Only then did she notice Irel huddled on the floor in a front corner. She rose to go to her, but Nubba shook her head and motioned Tria back, whispering, "She's all right. Don't pay any attention to her."

Before Tria could ask a question, Coral leaned forward. "If you haven't guessed, this is a war council."

She *had* guessed when she saw Kathyn. Verin must be here because she was Kathyn's roommate, as Taner was Coral's.

Kathyn's long blond hair hung loose over her shoulders. She twisted a strand around her fingers. Her eyes were the green of an angry sea. "Lina's turned my brother into a complete fool," she said. "He's totally unlike himself. He's sullen and short-tempered most of the time; he's secretive; he's neglecting his studies. And he wants nothing to do with me, though we've been close all our lives, and we've always confided in each other." With a lacy handkerchief she wiped away tears. "I can't reason with him."

"Oryon is the same," Taner interrupted. "I do not understand how he fell prey to Lina's spell." Her fingers tapped the ornate hilt of the sheathed dagger that hung from a belt of twisted leather.

Tria had learned that Taner came from an island of the far north, where people lived in tight-knit clans and hunted and fished for their livelihood. Every child on reaching puberty was sent out into the wilds to survive alone for two months. Many never returned. Those who did were presented with a special dagger with their names and deeds carved into the bone handle. The dagger was henceforth never out of reach of its owner's hand.

How and why Taner had traveled so far from home to attend Simonton School, Tria had not heard. But the girl was in her second year and had attained the second level.

"Oryon and I had an understanding," Taner said. Her eyes narrowed to angry slits. "Yet when we meet, he looks through me as if I were invisible. She has bespelled him. This I will tolerate no longer. I have waited, expecting Oryon to break free by his own power. He has not done so, though he has the strength. I think soon he will challenge Kress, and I fear that Kress will die."

"Don't underestimate my brother," Kathyn snapped. "It will be Oryon who dies."

"We're here to prevent anyone's dying," Verin said quickly. "We need to break her hold over all the fellows."

Tria resisted asking what they planned. She wanted no part of any plot.

Coral groaned and doubled over. "Nubba," she gasped.

"Irel. Get her out of here." She gestured toward the hunched figure. "I can't bear her pain."

"But we need her help," Kathyn objected.

"Has she consented to join us?" Taner asked, speaking as if Irel were not present.

Nubba nodded, but Tria wondered whether she and Irel really communicated or whether Irel agreed to Nubba's request merely to silence her.

"Take her to Kathyn's and my room," Verin said. "She can stay there until we have a plan worked out. Then we can tell her what it is, and she can tell us whether it will succeed."

"And if she says no, we must begin again?" Taner asked. "I do not wish to waste time so."

Coral stood. "Her pain is making me sick. If she stays, I'll throw up."

Nubba bent over Irel and whispered in her ear. The girl nodded and let Nubba help her to her feet and guide her from the room.

"It is not good that she felt so much sorrow," Taner said.

"It may not have anything to do with our plan," Kathyn said. "It may be something in the distant future of one of us."

"And is that less disturbing?" Taner snapped.

No one answered, and Taner seemed to expect no answer.

Verin explained to Tria. "Irel reads the future of every person she meets. She can't shut it out, and when she sees sorrow or tragedy, it upsets her. She came to the school hoping to learn how to close the images out."

"You mean she knows what's going to happen to each one of us?" Tria struggled to absorb that information. "She sees our whole future?"

"Yes, but Headmistress has forbidden her to tell anyone," Coral said, sitting up straight and massaging her temples. "She suffers terribly, having to keep all the knowledge inside."

Tria shuddered. Poor Irel! No wonder the girl acted so strange. "But if she can't tell anything she sees, how can she be a part of your plan?"

"She can't tell any individual what will happen to them or to someone else. But she can tell us whether the plan we form will succeed or fail. That isn't divulging anyone's future. All she needs to do is say 'yes' or 'no.' "

Tria frowned, not sure of the ethics of imparting even that much foreknowledge but agreeing that it would help to have it.

The door burst open and Nubba dashed in, panting. "We're too late!" she announced. "I saw Kress go into Lina's room. And Oryon is coming off the stairs."

They all jumped to their feet. Taner yanked her dagger from its sheath and headed for the door. Verin caught her arm. "Wait!" she said.

Coral and Kathyn looked at Tria. "It's your room, too," Kathyn said. "You've got to do something."

"The boys don't belong on this floor. Headmistress or Veronica will stop them."

"The stairs are supposed to be warded," Nubba wailed.

"We waste time." Taner broke free of Verin's grasp and rushed into the hall.

The rest swarmed after her, Tria trailing the others.

*I won't,* she thought, *I dare not use my power.*

Taner reached Tria's room and tugged at the door. Locked. As the others crowded around her, she inserted the blade of her dagger between door and frame, wriggled it back and forth, pried, muttered something about a spell, twisted the blade, and pushed again at the door. This time it opened. All six girls crowded into the tiny room.

A SCHOOL FOR SORCERY

Lina sat cross-legged on her bed, her textbook of Mandalic Studies on her lap. She looked up at her visitors, her lovely face registering shock and bewilderment.

Tria wasn't deceived. The book was a prop, the bewilderment an act. Lina never studied. But where were Kress and Oryon? Had Nubba been mistaken?

"They're here," Coral said, answering her unspoken question. "I sense them." Her voice was strained, her features contorted.

"But where are they?" Kathyn cried.

Nubba edged close to Tria. "What are they talking about?" she whispered. "Can't everybody see them? Oryon is standing over by the window, in front of the trunks. And there's Kress, trying to hide behind the clothes on your rack." She pointed to the front corner beside the vanity.

Tria stared where Nubba pointed, remembering the Shalreg, the monster only Nubba could see. Everyone thought the girl imagined things, but maybe she could perceive what others could not.

The others in front of her blocked Tria's view of the window area. She fixed her gaze on the corner beside the vanity. It *did* seem that her clothes had been shoved together on the rack, leaving a space that someone could crowd into.

Lina began shouting, making it hard to concentrate. "What's the meaning of this intrusion? Get out of my room! How dare you all burst in here like this!"

"They're with me, Lina," Tria called. "This is my room, too. Remember?"

Lina stood and peered over the heads of the other girls to glare at Tria. "You have no right to bring them here without asking me. How am I supposed to study?" She brandished her heavy textbook over Kathyn's head.

Kathyn swatted the book away. "Where's Kress?" she demanded.

"Your twin?" Lina continued her innocent act. "However should I know? Can't you keep track of him?"

"And where is Oryon?" Taner fondled her dagger as she spoke.

"Really, this is ridiculous!" Lina rolled her mascaraed eyes. "You can't think I have them hidden in here!"

"We know you do," Coral said. "I sense them."

Lina regarded the empath with a scornful curl of lip "Look around. Maybe they're under the beds. Or hiding in the chifforobe. Or stuffed under the desks."

"Kress, where are you hiding?" Kathyn called as she jerked open the door of the chifforobe and riffled through Lina's clothes.

"They're trying to hide," Nubba squealed. "But there's no place they can go. They're in plain sight."

"Of course they are, like your invisible creature." Lina advanced on the fat girl. "I suppose this is your doing. You've convinced the others you saw something that was merely a product of your childish imagination."

Nubba thrust out her lower lip. "I *do* see them," she insisted.

Taner bent to look under the beds. She straightened and sheathed her knife. "They aren't here," she grudgingly conceded.

But Tria pushed past Coral, Verin, and Nubba and eased herself between the vanity and her desk. She thrust her hand toward the apparently empty space in the corner under the clothes rack. Her palm pressed against warm flesh; although someone tried to shrink away from her, her fingers closed around an arm.

"They're here, all right," she called out. "I've found one."

At that, Taner shoved Lina roughly aside and strode toward the window, stopped abruptly in front of the trunks, and patted the air with her hand. The green silk scarf covering the trunk wrinkled and slid. Taner reached above it. "Ah-ha! He's climbed onto the trunks, but I've found the other," she said.

At Tria's touch Kress lost his shield of invisibility. He at least had the grace to look embarrassed. He did look ridiculous, cowering back among her dresses. She stepped aside to let him move out of the cramped corner.

Oryon, in black as always, managed to maintain his dignity as he stepped down from the trunks. He glared at Taner and tapped a slender black wand against the palm of his hand. The two curls that fell, one on each side of his forehead with his hair coming to a peak between them, gave him a demonic appearance.

A panther snarled. Nubba screamed. Coral fainted.

Kress squeezed past Tria and headed toward Oryon. In panther form Lina held the other girls at bay.

Verin was trying to calm Nubba. The panther sprang at them, while Kathyn stooped over Coral. Ignoring the cat and the knot of hysterical girls, Kress headed for Oryon. Taner moved to intercept him, her dagger held ready to strike.

Tria looked around for something with which to defend herself and her friends. The open Logic book on her desk caught her eye. She grabbed the large book up in both hands.

Her gaze swept across the open page. The dilemma she had been studying leaped out at her. *Power will be used either responsibly or irresponsibly. Therefore any use of power will produce either great good or great evil.*

*It can produce both together,* she thought with sudden understanding. *I'm forbidden to use my power, but if I don't, Oryon and Kress will hurt my friends. They may be bent on evil and I*

*intend good, but what we do can produce consequences both good and evil. I can't worry about those consequences. I can only hope for the best.*

She used her power to hurl the heavy Logic book at Kress. It struck his head. His knees buckled. Taner's dagger missed its aim and grazed his shoulder.

Tria focused on Lina's heavy bookends and sent one flying at the panther and the other at Oryon.

Oryon raised his wand. The bookend shattered. Its marble and gold fragments fell harmlessly to the floor.

The other struck the panther. It yowled and loosed its hold on Nubba. Taner leaped past Kress and threw herself at the panther. Oryon pointed his wand at her. She fell forward unconscious, but the force of her fall drove her dagger into the panther's haunch. With a snarl it twisted, and its claws raked Taner's face. Tria grabbed her desk chair to swing at the cat but set it down when Lina resumed human form.

"My thigh," Lina moaned, clutching the wound through her blood-soaked gown. "I'm bleeding to death. Help me."

Tria ignored her and concentrated on Oryon. Kathyn and Verin knelt beside Nubba and Coral. Behind Oryon, Kress lurched to his feet. Holding his head, he backed to the trunks and sat down on them. Oryon advanced on the one standing target.

"You shouldn't have interfered," he said as he pointed his wand at Tria. "We'll see whether your power is any match for mine."

Inches from Tria's face the tip of his black wand burst into flame. The heat seared her face. Her impulse was to back off, but the other girls had left her no room.

She stood perfectly still and summoned her power.

Oryon's angry face blurred. The blaze widened into a fiery curtain. She drew it between her and her adversary, shaped it,

A SCHOOL FOR SORCERY

spread it before her like a shield. Through it she could see Oryon only as a smoky shadow.

The shadow swayed; its arms inscribed dark designs. The fiery shield shrank into a sword. Oryon's black-gloved hand grasped the hilt and thrust toward Tria.

She spread the blade into a wispy fan, curled it away from her, rolled it into a glowing band, bent it around Oryon, and tightened it, forcing him to drop his arms to his sides.

The wand in his fingers flipped upward and touched the candescent circle. The band exploded into thousands of tiny sparks. The flickering swarm flew up toward the ceiling, then descended on Tria like a deadly rain.

Tria raised her hands over her head. Her thoughts directed the cascade of sparks into her cupped palms. She gritted her teeth to keep from crying out from the searing pain, held her hands in place, and tipped them to send the flame-shower fountaining back toward its maker.

Oryon lifted his wand and drew the flow of sparks to its tip. Passing his other hand over and through the firefall, he formed a blazing dragon the size of a housecat. He sent it flying toward Tria.

Hands burned, power weakened, Tria knew the battle was nearing its end. She had understood instinctively how to shape the fire, but as the dragon circled her head, her instincts failed. Strength drained from her like water from a sink. The dragon's hot wings fanned her face. It glided onto her shoulder. Its talons burned into her flesh; its hot breath ignited her hair.

Behind her someone—Taner?—cursed. She heard sounds of a scuffle. Someone reached from behind her to beat out the flames in her hair. Her power ceased to ebb and resumed its flow. Not strongly, but enough.

She focused on the dragon. It shrank to the size of a falcon.

E. ROSE SABIN

A sparrow. A dragonfly. She fixed her concentration on the tiny firebeast, reduced it to a glowworm. To a spark. This she flicked from her shoulder and ground beneath her shoe.

With the creature destroyed, she looked at Oryon. Kress had risen and stood behind his rival. He gripped Oryon's arms and pinioned them to his sides. He seemed to be using only his physical strength, not his power. Maybe being hit with the Logic book had brought him to his senses.

Slowly Tria turned to see how the other girls fared.

Taner sat on the floor directly behind Tria. Bloody scratches marred her face. She held her knife at Lina's throat.

Verin supported a shaking Coral, while Nubba clung in terror to Kathyn.

Behind them, in the open doorway, stood Veronica and Headmistress. Tria gasped. The blood drained from her face. How long had they been watching? Had they seen the whole battle? But if they had, surely Headmistress would have intervened.

As Tria stared foolishly, helplessly, at the tall Headmistress and the short, dumpy maid, Headmistress stepped inside the room, which seemed to enlarge to provide space for her.

"Mr. Klemmer, release Mr. Brew," she commanded. "He will do no more harm."

With clear reluctance, Kress released Oryon.

"Healer," she said to Verin. "You have permission to use your power to heal all wounds except the scratches across Miss Mayclan's face. Let her bear the scars as a reminder that she may not use her dagger."

Taner drew herself up proudly. "It is the custom of my clan to wear scars with pride."

Verin placed her hands on the gashes on Nubba's arms, pressed until the wounds closed and disappeared. Next, she moved to Lina's side. With a look of distaste she extended a hand, placed it on the girl's thigh. Headmistress watched her for a moment before turning to Nubba.

"Miss Balder," she addressed the quaking Nubba, "you will return to your room, and until further notice you are restricted to it. You may leave it only to attend classes, eat meals, and serve your assigned duties."

Nubba bowed her head in acceptance.

"Miss Snow, I judge you have suffered enough so that you will not again place yourself voluntarily in such a position. You may go to your room."

Coral nodded, and she and Nubba left. Verin placed her hands on Tria's burned shoulder and face. Her cool touch seemed to draw out the heat, smooth the blistered flesh. The pain eased. In moments, all evidence of the severe burns had vanished.

When Verin finished, Headmistress dismissed her to her room and turned again to Taner. "You also may leave, Miss Mayclan, but with this warning: a second use of your dagger will result in your expulsion."

Taner tossed her head in defiance and stalked past Headmistress and into the corridor.

While Veronica hovered in the background, Headmistress bestowed a long, chilling look on each of those remaining. "With the rest of you, I must talk at length. You will accompany me to my office."

She pivoted and marched through the door. One by one they fell into step behind her, with Veronica following as if to herd them along. Under other circumstances, Tria would have found the parade ludicrous. Now it reminded her of a funeral procession, and a deep foreboding filled her as she trudged through the silent halls.

E. ROSE SABIN

# 8

## DILEMMAS

The group gathered outside Headmistress's office. Headmistress took Kathyn inside and closed the door, leaving the rest waiting under Veronica's watchful gaze.

They stood in embarrassed silence, avoiding each other's eyes. Except for Lina. She winked at Kress, pouted when he turned his back on her, snuggled up to Oryon, who promptly moved away. Her spell over them seemed broken; if so, some good had come out of this disastrous mess. Tria glanced at Oryon. He shifted his gaze upward where a spider spun a web across the light fixture. Had he really tried to kill her? The whole bizarre episode was taking on a dreamlike quality.

She had no idea where her power or the knowledge to counter Oryon's attacks had come from. She had felt it pour into her as though from an outside source.

When her turn came to face Headmistress, she had to make her listen to her explanation. Otherwise Tria could be summarily dismissed from the school for violating the rules. The idea of going home to face her father and hear his "I told you so" was bad enough, but it was the thought of seeing her mother's disappointment that tied her stomach in knots. She *had* to keep her promise to her mother.

She had been defending herself and her friends. She would have to make Headmistress understand.

If only she knew what Headmistress was saying—doing—to Kathyn. It was taking so long! This waiting was like sitting on an anthill. Although Tria strained to hear, no sound penetrated the office door.

The door burst open. Kathyn dashed out, sobbing. Kress reached for her arm. She dodged him and ran up the stairs. Kress started after her.

"Mr. Klemmer." Veronica's call brought him to a halt. "You and Mr. Brew may enter the office."

Tria groaned. Another wait. And no way of knowing what Oryon and Kress would tell Headmistress. She gathered courage to say, "She ought to see us all together."

"It isn't necessary," Veronica answered.

"Why not?"

But Veronica clamped her lips tightly shut. Oryon and Kress trooped inside and the door was closed. Again Tria tried to hear the conversation within, thinking that male voices might carry, particularly if they were shouting. But she heard not a sound.

Time dragged. Lina made a great show of acting bored and put upon, but the performance was wasted on Veronica, who stared off into space and hummed a maddeningly cheerful tune.

At last the door opened. Oryon stormed out, face dark with anger. Kress followed, pale and shaken. Both headed down the corridor to the boys' quarters, walking rapidly, not speaking.

"Ladies," Veronica said, "Headmistress will see you both." She ushered them into the office, and, to Tria's surprise, fol-

E. ROSE SABIN

98

lowed them in, closed the door, and leaned against it.

Two chairs were placed in front of Headmistress's desk. Tria sat in one, and Lina took the other.

As before, the desk lamp left Headmistress's face in shadow. Her hands rested in the circle of light, their thin fingers interlaced. She did not speak. Perhaps she was waiting for a confession. Or an explanation.

Lina would not be the first to speak. Tria would be the one to yield, to blunder through a defense that would most probably be ridiculed and rejected. Lina would witness her humiliation. And if she was allowed to tell the whole story, Lina might well deny it all. Whom would Headmistress believe?

Tria was considering how and where to begin when Headmistress spoke. "Ladies," she said, "you have placed me in a dilemma—in fact, in two dilemmas."

Tria started. Another lesson in logic?

Headmistress had her full attention as she explained. "Simonton School was established to teach the gifted to use their power responsibly. Careless and frivolous abuses of power such as you have demonstrated turn many normals against us. The aim of Simonton School is to make the normals aware of the positive force our graduates have become throughout the continent. To this end we make an effort to recruit a representative selection of gifted young people from all over Arucadi, taking special care to seek out the most highly talented and those with rare and unusual gifts." She could have been reading from the recruitment brochure.

She paused a moment, twisted her ring so that the orange gem sent its reflection dancing over the walls and ceiling. "Both of you," she continued slowly, as though weighing each word, "have exceptional power. You were selected to room together because you have similar strength, and one of you cannot dominate the other as she could a lesser talent. We were quite sure that, despite the restrictions placed on you, you would eventually test your strength against each other. We have tried to make you aware of the possible consequences of that action."

Her tone sharpened. "Miss Mueller, you have attempted to shift the balance of power by enticing Oryon Brew and Kress Klemmer into a contest of strength, knowing that you could siphon their psychic energy into yourself. You compounded your offense by tempting these two, using spells to enhance their attraction to you, though you had no romantic interest in either gentleman or in any of the other male students you similarly bespelled merely to sharpen your skills and conceal your true purpose. You cannot have thought that Simonton School would condone such behavior."

*But you* did *condone it*, Tria thought. *You let it go on until it came to a head. Why?*

"You did not expect the contest to be between Mr. Brew and Miss Tesserell rather than Mr. Klemmer. But you must surely have been delighted by that unexpected development, since it meant you could not only absorb the power but by doing so could ensure the defeat of your rival."

Tria recalled the sudden weakness that had nearly cost her life. So Lina had been responsible. But someone, possibly Taner, had stopped her, either knowing what Lina was doing, or by a fortunate distraction.

Tria cast a glance at Lina to see how she was reacting. She expected to see Lina's usual expression of defiance. Instead, Lina leaned forward, lips parted, eyes wide. Her rapt attention was that of a student hearing a fascinating lecture; it contained no hint of contrition.

"Miss Tesserell."

Tria's gaze jerked back to the shadowy face behind the desk.

"Miss Tesserell, you have demonstrated a measure of re-

straint in the face of temptation. You resisted until you let yourself be manipulated into a situation where power seemed your only recourse. Although you employed it in self-defense, through ignorance you very nearly brought about disaster. I did not wish you to wield your power until you knew better how to control it and when to use it safely." She sighed. "You have not learned, yet I can restrict you no longer. That is one of my dilemmas. I would be remiss in forbidding you to defend yourself. I well know, however, that you risk the corruption of your power each time you resort to it."

Again she paused, toyed with her ring. When she spoke, her voice was softer, reflective, as if she were talking to herself. "When the gifted turn their power against each other, the entire Community is harmed. Talent is wasted. Our reputation suffers. Energy that could be devoted to good ends is wasted on destructiveness. And all too often we lose a valuable talent.

"It is my desire that you two learn to be friends, to work together, to apply your talent to the common good. But I cannot order you to do so. I can only hope.

"To encourage that result, and to place you under closer supervision, I am removing you both from regular work details—and, yes, I know, Miss Mueller, that you have exercised your gift to remove yourself from the lists. I am assigning you both to work with Veronica for two hours daily, carrying out any chores she sets."

"I don't intend to serve as a maid," Lina declared.

"You'll do as I order you, or you will leave the school," Headmistress said.

"Very well. I shall leave. I made a mistake in coming here. Your foolish classes bore me, and all your stupid regulations make the place a prison."

Again Headmistress sighed. "You may leave if you wish, but that brings me to my second dilemma. You came here of your

A SCHOOL FOR SORCERY

own free will to develop your gift. By leaving, you reject the opportunity to develop your talent according to ethical standards. I have the authority to strip you of your talent to prevent future harm to the Community. I consider it an abuse of power to exercise that authority, yet if I do not do so, I allow you to abuse *your* power. If I do not limit your freedom, I endanger the freedom of the Community."

"You cannot possibly do such a thing," Lina said.

"I will show you—both of you—that I can."

Tria felt a sudden darkening, as though an inner light had been extinguished. Something like a wind rushed through her mind. It seemed to flow toward Veronica, not toward Headmistress. She tried to grasp the significance of that flow, but her thoughts were hazy. She felt confused, disoriented, stupid. The world became a dull, dreary place.

Lina let out a loud moan and slumped in her chair.

The woman behind the desk said, "Veronica will escort you back to your room. At this time tomorrow your power will be restored. Then you must decide whether to leave or stay. If you prefer to leave, you will be allowed to do so, but your gifts will be permanently destroyed, and you will spend the rest of your lives as normals."

Lina did not leave the school. If her twenty-four hours as a normal were like Tria's, she *could* not leave. Tria shuddered at the memory of that nightmarish day. The lostness. The emptiness. The feeling of helplessness, of imprisonment. Even though her father had forbidden her to use her power, it had always been there, a familiar friend, imparting a sense of strength and wholeness. When that was taken from her, it awakened sympathy for those who had no such power. How could they bear to lead their whole lives like that? She understood, she thought, the jealousy, the sense of being cheated,

E. ROSE SABIN

which had led her father to deny and squelch first her mother's talent and then hers. Her new understanding caused her to work harder in her classes, determined to excel, to become a builder of bridges between normals and gifted.

Whether Lina had similar feelings, Tria had no idea. She said little, but with uncharacteristic meekness she joined Tria in trailing around after Veronica for two hours every afternoon. It occurred to Tria that before being assigned to this duty she had never seen Veronica performing any housekeeping task other than serving the meals, though now the little maid set them an example of diligent toil.

On the maid's instruction they dusted the furniture in the first-floor parlor, swept and straightened classrooms, washed chalkboards, emptied wastebaskets. Lina worked hard without resorting to her power. And although, for the most part, they worked in silence, it was a shared silence that created between them a new sense of camaraderie. Tria felt it, and she was sure that Lina did, too.

At night Tria slept soundly, no longer concerned that Lina was a threat to her.

As days passed, Tria saw a difference in the school's appearance. The dust was gone, the cobwebs wiped away. The hardwood floors, waxed and polished, acquired an amazing sheen. When they set themselves the task of scrubbing windows inside and out, their efforts brought light and warmth into the building, investing it with new dignity. In the parlor the oil portrait of Lesley Simonton seemed brighter, less brooding, as though the young man approved the changes they had wrought in the school that bore his name.

And Tria became more convinced each day that cleaning was not Veronica's usual pursuit but that she engaged in these chores solely for the benefit of her two charges.

"It's not fair," Nubba groaned one evening when they were

studying Metaphysical Theory in Nubba's room. "You saved our lives, Lina nearly got us all killed, and the two of you have to serve the same punishment. It is not fair."

Tria shrugged. "I don't mind the work. It's not as hard as what I did every day at home."

"That doesn't matter," Nubba insisted. "You shouldn't have to do it. And Lina's punishment should be far worse. She got off easy."

"She's behaving herself. That's the important thing, isn't it? In the courtyard yesterday I saw Kress and Oryon talking and laughing together like old friends. They've forgotten their feud. Doesn't that make it all worthwhile?"

Nubba frowned. "And what punishment did *they* receive, I'd like to know! Kress won't tell even Kathyn what Headmistress said to them."

"And has Kathyn told you what she said to her?"

"Well, not everything," Nubba admitted. "Only that her power is no longer linked with Kress's, and she has to let him go his own way. She has to develop her talent apart from him. She was upset about that, but I think there was more, something she hasn't told me, or anybody else."

*And why should she?* It must gall Nubba to know of secrets she couldn't ferret out.

Tria glanced at Irel, sitting silently at her desk, studying as if she were alone in the room. How it must torture Nubba to live with that quiet, secretive person and never be privy to any of her hidden knowledge.

Could Headmistress have assigned Irel to be Nubba's roommate to provide the nosy one with a constant reminder that not all curiosity could be satisfied?

Nubba broke into her thoughts. "Here's another bit of important information. It isn't such a good thing that Oryon and Kress are friends. They've joined forces. Against you. Taner told me they blame you for humiliating them and getting them into trouble with Headmistress. And for making them look like weaklings."

Tria stared. "Taner told you this?"

"Yes. She and Oryon are friends again, though I don't think they're any more than that—if they ever were. I never did believe Taner's claim that Oryon was her beau. I—"

"Never mind that," Tria snapped. "Tell me what you mean about their 'joining forces' against me. What are they planning?"

"I only know what I told you. Oh, and they're plotting against Lina, too, but of course she deserves it. Taner doesn't know any more. She said to warn you to be careful."

Tria slammed her textbook shut. "I'm sick of this nonsense! I thought it was over. Is it going to start again?"

She stood, letting her notebook and pencil fall to the floor. On a sudden impulse, she walked to Irel's desk. "Tell me, Irel, am I really in danger?"

The girl hung her head and clutched the edges of her book as though it were a life preserver.

"Come on, Irel. Say yes or no. You can do that."

"Yes," Irel whispered.

"Yes? I'm in danger?"

The girl nodded. Her hands shook.

"What can I do?" Tria's anguished cry escaped of its own volition. She did not expect an answer.

But Irel, gazing straight in front of her, said clearly, "Talk to Veronica."

The next day she and Lina were scrubbing the stairs under Veronica's tutelage. Tria had watched for a chance to speak to the maid where Lina could not hear, but their duty time was near its end before the chance came. Veronica sent Lina to empty and rinse the scrub bucket while Tria gave a finishing polish to the waxed banister.

When Lina was out of earshot, Tria spoke quickly. "Veronica, I've learned that I have enemies who intend to turn their power against me, and I was told to ask you for advice on how to stop them."

Veronica nodded as though accustomed to such questions. "And is the threat to you alone, or is it also to Lina?"

So it had done no good to avoid naming the plotters. Veronica's question indicated that she knew exactly what Tria had been referring to.

Tria confessed that the threat included Lina and that she had not talked to Lina about it.

"Do so," Veronica said in a tone that made the brief counsel sound more like an order. "Lina will not be easy to work with, but if you can persuade her to cooperate, you will gain a powerful ally, and you may curb her lawlessness."

Absently Tria polished the rounded end of the banister at the top of the third-floor stairs. Frowning, she said slowly, "But suppose she won't cooperate. Or that she insists on using methods I can't accept? What then?"

"In that case, I recommend that you seek both safety and wisdom by ascending the stairs to the next level."

Tria stopped polishing and looked at Veronica. Was she joking? Her expression was serious.

"I don't understand. This is the last stairway, isn't it? This is the top floor. Or is there an attic?"

"Tch, tch," Veronica clucked. "Have you been sleeping through your Metaphysical Theory class?"

Tria felt herself blush. "I remember Old Tum—I mean, Master Tumberlis saying that our minds can encompass seven levels, though most people discover only two or three." She recalled something else. "He also said that the dimensions of existence are infinite. But that can't have anything to do with what you are trying to tell me."

Veronica looked amused. "Did he not also say that Simonton School is a microcosm of the multidimensional universe?"

Tria frowned, wondering how Veronica knew all this. "Yes," she said, "but I didn't understand. What does it mean?"

For answer, Veronica waved her hand at the familiar hall. Tria saw Lina passing Nubba's room as she came toward them. Veronica must merely be signaling the end of the conversation.

"Look harder," Veronica whispered.

Tria peered down the corridor. For a mere second she thought she glimpsed a long, curving stairway rising upward into darkness. She blinked and the vision vanished. Had she really seen it?

Lina reached them and handed Veronica the clean bucket.

As Veronica accepted it, she said, "You have completed your assigned duty with me. As of tomorrow you will return to the regular work detail."

Tria could not suppress a cry of dismay, but Lina tossed her head. "About time," she said.

"And you will fulfill those duties this time, Miss Mueller."

"I suppose so," Lina said unconcernedly. She turned and ambled toward her room.

"No, she will not be easy to work with," Veronica said softly to Tria. "But you must make the attempt."

Swinging the bucket, she headed downstairs, leaving Tria with a hundred unanswered questions and a large mixture of doubt and dread.

# 9

## INVITATION

Tria stood by the courtyard fountain, which had been shut off and drained for the winter. Wilce had stopped her on her way to her first class and asked her to meet him at the fountain at break. They'd be able to talk privately; few students spent their break time in the courtyard since the weather had turned cold and blustery. Most stayed inside in a heated classroom and studied for the end-of-term exams they faced within the week.

Tria should be studying, too. She wasn't worried about either Mistress Dova's class or Master San Marté's. Her grades in Ethics and in Arcane Rituals were excellent. But her two classes with Old Tumbles were another matter. She'd have to cram to pass the Logic final, and Metaphysical Theory required the memorization of page after page of notes.

She pushed study and exams from her thoughts as Wilce strode toward her, hands in the pockets of his plaid wool jacket, a big grin on his handsome face.

"Hi, Tria. Thanks for coming."

"Glad to, Wilce. What's up?"

"Not much." He unpocketed a hand and ran his fingers

through his thick blond hair. "I, uh, wanted to ask you if you'd go to the Midwinter Ball with me."

Suddenly weak-kneed, Tria sat on the fountain's rim. Wilce sat beside her, a worried look in his brown eyes.

*He thinks I'm going to turn him down,* she thought. *I've got to say something.*

But words would not come. She wanted to blurt out an eager acceptance, and instead she sat tongue-tied.

He placed his hand on hers, his touch warm, reassuring. "I understand if you've already made other plans," he said. "I should have asked you weeks ago. I've always been a procrastinator. I kept thinking we'd draw the same duty detail again and I could talk to you then, but it didn't happen."

She took a deep breath, smiled at him. "I haven't made other plans. I'd love to go with you."

He beamed, and his fingers closed around hers. "That's wonderful! So we have a date."

A date! With Wilce! Tria could hardly believe it. When break was over, she floated to Ethics class and heard not a word of the lecture but sat enclosed in a warm glow, thinking of Wilce and the dance and how happy she was and how well things were going for her and how wrong she'd been about Simonton School.

She'd had no more disagreeable encounters with Headmistress since the night of her battle with Oryon. Headmistress nodded pleasantly when they met and on rare occasions even smiled at her. To her amazement, Lina had agreed to cooperate in a joint defense against Oryon and Kress. But the prophesied attack had never come about. The boys were cool toward them, but gave no evidence of mounting a sinister plot against them.

Tria purposely avoided the girls who had drawn her into the battle. She had classes with Nubba and Coral, so she saw and spoke to them but did not invite their confidences. She rarely saw Kathyn, Taner, and Verin unless she happened to share a work detail with one of them, and that had not happened for several weeks.

Tria spent her time with friends who focused on classes and friendships rather than on conspiracies and battles. Rehanne Zalos had become the closest of these new friends.

When class finally ended, she rushed to find Rehanne, stopped her on her way to the dining hall, drew her aside into the parlor, and clutched her hands.

"Wilce asked to take me to the ball!" The news burst from her, refusing to wait and be imparted in a dignified manner. She bounced up and down, her joy demanding motion, demanding to be shared.

Rehanne's wide smile answered hers. Her friend gave her a big hug. "That's wonderful, Tria! More wonderful than I think you realize."

Tria pulled free of Rehanne's embrace and regarded her friend. "What do you mean?"

Rehanne shrugged. "This year not many are going as couples. Most of us are just—going. Last year most of the fellows invited girls. But not this year.

"Oh, the third-year students are going as couples," she went on in a rapid speech that too clearly hid some hurt. "Evyar and Adeen intend to get married after graduation, and Helena and Cleance are always together. Everyone expects them to be named King and Queen of Winter. But the first- and second-year fellows are holding back. Taner is furious because Oryon hasn't mentioned the dance to her. She's too proud to ask him. Elspeth did ask Palmer, and he said that of course he'd dance with her, but 'the men have decided to go as a group this year.' *Men!* Isn't that ridiculous?" Her smile changed to a frown, and Tria heard the hurt in her voice as she added, "I keep hoping Gray will ask me, but he hasn't, so I guess I'll tag along with the other girls."

"You could always use your gift of coercion to give him a little mental nudge," Tria said, teasing.

"You know I'd never do that." Rehanne sighed. "But don't think I haven't been tempted. It would be so easy—but it would be wrong, and if he ever found out or even guessed, he'd be through with me forever."

"Oh, I doubt that. But he'll ask you. It's not too late. Wilce said he'd meant to ask me earlier and hadn't got up the nerve. That's probably all it is with Gray and the others. You wait. They'll be falling all over themselves to invite dates, now that Wilce has broken the ice." She hugged Rehanne again, wanting to erase her doubt, wanting her friend to share her joy.

But Tria could see the uncertainty behind Rehanne's smile, and her friend only said, "Come on, we'll be late for lunch."

As they hurried toward the dining hall, Tria resolved to see Wilce and ask him to speak to Gray. Probably a word from Wilce would be all the prodding Gray needed, and Rehanne need never know.

Her happiness restored by that resolve, Tria scarcely noticed that the only table with two empty places was the one at which Lina sat, along with Petra. She and Rehanne greeted them and sat down, only to have to stand again for the noon blessing, led today by Master Hawke.

Tria echoed the words of thanksgiving in her heart, scarcely beginning to express her gratitude when Master Hawke concluded the prayer.

Veronica served the food, and Tria was astounded to see a platter of roast pork set before her, the succulent meat swimming in rich gravy. The cooks must be celebrating her good fortune. She stared at the heaping dishes of vegetables served with the roast. For once, the harvest from the student-tended garden graced the student tables.

"Is this a holiday or something?" Tria asked, piling her plate high with the delicious fare. Her question was answered by puzzled negatives and blank looks. "The food, I mean. It's so different today."

Petra peered at Tria's plate. "Different? How? It's the same slop they always serve."

Rehanne shrugged. "They're being generous with the fresh vegetables while they last, I suppose. We'll have preserved and canned food all through the winter."

Lina said, "The food has not changed. Only your perception of it is different."

The smirk on her roommate's face kept Tria from asking more questions. She didn't care to give Lina a chance to show off. Instead, she let Rehanne guide the conversation to other matters. But later, in their room, she asked Lina what she'd meant.

Lina sat cross-legged on her bed, her white dressing robe billowing around her. "So much here is clothed with illusion," she said. "I suppose the intention is to test us to see how long it takes each one to perceive the reality beneath the illusion. I saw through the deception immediately. It's a child's game, really."

"You mean, the delicious lunch we had today is no different from what they've been serving all along? You mean the meals haven't been overcooked cabbage and tasteless, sticky rice, and dry fish cakes, and tough, stringy chicken, and half-raw turnips and—"

"Ugh! You've been letting yourself accept that kind of garbage as food?" Lina wrinkled her dainty nose. "What a fool you've been! Haven't you learned to look beneath the surface of things? Don't you know how to test for the presence of illusion?"

Lina's disdainful tone angered Tria. She answered with a shrug, not wanting to confess her ignorance.

"I suppose I'll have to teach you." Lina's show of disgust did not conceal the triumph that lit her eyes and played with the corners of her mouth.

"No, thanks," Tria snapped. "I'll figure it out for myself. If you learned it, I'm sure it can't be difficult."

Lina scowled and lapsed into a sullen silence. Tria felt guilty. She should apologize, but she was too angry with Lina for spoiling her euphoric mood. She gathered her books and left to study with Rehanne.

That evening Tria found Wilce in the library studying for exams. She slipped into the seat next to him and in whispers asked him to talk to Gray about inviting Rehanne to the ball.

Wilce pushed away the book he'd been reading. "Don't ask me to butt in on another fellow's business." He sounded cross and a little guilty, a reaction she hadn't expected. "Some of the guys are putting pressure on the rest to go alone this year. It makes sense, really. It's not as if you girls needed transportation. All any of us have to do is walk downstairs to the dining hall. We'll all be there, with or without dates. And a lot of the guys can't afford to order a corsage and buy a date gift."

"Date gifts?" Tria asked, puzzled.

"It's a Simonton tradition," he explained. "When a fellow asks a girl to the Midwinter Ball, he buys a special gift to give her just before the ball ends, while the band plays the final song."

"Wilce, I don't need a corsage or a date gift, and neither does Rehanne. But the Midwinter Ball is the biggest event of the year, and another Simonton tradition is for the students to go as couples."

"Well, that tradition is going to be broken this year. A lot of the guys feel it's time to make new traditions."

"If you feel that way, why did you invite me? Why didn't you go along with what the other boys decided?"

He hesitated, looking embarrassed, not answering. Tria held her breath. Had she gone too far? Would he—could he—uninvite her?

Wilce took her hand and said, "You're special, Tria. You never flaunt your power, and you go out of your way to help others. You're the only one who has patience with Nubba when she gets out of work by screaming about her monster. And the way you tamed Lina . . ."

Tria laughed. "I wouldn't call her 'tamed.' I'm not sure she hasn't simply changed her tactics."

"Whatever you say. You know how to handle her. All right, I'll speak to Gray. I know he wanted to ask Rehanne. I'll convince him not to let the others influence him."

# 10

## Excursion

The excursion to Millville was Lina's idea. "Tomorrow's Freeday," she said. "We can take the early morning bus to Millville. We need a break from studying for exams."

"But you haven't studied," Tria said, looking up from the notes spread across her desk. "You never study."

"So? You do."

"You said 'we.' "

Hands on her hips, Lina gave Tria an exasperated look. "All right, then, if you insist on precision. *You* need a break and *I* want one, whether I need it or not. I haven't been to Millville in weeks."

"You went Freeday before last," she reminded Lina. "That's not weeks."

"It certainly is. It's two weeks. That's long enough for me, and you've *never* gone. You stay holed up here like a badger."

"Lina, I just don't see any point in going. You know I don't have money for shopping."

"Well, you're going to the ball, and you have nothing suitable for it. I can lend you a dress, but you have to have decent accessories."

"I haven't asked to borrow anything from you. Now let me work." Tria picked up her pencil and went back to her notes.

Lina snatched the pencil from her hand and threw it across the room. "Tria Tesserell, you are the most stubborn creature ever. Here I am, trying to be nice to you, and you won't even listen. Put those stupid notes away and pay attention. You *are* going with us to Millville tomorrow."

"Us? Who's 'us'?"

"You, me, Kathyn, Elspeth, Bettina, Petra, Norietta, and probably Eula and Coral and Verin."

So this really was to be a grand excursion! "What about Rehanne?" Tria asked. "And Nubba?"

Lina's eyes gleamed with mischief. "Oh, yes, I forgot to mention Rehanne," she said. "Now that Gray's asked her to the ball, she'll want to shop. As for Nubba, you can invite her if you want."

She had fallen neatly into Lina's trap. She would have to go to keep poor Nubba from being left out. Nubba would be deeply hurt if she was not invited when all the other first- and second-year girls except Irel and Taner were going. Irel would never go anywhere with the others, and Taner's refusal to have anything to do with the ball doubtless included shopping for it, but everyone knew that Nubba would rather die than miss the ball.

"All right," Tria conceded, "I'll ask Nubba if she wants to go, and if she does, then I'll go, too."

Lina turned away, but the mirror reflected her triumphant smile. Of course there was no doubt as to how Nubba would respond.

The wind buffeted them, making them grab at their long skirts as they got off the bus. Although the air was cold, Tria felt warm and comfortable in the midst of her friends. She was glad Lina had made her come. Chattering and giggling, they headed down the sidewalk while the Millville folks gawked.

It was certainly not unusual for Simonton students to visit Millville, but Tria guessed that the townspeople were not accustomed to having so many descend on them at once. Several of the people they passed looked alarmed. Mothers grabbed children and held them tightly by the hands or lifted them into their arms.

"We should separate into twos and threes," Tria suggested. "It makes people nervous to see this many gifted all together. They probably think we're planning something."

"Well, we are. We're planning to shop," Lina said with a malicious grin.

But the others agreed with Tria, and the girls separated, arranging to meet for lunch at the Sunshine Café. Tria stayed with Rehanne and Nubba, Lina walked off with Kathyn and Eula, and the remaining six broke up into twos. Millville was not a large town. They would run into each other often, but they all headed in different directions for now.

Bare-limbed trees lined the space between the street and sidewalk, their fallen leaves heaped on the ground beneath them. The buildings along Main Street were old, many of red brick, others of weathered wood. But the shops all boasted show windows decorated with gaily colored lights, and their displays were often arranged in snow scenes. Nubba bounced along, bubbling with excitement. Rehanne strolled beside Tria and paused to gaze into each window. Tria enjoyed lingering to admire the displays as much as Rehanne. But Nubba kept getting ahead of them, leaving Tria torn between hurrying to catch up with her or lagging behind with Rehanne and being subjected to Nubba's impatient calls.

Nubba was well ahead of them when she gave a loud shout and disappeared into a shop doorway. Tria hurried forward,

A SCHOOL FOR SORCERY

but even before she reached the door, the odors of fresh baked bread, cinnamon and other spices, and rich chocolate told her that Nubba had found a bakery.

And such a bakery! A miniature town adorned the window, its houses made of ginger cakes, with windows drawn with yellow icing to portray lamplight within. Spun-sugar snow covered the ground; gumdrop bushes surrounded the houses; and licorice-stick lampposts lined the chocolate-square streets. There were even tiny figures populating the village.

"Now that's magic!" Tria breathed in awe as Rehanne joined her. "Look, even the little people look like they're made of some kind of candy."

"They are," Rehanne told her. "They're marzipan. That's made of crushed almonds and sugar and . . . and egg whites, I think. It's yummy. And look at those marshmallow snow-men!"

They still stood entranced when Nubba emerged, laden with an armful of paper-wrapped delights.

"Here," she said happily, thrusting one sticky packet into Tria's hands and offering a second to Rehanne. "My treat. It's my thank you for being my friends."

Surprised, Tria lifted the covering paper and saw a flaky horn oozing creamy filling, a cinnamon bun thick with icing, and two delicately decorated petit fours.

"Nubba, you shouldn't have! Why, we'll spoil our lunch if we eat all this."

Nubba laughed. "This is better than the café food, and anyway we'll walk it off by lunchtime." Opening her own packet, she took a big bite of the cinnamon bun.

"Thanks, Nubba," Rehanne said, with a wry glance at Tria, as she picked up a petit four.

The cream horn was delicious, but Tria knew she'd never be able to eat the rest of the sweets. When they resumed their

E. ROSE SABIN

stroll along the street, she stayed back with Rehanne and let Nubba get well ahead of them. When they came upon two small boys staring wistfully at a toy store display, Tria nudged Rehanne and offered the rest of her sweets to one of the boys. Gratefully, Rehanne gave her goodies to the second boy, putting a finger to her lips to caution silence.

The children eagerly grabbed their prizes and ran off. Tria and Rehanne grinned at each other and hurried on after Nubba. They needed to exchange no words to assure each other that their friend would never know how they had disposed of her largesse.

Except for Nubba's purchase of the sweets, they were content merely to browse and buy nothing. When they reached the point at which the shops ended and gave way to offices and private homes, they turned around and headed back toward the Sunshine Café. They'd covered only a block and a half when Kathyn came running toward them, beckoning, her face beaming.

They joined her, and when she'd caught her breath, she said, "Guess who we just saw and what they're doing!"

Tria shook her head and Rehanne shrugged.

"We saw Wilce and Gray going into a jewelry store. They didn't see us—we ducked out of sight. Then we peeped into the window. We couldn't see what they were buying, but I'm sure they're getting date gifts for you two." She indicated Tria and Rehanne with nods of her head. "If you hurry you might sneak a peek and see what they're buying."

"We told them we didn't want date gifts. They're probably buying presents for someone in their family."

"No, I'm sure they wouldn't ask you to the ball and not buy you a date gift," Kathyn said.

"Let's hurry!" Nubba said, practically dancing. "I'll bet Wilce will get something real special for you."

A SCHOOL FOR SORCERY

"No," Rehanne said, placing a restraining hand on Nubba's arm. "I don't want to know what Gray is getting for me. I want to be surprised. Don't you, Tria?"

Tria nodded. "Definitely, I want to be surprised," she said. "Kathyn, you get Lina and Eula right now. Tell them not to dare spy on the boys."

Kathyn looked disappointed, but she said, "I'll tell them. They may not want to come. Lina wanted to go into the store—to buy something for herself, I mean." She added the last hastily when Tria glared at her.

"I'll go back with you," Nubba said, starting off.

Tria caught her arm and hauled her back. "No, you don't. I know you'd try to see what they bought. I mean it when I say I don't want to know. I want to be surprised. And I don't mean for any of the rest of you to know either."

Kathyn jogged back while Tria and Rehanne waited with a much put-out Nubba. In only a few moments Kathyn returned with Lina and Eula, both carrying shopping bags. Tria had expected her roommate to be angry, but Lina was laughing.

"I knew what you'd say," she said on reaching them. "I even had a bet with Eula. And don't worry, I don't know what they bought, though I could have found out easily enough. I do know one thing, though. That jewelry store doesn't sell cheap stuff. You're both lucky, especially since most of us won't get any gift at all."

Lina was acting as though she didn't care, but Tria detected a hint of jealousy in her roommate's green eyes. "They shouldn't give us gifts," Tria said. "I don't care if it is a tradition. With so few of the boys inviting girls this year, it isn't right for just a few of us to be treated so specially."

"If you really feel that way, you shouldn't have accepted the date," Lina said cattily. "But you did, so you might as well take all that goes with it. Now, what have you bought so far?"

Tria hesitated. Lina knew very well that she had no money for shopping. She suspected that her roommate was trying to embarrass her, and it was hard to resist giving a sharp retort. But this day was too enjoyable to spoil by sparring with Lina.

"We've just been window shopping," she said. "I haven't found anything I want to buy."

"Well, then, it's good I've found you," Lina said. "I can help you look."

To Tria's profound relief, Rehanne intervened to say, "Not now. It's almost time to meet the others for lunch. We need to head for the café."

Lina grudgingly agreed, and they set off toward the café. They'd gotten near enough to see Coral, Verin, Petra, and Elspeth waiting outside when they heard shouts and screams coming from a side street.

Tria gave the others a single quick glance and sped toward the sound, sure her friends would follow.

The first thing Tria saw when she rounded the corner was a large dog in the center of the street, its yellow fur bristling, ears laid back, teeth bared, muscles tensed for a spring. Its head swayed back and forth as if it could not make up its mind where or on what to vent its rage. It opened its mouth and let out a furious howl. Only its indecision held it back.

On one side of it two terrified boys—the same two to whom she and Rehanne had given the sweets—cowered at the base of a tree, its branches too high above them to reach. On the other side stood Oryon and Kress, laughing, baiting the dog with a stick. Behind them, Davy, Jerrol, and Fenton lounged against the side of a building, watching.

Following Tria's fleeting thought that the whole school must be in Millville came the realization that the dog should not be in doubt about whom to charge. It was obvious who was teasing it. But when it crouched to spring at Oryon and Kress, something confused it, made it shake its head and turn toward the little boys.

Oryon and Kress were using power. Tria could feel the currents. They were tormenting the animal, then diverting its fury to the hapless boys.

Other people were gathering, and one man ran toward the boys to protect them, while another picked up a heavy stone and moved toward the dog.

The maddened animal leaped. The man snatched one boy out of its way, but it landed on the other, and its teeth ripped into his shoulder.

Tria confronted Oryon and Kress. "Stop it!" she said. "How dare you!"

Oryon raised his brows in mock surprise. "Stop what?" he asked. "Just what is it you think we're doing?"

Kress paid her no attention; he remained focused on the dog. So he was the one working the magic, and she had to break his concentration.

Rehanne stepped up beside her. "I'll help," she whispered.

Lina slipped behind a cluster of high bushes.

Tria gathered a ball of light and tossed it at Kress's face. Gasps rose from the gathering crowd, but Kress never blinked. "Witches!" someone shouted.

Kathyn pushed both Tria and Rehanne out of the way and launched herself at her twin, beating Kress on his chest and shoving him backward toward Davy and the others. "Headmistress told you not to draw power," she shouted. "I'm forbidden to let you, so why aren't they?" She glared at Davy, Jerrol, and Fenton, who returned puzzled looks. She swung back to her twin. "They don't know, do they? You don't even bother to ask permission anymore."

She might have said more, but a black panther glided out

from the bushes and, snarling, pounced on the dog, tearing it from its prey.

The dog yipped and yelped, twisting beneath the panther's weight. The panther slipped off its back, the dog ran, and the panther darted behind the bushes. A moment later Lina strolled out and joined Tria and Rehanne. Eula and Elspeth sprinted after the dog, and Tria recalled that Eula had the gift of calming animals.

Tria felt as much as saw the crowd forming around them. Oryon shrugged and stepped back to join Kress. He raised his voice and said, "We were only trying to keep the dog away from us. We didn't mean to send him toward the little boys."

It was clear that the townspeople didn't believe him, no matter how much injured innocence he put into his voice. Observers must have seen that he and Kress had done nothing to help the two threatened youngsters.

"We're in real trouble now," Kathyn told Kress. "When word of this gets back to Headmistress, we'll all be punished. She'll probably cancel the ball."

"So?" Kress said defiantly.

But Oryon again addressed the crowd. "Look. The child is all right. No one got hurt."

Tria turned with the others to look. She had seen the dog tear the boy's shoulder open. Verin was holding the child, her hand pressed over the injured shoulder. "He's right," she said. "Only his shirt is torn." She moved her hand away to show the unblemished skin beneath it.

She had healed the boy, of course.

"I know that dog," a man said, stepping forward. "It's always been a gentle animal. Never seen it act that way before. What got into it?"

"And what was that thing that attacked it?" a woman asked.

"What does it matter?" Lina said. "It saved the boy, didn't it?"

Eula and Elspeth returned at that moment, leading the dog, now calm and wagging its tail, despite the long scratches on its back.

Verin handed the child to a man who seemed to be his father. She went to the dog and stroked it, running her hands over its back. When she stepped away from it, the bloody scratches were gone.

Again people in the crowd murmured of witchcraft.

"We can't please them, can we?" The voice that murmured into Tria's ear was Oryon's. "They don't like us any better when we do good than when we do harm. So there's really no point in being good."

She cast him a withering glance. "Nobody even thought of bothering us until you started making trouble. Did you mean to goad that dog into killing that child?"

"Of course not. We would have stopped it if you hadn't come along. You were the one who drew everyone's attention. You and Lina with her needless theatrics."

"Needless! She saved that boy's life!"

"Which would not have been in danger if my dear sister hadn't broken my concentration," Kress said.

Tria snorted and looked away from him to study the crowd. She estimated the number of people around them at around two dozen, and although no one had yet made any threatening moves toward them, she felt it was only a matter of minutes before they did.

The others, too, were aware of the growing danger. Lina snarled. "Don't change," Tria warned.

Rehanne's eyes were shut, her face set in concentration. Tria was sure that she was exerting her talent of coercion in an attempt to control the throng, but the crowd was too large for that.

Davy and Fenton looked scared, but Jerrol stepped out in front. A man raised a menacing fist—and froze. Jerrol's talent held him immobile. But the act enraged the mob, and Jerrol was far from strong enough to hold them all. People were shouting now and pressing forward. Tria saw peace officers join the crowd and move through it toward them. It was clear from the direction of their movement and their grim expressions that they were there not to control the crowd but to warn and possibly arrest the objects of the crowd's anger.

She glanced at Oryon, who still stood beside her. He was breathing deeply, and his dark eyes sparkled. *He's enjoying this*, she thought.

Then, inexplicably, the shouts lessened, the group stopped moving forward, and many turned away from their targets. The peace officers drew back. At first Tria thought they were all reacting to something Oryon had done. But his face had darkened; his brows had drawn together in an angry frown. "Meddlers!" he muttered. "Spoilsports."

He was taller than she and could see over the heads of the crowd. She stood on tiptoe but still was not tall enough to see what had turned the mob and aroused Oryon's anger.

Like her twin, Kathyn was tall, the tallest of the girls. Her relieved laughter comforted Tria. "It's Wilce and Gray," she said. "We're saved."

The crowd parted, and Tria could see them. Wilce simply moved among the people, speaking softly. Tria did not have to hear what he said to know that along with his words he was spreading his calming influence, using his peacemaking talent to defuse the tension.

And Gray! Gray had stopped beside a pile of leaves and

was using his power to lift the leaves into the air and shape them into likenesses of people in the crowd. Men and women cried out, not in anger but in delight, to see someone's face briefly reproduced, only to have the portrait disintegrate and then reform into a new likeness.

With everyone, including the peace officers, focusing their attention on Gray and his ephemeral sculptures, Wilce reached his fellow students.

He smiled, and Tria's heart warmed, sure that the smile was meant especially for her.

"Go while Gray has them all distracted," he told them all. "Get to the bus stop and take the next bus back to school. Those peace officers won't be diverted for long."

"Who gave you the right to order us around?" Kress demanded.

But Oryon said, "No, he's right. It's time to go." Then his lips curled in a sneer and he said, "We'll finish this another time."

# 11

## MIDWINTER BALL

Either hold still or I'm going to walk out and leave you like this," Lina said through a mouthful of pins.

"Sorry." Tria straightened and held out her arms so that Lina could scoot around her, pinning the hem in the full blue skirt.

"If you'd use your power for this, it would be a lot easier."

"And wouldn't I look cute when my dress fell apart on the middle of the dance floor. Come on, you're almost all the way around."

"I've got another third to go, and if you keep wiggling I'll never finish. I don't know why I offered to do this."

Tria didn't know either. Despite Lina's insistence that she could not wear a "peasant outfit" to the Midwinter Ball, she had resolved not to accept Lina's offer of one of her own expensive frocks, but that resolve weakened when she saw the gown. It was glorious, its soft silk chiffon swirling like a cloud around her.

Because she was taller and heavier than Lina, the dress had to be altered. Fortunately, and unexpectedly, Lina proved skilled with needle and thread, able to let out darts and the generous seams, as well as take out and redo the hem. She'd agreed to do the alterations after Tria flatly refused to use her power to adjust the dress to the desired size.

"The dress brings out the blue of your eyes. You can have it."

"Thanks, Lina. It is gorgeous. But I couldn't keep it. It's too expensive."

Lina shrugged. "I have plenty of others. And the color's not as flattering to me as it is to you. Besides, I'm not going to do all this work only to have to rip it all out and put it back the way it was."

"You wouldn't have to," Tria said with a wicked grin. "You could use your power."

The day of the dance dawned cold and snowy. The sun came out in midmorning and melted the snow to slush. Clouds drifted in and thickened, and by evening the slush turned to ice. Perfect weather for the Midwinter Ball.

In a cloud of blue chiffon, Tria descended the stairs, her hand resting on Wilce's arm. How fine he looked in his ruffled white shirt and black tuxedo!

Behind them, to Tria's deep satisfaction, Gray escorted Rehanne, her plain features radiant, her cheeks reflecting the rose of her organdy gown.

Tria touched her fingertips to the rosebud-and-carnation corsage that graced her shoulder, its pleasing perfume drifting to her face like a promise. She thought of the gift Wilce would present to her at the evening's final dance. No matter what it was, she was sure it would delight her. Aglow with anticipation, she felt confident, graceful, no more the ignorant little country girl she'd been.

As she entered the dining hall with Wilce, she noted the envious gazes of the girls who had come without escorts. Her sympathy for them did not prevent a welling of pride.

Her thoughts were so focused on her own transformed appearance, it was a moment before she noticed and gasped at the transformation wrought on the dining hall. It had become a vast ballroom, lavishly decorated with glittering snowbanks, its far wall a glass-blue glacier, streamers of stars sweeping down from the high ceiling to bathe the room in a sparkling silver light.

Tria could scarcely remember the required courteous responses as she and Wilce were greeted by each faculty member in the formal reception line that stretched from the doors toward the center of the room.

Master Tumberlis's long-tailed coat was shiny at the elbows and the lapels were worn, but he bowed and kissed her hand with a dignity that brought tears to her eyes. They received an effusive welcome from Master San Marté, attired in a mauve tuxedo with pink lace cuffs and shirtfront. Mistress Dova was elegant in gold lamé, Mistress Blake lovely in a confection of lavender moiré. Master Hawke wore an imposing black cape and red silk cravat. Aletheia looked more ethereal than ever draped in diaphanous white. At the end of the line, Headmistress stood in a straight black gown, its severe lines offset by a glittering jetbead trim.

Headmistress greeted Tria warmly, beaming approval of her association with Wilce. At last she felt that her early transgressions were forgiven, and she basked in Headmistress's smile.

The musicians caught her attention. Pulling Wilce along, she hurried across the room for a closer look. Crowded onto a small stage at the base of the glacier, the seven members of the band wore penguin costumes made with real feathers. Beaked and feathered masks completed the illusion.

Tria clapped her hands in delight, and as if waiting for that signal, the musicians picked up their instruments and the music began.

Wilce led her onto the dance floor. She hoped she wouldn't disgrace herself. "I'm not much of a dancer," she said.

"Don't worry. Just follow me."

One hand firm against her back, he guided her through the uncomplicated pattern of the waltz. At first she watched her feet and counted to herself, "One—two—three; one—two—three." Soon she learned to anticipate his moves by the motion of his shoulder on which her hand rested. She lifted her gaze and met Wilce's approving smile. Gray and Rehanne glided past them, Rehanne's lovely turquoise eyes broadcasting her happiness.

"I'm glad you convinced me to talk Gray into taking Rehanne," Wilce said, speaking low, his lips beside her ear. "The guys that insisted on coming alone are crazy. They don't know what they're missing."

"I wish they'd get here." The envious glances of the unescorted girls dampened her joy. Besides Wilce and Tria and Gray and Rehanne, only four other couples were on the floor. Palmer had relented and invited Elspeth after Gray asked Rehanne. Seeing the two dancing cheek-to-cheek made Tria wonder why Palmer had been so reluctant. The other couples were third-year students.

"Guess the rest of the fellows are waiting to make a grand entrance."

For the moment Wilce's explanation satisfied her. Giddy with joy and the warmth of his arms, Tria shut her eyes and let the music waft her along a stream of stars, galaxies whirling around her, barren planets bursting into glorious life as she passed.

The music stopped and silence dispelled her dream. The

other boys had not yet come. All the girls were present except Irel, who never attended parties, and Taner, who had declared the ball "a foolish custom." Over half the school's male students were missing.

The band struck up a lively fox-trot. Tria urged Wilce to ask Nubba to dance. From the sidelines, she admired the graceful way in which he avoided Nubba's clumsy feet without losing the rhythm of the dance. Gray danced with Coral, and Palmer with Kathyn. The third-year students exchanged partners only among themselves. Lina, in shimmering green, prowled around the edges of the crowd like a cat stalking its prey.

The faculty receiving line disbanded. Old Tumbles wandered over to the refreshment table. Master San Marté danced with Aletheia, while Master Hawke claimed Mistress Blake as his first dance partner. Mistress Dova and Headmistress resisted the music's appeal and remained near the door, no doubt waiting for the late arrivals.

Where were they? All around her Tria heard strained whispers: "Aren't they coming?" "They wouldn't ruin the Midwinter Ball, would they?" "Why are they so late?"

The music ended, the dancers drifted from the floor, and in the silence someone said, "Here they come!"

Jerrol and Davy herded four other boys inside, separated from them, and greeted Headmistress and Mistress Dova. Too far away to hear their conversation, Tria was alarmed to see the two women back slowly toward the wall and stand as stiff and unmoving as statues.

Kress sauntered in, tall and resplendent in a swallowtail coat. A masked woman in a daring backless and strapless silver gown leaned on his arm. Oryon, in black tuxedo and black silk shirt, escorted a woman dressed in low-cut clinging scarlet. She too wore a full face mask.

A SCHOOL FOR SORCERY

Reece and Fenton swaggered in behind the two couples. Britnor entered last and closed the ballroom doors. The band struck up a lively melody, and Kress and Oryon paraded their partners onto the dance floor. No other couples moved to join them.

Wilce came up beside Tria and grabbed her elbow. "Those women aren't students. There's going to be trouble. I'm taking you out of here."

Tria shook her head. "They have no right to spoil the ball for everyone."

"But they will. That's what they intend. It's their revenge on Headmistress for punishing them and on you girls for humiliating them and for spoiling their fun in Millville."

"But they seemed to be over all that," Tria objected.

"They haven't forgotten." Wilce's worried gaze focused on the conspirators. "I should have realized they were planning more than a joke. But I never talked to Oryon or Kress. And the others probably think it is some sort of joke. Jerrol is Oryon's roommate, so Oryon can twist him around. Fenton never takes anything seriously. Davy'd go along with Fenton. Reece and Britnor are looking to expand their power. Maybe they think this is the way to do it. But they're in over their heads." He tugged at her arm. "An explosion's coming. Let's go before things get rough."

"We can't go," she snapped. "They've done something to Mistress Dova and Headmistress."

"Just let me get you safely out of here, and I'll come back and do what I can."

"I'm not leaving. Whatever they've planned, we've got to face it." She looked around, spotted Lina pushing toward her through the crowd, and went to meet her, drawing Wilce with her.

"This is it," Lina said. "The attack they threatened. You ready?"

Tria shook her head. "I didn't expect it here in front of everybody. It'll be hard to defend ourselves. But we'll have to do whatever we can to stop them."

The dance ended. Kress and Oryon bowed low; their partners curtsied. With a flourish the women removed their masks, revealing grinning death's-heads.

# 12

## CHALLENGE

Lina's sharp intake of breath was followed by an unbelieving whisper. "Dire Women! They've summoned Dire Women!"

The catgirl's tone sounded far too admiring for Tria's liking. Tria tore her gaze from the frightful apparitions to cast a sharp glance at her roommate. Lina's face was pale as her eyes followed the movements of the dreadful women.

With a sound like the crack of a bullwhip, leathery wings unfurled from the Dire Women's bare backs. The creatures rose into the air and flapped around the room, weaving in and out among the strands of fairy lights like ugly moths, defiling the beauty that had given Tria such delight. Kress and Oryon, Davy, Jerrol, and Fenton spread out on the empty dance floor and, facing the trembling crowd, took positions at the points of an invisible pentagram. Britnor and Reece guarded the doors, allowing no one to leave.

"They've lost their minds," Wilce said, reminding Tria of his presence at her side. His voice was taut, brittle, and he seemed to be talking more to himself than to her. "I should have sensed their trickery. Maybe if I can get to them, use my gift . . ."

"No, it's too late for that." Tria clasped his hand as panic erupted. "Stay here and try to calm things down around us."

But the girls' screams grew louder, and no one, not even the faculty, seemed to know what to do.

Master San Marté backed into a corner and fanned a silk handkerchief about as though to ward off the evil.

Master Tumberlis collapsed, clutching his chest. Verin knelt beside him. She beckoned to fellow healer Salor Tribane, who had arrived with the other boys. Looking ashamed, he joined her and placed his hands over the old man's.

Mistress Dova climbed onto an artificial snowbank and shouted in an arcane tongue—probably a spell, but as far as Tria could see, it produced no effect.

Aletheia, her gaze fixed on the Dire Women, stood on tip-toe, poised as though ready to follow them into another dimension.

Master Hawke traced glowing symbols into the air with his cane. They hung like pretty ornaments, then faded slowly away with no noticeable result.

Headmistress stood as though carved in stone.

Above all the other tumult, Nubba could be heard shrieking about the Shalreg.

Tria groaned. "Don't tell me that's here, too."

She caught sight of Rehanne near the refreshment table, clinging to Gray's arm. Pulling Wilce with her, Tria struck out in that direction. The scarlet-gowned Dire Woman circled above the refreshment table. She swooped down and caught hold of Gray. Rehanne tried to pull him free, but the woman tore him from her grasp and lifted him into the air as an owl might lift a field mouse.

Above the screams of terror Tria heard the flap of wings. The silver-gowned creature dove toward Wilce.

"Oh, no, you don't!" Tria shouted, jumping in front of

E. ROSE SABIN

Wilce. She flung up her arms to ward off the Dire Woman.

Someone yelled, "Use your power, Tria!"

She could not. Now, when she most needed it, her power deserted her. Surrounded by noise and panic, she couldn't concentrate, couldn't act. A batlike wing slapped at her arms and face and, with a single powerful stroke, brushed her aside as if she had been a feather.

By the time she recovered her balance, the Dire Woman had snatched Wilce and borne him up toward the ceiling, above the reach of the crowd.

In helpless horror Tria watched the women fly back and forth. They met and hovered a wingspan apart above the center of the room. Wilce and Gray dangled limply in their grasp. Tria couldn't tell whether they were unconscious—or dead.

With every gaze fixed on them and the astonished crowd holding its collective breath, the Dire Women and their prey vanished. One instant the hideous wings flapped, the skull faces grinned maliciously; the next instant—nothing but white ceiling, empty space, and silence.

"Where did they go?" Rehanne's anguished cry shattered the stillness.

As though a spell had broken, the room filled again with noise. The five who formed the pentagram relaxed their rigid stance and moved closer together.

Lina stepped forward. As she moved, her body metamorphosed into her panther shape. She bounded toward Jerrol, the nearest of the five. With a snarl she leapt for his throat.

Kathyn ran toward Kress. Tria headed for Oryon. The room crackled and sparked with spells and counterspells as students and faculty shook off their stunned state. The simultaneous unleashing of so much power created currents and crosscurrents. Lights flashed, the room became unbearably hot, odors of sulfur and attar of roses mingled in a nauseous pastiche.

A SCHOOL FOR SORCERY

Tria's flesh crawled; her hair stood on end. Her pace slowed; she struggled as though plowing through deep mud.

Lina tumbled to the floor, restored to her human shape. Jerrol, blood pouring through the hand he clamped to his neck, stood as if dazed, then slowly crumpled.

The storm of conflicting magics gained hurricane force. It shoved Tria back, kept her from reaching Oryon.

"Hold!" Headmistress's voice cut across the confusion. "Withdraw your power."

The babble died away; the varicolored glows faded. In the lull, Kathyn's angry voice rang out. "Headmistress was right about you, Kress. She said you were weak. I didn't want to believe it. She said I had to stop letting you draw power from me, or I'd be dragged down with you. She should have told all your friends the same thing."

She stopped and looked around, as though suddenly aware of the stillness. When Kathyn turned her head, Kress slapped her cheek, the sharp blow echoing through the room. She spat on him and walked away.

Headmistress strode into the center of the room. She stopped beside Jerrol, bent down, and placed a hand on his torn neck. His breath was coming in ragged gasps, but it eased beneath Headmistress's touch, and when she stood, the gaping wound was gone. Lina, still sitting on the floor, scowled and scooted toward Tria.

Headmistress confronted the rest of the miscreants. "You will produce Wilce Riverman and Gray Becq at once."

Davy shifted from foot to foot; Fenton backed off several steps as if to distance himself from the rest; Reece wiped sweat from his face. All three looked nervously at Oryon and Kress. Britnor drew a warding sign in the air in front of him.

Kress gazed after his twin, his face flushed with anger, his fists clenched. He did not look at Headmistress, did not seem aware of her presence.

Unlike his companions, Oryon met Headmistress's gaze without flinching. He swaggered from the center of the group to place himself in front of the others, face to face with Headmistress, his lips curling in a defiant sneer. "You're more powerful than I," he said. "You bring them back."

Watching Headmistress, Tria thought she saw a nervous tic flicker across one cheek. But the woman addressed them in a firm voice. "As you know, I have the authority and the ability to strip you of your power. If you do not immediately restore Mr. Riverman and Mr. Becq, you—all of you—" she paused to strafe all the conspirators with her glare, "will be deprived of your gifts and sent home in disgrace."

At that threat, Kress wrenched his gaze from Kathyn and cast a worried glance at Oryon. Britnor's hands developed a noticeable tremor.

Oryon said smoothly with a hint of laughter, "Ah, but if you do that, we won't be able to restore Wilce and Gray, will we? You will have to find them yourself."

"And you think I cannot?"

Headmistress was sparring with him. Tria gritted her teeth. *Come on*, she thought. *Bring back Wilce and Gray, and give these criminals the punishment they deserve.*

But Headmistress said, "You are wrong if you think your cleverness will save you. Consider carefully what you do."

"I have considered." Oryon's arrogant lift of his chin made Tria seethe. "I will not do as you ask, nor will Kress."

Tria gasped at his audacity. He had to be convinced that he had no reason to fear Headmistress. As she waited for Headmistress to prove him wrong, he continued. "What was done here tonight was our work, Kress's and mine. The others, as you well know, do not have the power. They were merely assisting in what they thought would be a practical joke."

Reece nodded his head vigorously. Davy looked ill. Jerrol rubbed his healed neck and stared at the floor.

Headmistress turned to Kress. "Mr. Klemmer, do you agree to share responsibility with Mr. Brew for what has happened, and do you also absolve these others of blame?"

Kress hesitated, glanced at Oryon, cleared his throat, and said, "Yes, I do."

"So be it," Headmistress responded. "On your heads be the consequences of your actions. I ask you once more—both of you. Restore the two who were spirited away by your illicit actions."

Oryon snorted. "I reject the concept of 'illicit,' " he said. "One may do what one has the power to do, regardless of Master San Marté's babblings about ethics."

Gasps and shocked whispers rustled through the room.

Oryon raised his hand, commanding silence. "Now I will instruct *you*, mistress. I—we—will not restore Wilce and Gray. Instead, I challenge you to restore *Mr.* Becq and *Mr.* Riverman. I will grant you the generous term of one year in which to do so. If you succeed before the end of that time, Mr. Klemmer and I will accept our punishment. If you fail, Mr. Becq and Mr. Riverman will perish, and we will reorganize this school under our rules and our administration. And *you*, esteemed Headmistress, will be stripped of *your* power."

He stepped back and looked up at Headmistress, his arms crossed over his chest.

The ballroom doors swung open and Veronica walked in. Tria took note of Headmistress's reaction; she was sure relief registered in her eyes.

"We will conclude this matter in private," Headmistress announced. "All students except Mr. Brew, Mr. Klemmer, Miss

Mueller, and Miss Tesserell are dismissed to your rooms. I am sorry this special event has been ruined for you. Faculty, you will please conduct the musicians to their bus and monitor to be certain all students reach their rooms without further incident and that no one indulges in unauthorized use of power."

The faculty moved quickly to obey her. Aletheia was not with the others. Tria wondered whether she could have followed the Dire Women. Maybe she would retrieve Wilce and Gray, though Tria doubted that she had the strength

The students were slow to stir. Clearly, they wanted to see the outcome of Oryon's bold challenge. It took some time for the five faculty members, prodding and pushing, to move them through the doors. Kress's and Oryon's five companions slunk away with the rest.

Rehanne broke away from the departing crowd and ran to Headmistress. "I won't leave," she said. "Not until I know what you're going to do about Gray. I came with him, so I'm involved in this."

Headmistress frowned and shook her head, but Veronica walked up to them and lightly touched Headmistress's elbow.

Headmistress gave Veronica a swift glance and turned back to Rehanne. "Very well, if that is your wish."

Tria wondered what signal had passed between Headmistress and Veronica.

Lina stood beside Tria. "I don't like this," she whispered.

Oryon continued to regard Headmistress with a supercilious smirk, while Kress glowered at her.

Headmistress stepped back. Her gaze scanned the faces of all five students, lingered on Tria, then fastened on Oryon. "Mr. Brew, professional ethics prevent me from merely dismissing your challenge. I am obliged to address it, though I need not accept it. First, I must offer you the opportunity to revoke the challenge. If you do not, you will have no right of appeal. Upon your defeat, you will be stripped of your power and banished from this school. You will also be held legally accountable for any injury suffered by Mr. Becq and Mr. Riverman, so that you may face imprisonment for your crime. Do you understand this?"

"Of course I understand it," Oryon growled. "You're stalling."

"Not at all. I am following the code of conduct that you spurn. You have stated before witnesses your full awareness of the consequences of your action. What of Mr. Klemmer?" She fixed her gaze on Kress. "Do you also understand?"

Beads of perspiration lined Kress's upper lip. He answered too loudly, "Yes. I understand perfectly. Get on with it."

"I shall, although this unfortunate matter is not one which can be quickly resolved." Headmistress sighed and looked down at Veronica, who nodded as though another signal had been exchanged.

"Mr. Brew, I cannot accept your challenge. Although you doubt it, I have access to power much greater than yours. The contest would be most unfair."

Weak-kneed with relief, Tria waited for Headmistress to restore Wilce and Gray and wreak the promised punishment on Oryon and Kress.

She did not. She paused and said, "I shall not dismiss your challenge. I shall transfer it to Miss Mueller and Miss Tesserell. And Miss Zalos." She nodded at Rehanne. "They are your peers, and they have strong cause to desire your defeat." She looked at the three girls. "Do you accept?"

"And what will happen if we don't?" Tria demanded indignantly. "Will you abandon Wilce and Gray?"

Before Headmistress could answer, Lina said, "We accept."

Headmistress said, "I cannot bring your two friends back.

E. Rose Sabin

144

I can only punish these two who are to blame for their loss. If you wish their restoration, you must accomplish it yourselves."

So! Headmistress confirmed her lack of power. At least to some extent she *was* a fraud. Wilce and Gray were lost if Tria didn't accept this dangerous and possibly futile quest. Lina had agreed, not out of concern for the lost ones, Tria felt sure, but out of pride. Tria cared nothing for *her* pride. But she could not abandon Wilce and Gray. "I accept," she said, her voice steady.

"And you, Miss Zalos?"

Rehanne inhaled audibly. "I accept, too," she said.

# 13

## THEFT OF THE *B*REYADON

Heedless of her lovely ball dress, Tria leaned against the side of her desk and frowned at Lina. The catgirl perched on the edge of her trunk and tapped her long nails against its metal band.

"There's nothing we can do tonight," Lina stated in a flat voice. "Our power is at low ebb; we're worn out, and we have nothing here to work with."

"We can plan," Tria insisted, refusing despite her weariness to admit that Lina was right.

Lina snorted. "What kind of plans are we likely to come up with when we're both too tired to think straight?"

"I wouldn't be able to sleep. Could you?"

"Certainly. It's the logical thing to do. We're confined to our room; Rehanne can't join us, and she should be in on any plans we make. We have a whole year; we can afford one good night's sleep before we launch our attack."

"It's a search, not an attack," Tria countered. "And I can't bear to think of Wilce and Gray in the clutches of those horrid things a single night. Of course *you* don't care; Wilce means nothing to you."

Lina pushed herself away from the trunk. "That's precisely why I can think more clearly than you can." She unfastened her gown and stepped out of it, leaving the stylish green confection puddled on the floor. "You're crazy if you think the rescue is going to be so easy you can accomplish it tonight." In her underclothes she marched past Tria, sat at the dressing table, and brushed her thick, dark hair.

Tria turned and glared at Lina's mirror image. "I've got to try. I've got to do *something.*"

"Tria, think!" Lina wielded the brush vigorously as she spoke. "Oryon is clever, and he's tremendously talented. He has to be utterly sure of himself to have done what he did—challenging Headmistress, giving a whole year to find Wilce and Gray. He thinks he has a foolproof scheme. I'm betting he's wrong. He's overconfident, and whatever secret ritual he used we can discover. But I don't think it's going to be easy or that we're going to do it right away." She set her brush down and met Tria's gaze. "I'd guess it'll take weeks, maybe months. After all that time in the Dire Realms, Wilce and Gray, if they're still alive, will be changed into something you might not *want* back."

Tria shuddered. Tears welled in her eyes. "I can't let that happen. That's why I can't wait." She rose and stood behind Lina. "You know, neither Wilce nor Gray have talents that will help them fight those creatures. How can truth-reading or peace-bringing help Wilce escape Dire Women? And Gray! He only uses his power to create fleeting works of art. Maybe that's why the Dire Women chose them: they knew they couldn't fight back. Lina, we're their only hope!"

Lina sighed. "Well, I'll tell you this, if you haven't already figured it out for yourself. Kress is the weak spot in Oryon's design, as Kathyn so dramatically pointed out. I intend to work on him, find out what he knows, get him to change sides." She stood and stretched. "So you have my plan. That's all you'll get from me tonight."

In brooding silence, Tria watched her roommate finish getting ready for bed. Lina turned off the overhead light and her desk lamp, leaving only Tria's lamp lit. She snuggled under her quilt and settled on her side, her back to Tria. Minutes later her slow, deep breathing showed that she slept.

Slowly Tria removed the blue chiffon gown. Hating the sight of it, she hung it in Lina's chifforobe and put on her nightgown, lay on her bed on top of the blanket, and tried to think.

Her thoughts flew about like frightened sparrows, converging, scattering, swerving, swooping down on an idea only to flutter off in another direction.

A word popped into her mind and her errant thoughts swarmed onto it. "The *Breyadon*," she said aloud, earning a sleepy grunt from Lina.

*The mage's book*, she thought. *The verse. I have to remember the verse. If I can get back to the crystal place, the wise man will tell me what to do.*

She sat up and tried to remember the words she had repeated after Mistress Dova, whispering them, not wanting to wake Lina. "*Bororave Anthrillosor.*" She remembered clearly that first line. "*Laysa Grilden Madramor.*" She thought she had the second line right, but she wasn't sure. "*Vernee . . .*" She couldn't remember the rest of the third line. She tried several combinations of syllables, but none sounded quite right. Did it matter? Could it be that only the final line, the one she'd mixed up in class, provided the key?

She tried repeating that line. "*Reven Misi Ish Shathor.*" No, that wasn't it. "*Renev Simi Shath Ishtor.*" No, not that either. "*Vener Simi Ish Thator.*" Wrong.

She tried all the combinations she could devise. One of them must be right, but nothing happened. Each failure brought her closer to tears.

Finally, shivering with cold, sobbing from frustration and exhaustion, she crawled under her covers and huddled in sleepless misery. A single thought consoled her. *Tomorrow I'll find Mistress Dova, tell her the truth about what happened that day, and persuade her to show me the book. She'll help me; I'm sure she will.*

The day after the Midwinter Ball marked the beginning of the three-week winter holiday. More than half of the first- and second-year students left to spend the holiday at home, and four of those gave notice that because of the disaster at the ball they would not return for the second semester. The third-year students carried on as though nothing of consequence had occurred. *And why shouldn't they?* Tria thought bitterly. They would complete their studies and be graduated before the year's span of Oryon's challenge ended.

A few students remained at school throughout the holiday period—Tria, because she could not afford the trip, and Taner, because she lived too far away to make the long journey. Lina and Rehanne canceled their plans to return home. Oryon and Kress were staying, and Kathyn also decided to stay, explaining that she was too shamed by Kress's behavior to face their parents.

Some faculty members spent the vacation away from the school. When in the early morning Tria visited the faculty residence hall to arrange an appointment with her, Mistress Dova had left. Also gone were Master Hawke and Mistress Blake, the instructors Tria considered most likely to provide assistance in the search. Aletheia was not to be found, and no one seemed to know whether she had also left on vacation or had never returned after her disappearance from the ball. Tria left a message requesting an appointment with her, should the Transdimensional Studies mistress return.

Not knowing what else to do, Tria went to Headmistress. After only a few minutes' wait, she was admitted to the second-floor office. Headmistress was seated behind her cluttered desk and, as before, the sparkling gem in her ring was her most visible feature.

She spoke from the shadows. "I trust, Miss Tesserell, that you have not come to withdraw your acceptance of Mr. Brew's challenge."

Taken aback by the unwarranted suspicion, Tria spluttered an indignant denial.

Headmistress cut her short with a wave of the ringed hand. "Very well. Your loyalty to Mr. Riverman is admirable. I should not have questioned your resolve. I must tell you, however, that I can offer you no help on your quest. Much as I wish you well, I have agreed not to interfere in any way with the contest between the two factions."

Tria dug her nails into her palms to control her fury. Headmistress was making this affair sound like a sports event. "I came only for information." Tria fought to keep her voice level. "I need to know where I can find a copy of the *Breyadon*. I went this morning to ask Mistress Dova for permission to look at hers, but she had already left."

"May I ask how you expect the *Breyadon* to benefit you? You surely cannot read it."

Headmistress's cold tone fueled Tria's anger. The woman should realize that she was doing her best to save Wilce and Gray, and that if she failed, Oryon and Kress might well carry out their threat to destroy Headmistress and her school. Tria refused to confide in someone with such an insufferably arrogant attitude. "I need it," she snapped. "If you can't interfere in the contest, that's all you need to know."

"You are correct, Miss Tesserell," Headmistress said in a warmer tone. "I'm sorry that it must be this way. You have undertaken a daunting and lonely task. I once faced a similar mission; I *do* understand. But I can give you no aid. I do not own or have access to a copy of the *Breyadon*. Mistress Dova's copy is the only one I know of in this area. It is her prized possession. The original is kept in a vault beneath the Shrine of Lady Kyla at Hillcross, where the rector alone has access. You will have to await Mistress Dova's return and make your request to her."

"But she won't be back for three weeks," Tria objected, her heart sinking. "And I only want to look at the book; I won't take it anywhere. Can't you let me into her rooms? You must have a master key."

Headmistress stood and frowned down at Tria. "I have no right to allow you to enter someone else's private quarters. Nor should you request such a thing, Miss Tesserell. You and Mr. Brew are closely matched in power, but this contest is more about moral values than power. Your hope of victory rests on your maintaining the ethical advantage. I charge you to keep that truth firmly in mind."

Tria was not convinced that the good side would win, but she did not argue that point. Instead, she asked, "How can you say we're closely matched when I'm only first level and by now he's probably gone beyond second?"

"The levels are not determined solely by strength," Headmistress said. "You have achieved second level, and Mr. Brew, despite his arrogant claims, has not yet passed beyond that level."

E. ROSE SABIN

Second level! That was something. *But not enough*, Tria thought as she left Headmistress's office. *Not nearly enough.*

Tria tried to find a comfortable position on the cold, hard floor. She leaned her back against her bed's metal rim and cast a sorrowful glance at Lina's carpet, rolled up between the desks. It would have provided a bit of warmth and softer seating, but comfort had little importance. Although it might take on greater priority if they had to sit like this for several hours, as Tria feared they would. None of them had worked this spell before—Tria had never worked *any* spell—but Rehanne insisted she knew how.

The floor between their outstretched legs was covered with a thick layer of dirt, dug secretly from under the snow in the garden that afternoon and stealthily lofted to the room in buckets by Tria's and Lina's power. The other materials had been easier to acquire. The candles and porcelain bowl they'd found in the kitchen. They'd broken icicles from tree branches and melted them for rainwater. For the gemstone, Lina provided a ruby earring. Rehanne found a supply of incense in the assembly hall. The sprig of mistletoe had come from the holiday decorations in the parlor. Tria wondered whether materials gathered from such mundane sources could work, but Rehanne assured her they would.

"This spell doesn't require exotic ingredients," Rehanne said. "The key ingredient is our own breath. That and the rainwater. We'll have no problem."

The spell was Rehanne's idea, conceived when Tria explained her need for the *Breyadon* and described her unfruitful interview with Headmistress. Lina had suggested they sneak into the faculty residence hall and steal the book. But Tria reminded her of Headmistress's caution about ethics, and when Lina ridiculed the notion, Rehanne sided with Tria. But there *was* a way, Rehanne said, of getting into Mistress Dova's rooms, finding her copy of the *Breyadon*, and reading the incantation. They could perform a "spirit search," working a spell that would allow one of them to go in spirit to Mistress Dova's apartment, in that form find and read the needed spell, and then return to her own body.

Tria questioned the morality of even that type of illicit entry. But her need and the enthusiasm of Rehanne and Lina persuaded her to agree to the attempt, despite her strong mistrust of spells.

The room door was locked, the room warded. The mirror on the back of the door was covered with one of Tria's heavy plaid headscarves. A black cape of Lina's was draped over the dressing table mirror; a blanket cloaked the chifforobe mirror. Rehanne explained the importance of covering mirrors: "Mirrored reflections of the working of a spell can change its outcome, either reversing or doubling the effect."

They had spread the dirt out on the floor and smoothed it, painstakingly removing stones, pebbles, bits of sticks and leaves. Rehanne had drawn mystical runes in the cleansed sand.

The preparations took all afternoon. They had worked through the supper hour. At last, all was ready; it was time to begin.

Rehanne burned the incense, ladening the air with its cloyingly sweet smell. She lit the candle and set it in the center of the circle. Before it she placed the white porcelain bowl filled with rainwater. The ruby earring and the sprig of mistletoe lay beside the bowl.

After turning off the room lights so that the only illumination came from the candle, Rehanne began to chant. Her voice rose and fell in hypnotic rhythm.

*"Hoos Husaroo Ushiu,*
*Hoos Husaroo Avial,*
*Koosh Illom Chucanel,*
*Chitálcat, Shroocané."*

Tria's heart thudded; her hands were sweating. She rubbed them surreptitiously on her white dress. The little she knew of spells made her fear that her nervousness and qualms about ethics would hinder the magic. She tried to compose herself and blank her mind, letting the sound of the chant replace her thoughts. But a cramp in her leg defeated her attempt. She shifted her weight from one side to the other. Rehanne paused in her chanting and gave Tria a warning glance.

*I know,* Tria thought. *I'm acting like someone who never practiced meditation. I ought to be able to concentrate, especially when it's so important.*

But that was the problem. This was no mere exercise, no class experiment. This was real, and so much hinged on it. If it failed, she more than the others would be responsible for the consequences, because reading the *Breyadon* had been her idea, and she was the one too filled with impatience to await Mistress Dova's return.

She flexed her bare feet, stretched her toes, willed her leg muscles to relax. She listened to the chant.

*"Chitálcat, Chucoomakwic*
*U-lu Mucamob, Shroocané."*

The words were in one of the "hidden" languages developed by the ancient mages. Two or three of the better known languages were offered to the school's upper-level students, taught by Mistress Dova or Master Hawke, but Tria did not think Rehanne had taken such a course. It must have been part of the lore passed on to Rehanne by her gifted grandmother. Tria envied Rehanne the experience of being encouraged and trained by a family member instead of being forbidden to use

A School for Sorcery

her powers as Tria had been, even by her gifted mother.

She forced her rebellious thoughts back to the business at hand. Rehanne stopped chanting, picked up the earring, and nodded at Lina and Tria. She dipped the ruby earring into the water, touched it to Tria's forehead, then to Lina's and to her own. Next she dipped the mistletoe into the water and sprinkled it over the runes drawn in the sand as she resumed the chant.

*"Pezon Garal, Chitálcat,*
*Sa-kitok, Chucoomakwic,*
*Pes Al U-cu Mucamob*
*Pes Al Shpayalol Agab."*

When she finished speaking, she picked up the bowl and held it briefly over the candle, then set it down. At her signal Tria and Lina leaned forward together with Rehanne, and they all breathed softly onto the water, stirring it so that faint ripples played across the surface.

While Tria and Lina sat quietly, staring into the bowl, Rehanne resumed the chant.

Her gaze fixed on the water, Tria felt herself caught up in the rhythm of the chant. The room receded, leaving her suspended in emptiness, a silver haze around her, the chant sustaining her, sweeping her with it like a sail on a raft.

*"Hoos Kamé, Shroocané, Shibaltá."*

Shadows formed around her. She floated through them before they could resolve into distinct shapes. Dimly aware at first of Lina and Rehanne beside her, she lost the sense of their presence when she passed through a zone of intense cold. Although she endured the cold only a few seconds before being carried beyond it, it left her shivering, feeling she had crossed the barrier between life and death.

She no longer heard Rehanne's voice; an utter, frightful silence surrounded her. She felt stranded outside time and space in a state of nonbeing where nothing *was*, yet everything was possible. The tension of utter potentiality stretched her, expanded her like a fragile bubble.

The bubble burst. Walls, carpet, furniture, sound, smells all winked into being around her.

She stood in a small, comfortable sitting room. No light was turned on, yet she could see, as clearly as though it were day, the blue-and-violet-flowered davenport along one wall, a low davenport table of brown mahogany in front of it, the dusky rose wing rocker by the bookcase, the brass floor lamp beside it. It was a pleasant, homey room, smelling of flowers and furniture polish and old books. The faint strains of violin music came from another apartment.

Tria pulled a book from the bookcase and glanced at the flyleaf. Mistress Dova's signature erased any doubt that she had reached her destination. Tria scanned the titles of the books on the shelves but did not linger. Mistress Dova would keep the *Breyadon* in a special place, not with her other books.

Tria soon satisfied herself that the treasured volume was not in the sitting room. A short hall gave access to a study and a bedroom. Tria guessed she would find the *Breyadon* in the study.

Bookshelves lined one wall. The neat arrangement of books within it made it easy for Tria to confirm that it held many scholarly tomes but no volume of magic. A rolltop desk offered a more likely repository. It was closed and locked, but Tria found that no hindrance. Although she seemed to have a physical form, walls and other barriers did not restrict her body. Her hands could reach through the locked desktop; her vision easily passed through it to focus on the objects and papers within. To her normal vision the interior of the desk would have been pitch black, but Tria's spirit vision seemed to carry its own illumination. She discovered how to send her gaze into books and stacked papers so slowly that she could read a single page at a time, exposing Mistress Dova's fine, precise handwriting in the ledger of her personal finances, the meticulously kept journal covering the current year, and a stack of letters neatly tied with a yellow ribbon. Tria resisted the temptation to read these items. She would not pry into Mistress Dova's personal life; she was not here for that purpose and would violate the instructor's privacy no more than she must to find the object of her search.

It was not in the desk. Nor was it in the small file filled with student papers. Tria had guessed wrong about the study; she moved on to the bedroom.

The book was not on the floor under the bed, hidden by the hand-embroidered coverlet. Nor was it in the chest of drawers or the dressing table. She turned to the chifforobe, lined with fresh-scented cedar, where clothes not taken for the journey hung in orderly fashion. A shelf above them held hats; pairs of shoes lined a rack below.

A force like a strong magnet tugged at Tria. The room began to fade around her. She was being drawn back to her physical body. And she had not found the book.

"No!" she exclaimed. Resisting the pull, she jumped onto the bed, stood on tiptoe, and peered over the ornamental rim around the top of the chifforobe, an inch or so below the ceiling. In that hidden refuge Tria saw the familiar flat wooden box. Straining to remain in the room, she looked into the book. It was much thicker than she'd remembered. It seemed impossible to locate in the hundreds of pages of undecipherable script the verse she wanted. In her despair, the book, the chifforobe, the walls dimmed and swam away.

She fought the tidal pull and concentrated on the book, speaking aloud its title: "*Breyadon.*" It surged back into focus. She plunged into it, frantically scanning the first page, the second, the next, easing her spirit vision page by page through the mystical tome, searching for the remembered words.

She stopped, stared at the line. "*Bororave Anthrillosor.*" And the next line: "*Laysa Grilden Madramor.*" She had it! She reread those lines to be sure, moved on to the third: "*Vernee Shushar Okravor.*"

"Ah-ha!"

The triumphant shout halted her reading. The words blurred, disappeared. Oryon's face floated in the void above the book.

"What treasure have you led me to? How accommodating of you!" Hands appeared out of the blackness, grasped the *Breyadon*, and lifted it from its box. Book, hands, face vanished, but Oryon's mocking laughter swirled around her. Tria stared at the empty box.

That damning sight remained imprinted on her vision when she sank into her body, felt its heaviness, the hard floor beneath her, the stiffness in her legs. The smell of melting wax tickled her nostrils; the guttering candle cast lurching shadows over the horror-stricken faces of her two companions.

"Did you see him?" Tria could barely speak.

Rehanne nodded glumly and Lina snarled.

"We were with you, though you couldn't see us," Rehanne said. "Only you could hunt for the book, but we were lending our strength to your search."

"And for what?" Tria asked bitterly. "I only led Oryon to the *Breyadon*. What will he do with it? And how will I explain to Mistress Dova? I've made everything worse."

"You found the incantation you were looking for," Lina said. "Can't you use it?"

"I found it, but I never had a chance to read the last line. And if Oryon finds it and does use it . . . We've got to get the book back from him!"

A SCHOOL FOR SORCERY

Lina stood and stretched. "The book is your problem. As far as I'm concerned, we gave your plan our best try and it failed. I intend to put *my* plan into operation now. You two can do what you want, but I am going after Kress."

E. ROSE SABIN

160

# 14

## A MESSAGE FROM WILCE

Each day that passed without progress toward their goal seemed an age. It galled Tria to see Oryon strut around as though he owned the school. And Kress no longer displayed any misgivings but swaggered through the halls ordering other students out of his way or demanding favors. Tria saw no evidence of the progress Lina claimed to be making in her campaign to win Kress's allegiance. In fact, she never saw Lina and Kress together, though Lina insisted that they met often.

Tria and Rehanne spent most days in the library researching spells and rituals and reading all they could find on the learning of the ancient mages. Tria chafed at the hours wasted poring over musty volumes, pursuing tenuous leads that produced only tired eyes and short tempers.

Those days of fruitless research seemed endless, but the three weeks between semesters were passing too quickly. Mistress Dova's imminent return threw Tria into a frenzy of indecision. They had accomplished nothing toward recovering the *Breyadon*. She should confess what she had done to Mistress Dova. But it was likely that the Arcane Studies instructor would not immediately discover the loss. Anyway, Oryon, not she, was guilty of the theft. She did not have to accept responsibility. But she had led Oryon to the book, though by what means he had invaded Rehanne's spell she was unable to fathom. If she kept silent, would Mistress Dova be able to trace the missing volume? And would her divinations lead her to Oryon or to Tria?

"We have to get the book back," Tria said repeatedly to Rehanne. But neither of them could find a way. None of the numerous spells for tracing lost articles seemed to apply to their situation. Spells for recovering stolen items emphasized identifying an unknown thief; none offered help when the thief was known but the whereabouts of the stolen item was a mystery.

The girls did not think it likely that Oryon would keep the book in his room where his roommate, Jerrol, might find it. Although Jerrol had helped Oryon on the night of the ball, he had since made clear that he was not in Oryon's confidence. But as the three weeks drew to a close and nothing else occurred to them, Tria and Rehanne decided to make sure Oryon did not have the *Breyadon* in his room.

At the supper hour the boys' floor would be deserted, and the wards would not yet be set. The girls checked to be sure all the boys in residence had responded to the supper bell. They passed into the corridor and located Oryon's room. Getting into it was suspiciously easy: it was neither locked nor warded. They conducted a rapid but thorough search. The room held few hiding places. Nothing was locked; there were no mysterious packages. The dresser contained only clothes, the desks only textbooks and papers done for courses. An oak armoire held both Oryon's and Jerrol's clothes and shoes, nothing more. The room was innocent of all magical paraphernalia except for Oryon's wand, which lay on his dresser. They found nothing suspicious, nothing even faintly sinister.

E. ROSE SABIN

Tria picked up the black wand and rolled it thoughtfully across the palm of her hand. Oryon was the only person she knew who used a wand. Was it only for effect, or did it actually enhance his power? She recalled how he had focused his power through it in their duel. She hadn't planned to remove anything from the room except the *Breyadon*, had they been lucky enough to find it. But if she could weaken Oryon by taking the wand . . .

She looked up, intending to ask Rehanne's advice, but a peculiar shifting of shadows drew her gaze to the mirror hanging on the back of the closed door. Instead of her own reflection in the glass, Oryon's face peered at her. His dark eyes bored into her, warning her off. She dropped the wand. Rehanne's startled scream told Tria that she, too, saw the face in the mirror.

The image faded away. The mirror reflected only Tria's own frightened likeness, yet she stared at it until Rehanne reached past her, opened the door, and dragged her from the room, leaving the wand lying on the floor.

The corridor was empty, and they passed through it and climbed the stairs to the third floor without meeting anyone. Not that it mattered, Tria reflected bitterly. Oryon knew what they'd done.

"How does he do it?" Tria asked after they'd described their adventure to Lina. Rehanne had already declared herself mystified by the mirror trick.

Lina shook her head. "That's the wrong question. What we need to know is, where is he getting the power to do it?"

Tria sat on her bed, legs curled to her side. She stared at Lina, startled that the catgirl had pointed out what she should have seen all along. She thought back to the duel she and Oryon had fought in this room. He'd been strong and the outcome had been close, but if he'd had then the power he possessed now, he would easily have defeated her. Somehow, between that night and the time of the Winter Ball, Oryon discovered a way to increase his power. Where had he found the knowledge or acquired the added talent? If they could learn his source . . .

"Have you wheedled any information from Kress? Can you get him to tell you where Oryon got his power?"

"I'm working on it. The thing is, he's afraid of Oryon. Of course, he doesn't admit it, but it's obvious."

Rehanne, seated at Tria's desk, said, "He wasn't, before the ball."

"So he knows about Oryon's source of strength, but Oryon isn't sharing it with him." A sense of excitement welled in Tria. "He must resent that. You're right, Lina. We've got to work on Kress."

"I've said that all along," the catgirl pointed out.

"You didn't tell us why."

"I didn't have it all worked out. It was clear enough that night that Kress was letting Oryon take the lead. He wouldn't have done that if they'd been equal in power."

Tria nodded. She'd seen that but hadn't thought through the implications of it. Her anxiety over Wilce had been clouding her mind.

"Kress has the ability to draw power from others," Lina went on. "He doesn't advertise the fact, but I recognized it long ago, since it's an ability I have, too. And Kathyn pointed it out in her tirade on the night of the ball. Whatever this new power of Oryon's is, Kress ought to be able to tap into it. But he can't, that's clear."

Tria's curiosity prompted her to ask, "How does it work—drawing power?"

Lina's long-nailed finger traced a circle on her spread. She didn't speak. Tria realized she had violated a taboo in asking the question. Drawing power was a proscribed talent unless one had the power donor's permission. She recalled Master San Marté's stern lecture on the subject. Yet Tria remembered all too well how Lina had used the talent on her during her struggle with Oryon. Headmistress had known, yet had awarded Lina the same punishment as Tria. And what had Kathyn said on the night of the ball? Something about Headmistress warning her not to let Kress draw power from her. Well, if she'd let him, he'd had her permission, so that wasn't forbidden, but Headmistress had known about it.

Headmistress made a great show of demanding rigid adherence to the rules, yet she allowed so many things to go unpunished.

Rehanne broke the awkward silence by asking, "Does Oryon have that same talent?"

"No. I'm sure he doesn't." Lina's quick reply revealed her relief at being able to avoid Tria's question. "Those who have that ability can always recognize it in someone else."

"Hmmmm. I wondered," Rehanne paused, rubbed her chin, "I just thought, maybe . . . could Oryon be drawing in all Wilce's and Gray's power and using it for his own ends?"

Tria straightened, slammed her feet against the floor. "By the seven levels! If he's doing that, he'll kill them!"

Lina looked pensive. Her fingers continued to pluck at the spread. "I suppose it's possible," she conceded. "If he has access to them, wherever they are. It wouldn't explain everything, though. He had to have power before that. Power enough to summon the Dire Women and to control them. And power to develop the ability to draw power, if that's what he's doing. Because I *know* he doesn't—or didn't—have that talent."

"Could he have stumbled onto a particularly effective spell for summoning the Dire Women?" Rehanne asked. "And could they have taught him to draw power? Don't Dire Lords have that ability?"

Tria shuddered, seeing again those voluptuous forms with the death's-head faces. "They're totally evil. Anything he learned from them . . ."

"*They* draw power. Yes, that's it!" Lina bubbled with enthusiasm. "They could draw power from Wilce and Gray and share it with Oryon. And Kress couldn't draw that kind of secondhand power. So it fits."

Tria jumped to her feet. "We've got to find Wilce and Gray before he destroys them." She began to pace the narrow space between the beds.

Lina watched her, green eyes narrowed to catlike slits. "If we could find the summoning spell he used, would you dare to try it?"

The question halted Tria in midstep. "Summon the Dire Women? And risk unleashing their evil? You know that's an absolutely forbidden use of power."

"Oryon did it."

Tria backed to her bed and sat down, Lina's wry comment echoing in her brain.

"And look what happened as a result," Rehanne said indignantly. "Don't listen to her, Tria."

"What happened was exactly what Oryon wanted to happen," Lina snapped. "If he could control them, why couldn't we? You say we have to get Wilce and Gray back right away. Well, the Dire Women took them. Wouldn't it be logical to have them bring them back?"

"We don't know how to do it." Tria's expressionless voice belied her inner turmoil. "None of the classes teach spells for invoking Dire Lords or Dire Women, and if the library has any books with that kind of spell, they're locked away where students can't use them."

E. ROSE SABIN

"The *Breyadon* was locked away, and we found it."

"And led Oryon to it," Rehanne said. "We can't use that spell again. It wouldn't do us any good anyway; it only works when we know what we're looking for."

"Besides, we're only guessing about what happened. We're only guessing that Oryon found a spell for summoning the Dire Women and that they are supplying his power, that they—" Tria choked on the words, "—that they are channeling Wilce's and Gray's power to him."

"But it makes sense, doesn't it?" Lina leaned forward, eyes shining. "It gives us something to work on."

"You already *have* something to work on." Rehanne glowered at the catgirl. "You're supposed to be working on Kress."

Lina nodded briskly, ignoring Rehanne's hostile tone. "Kress has to know about the summoning. Remember, Oryon needed his help—and Jerrol's, Davy's, and the others'—to keep things under control. Until the Dire Women disappeared with Gray and Wilce. Then suddenly Oryon could act on his own; he didn't need the others anymore."

Tria nodded, recalling the scene with vivid clarity. Lina was right. Oryon's power had increased at that time. And it had been growing ever since. They couldn't possibly stop him now—unless they used the same method he had used.

Rehanne stood and thrust the desk chair aside. "I won't have anything to do with summoning Dire Women," she said. "I'll do everything else I can to help, but not that. I'm going to my room. Tria, I'll talk to you in the morning."

*Away from Lina*, was the clear implication. Tria didn't say anything, and Rehanne left.

"So?" Lina said, as the echo of Rehanne's departing steps faded in the distance. "Are you willing to try it?"

"I don't know." Tria's head hurt. Her limbs felt heavy and cold. "I—I'll have to think about it."

"You're the one who's been in such a hurry." Lina's lip curled. "All right, think about it. You'll see it's the only way."

Tria left the room early, while Lina still slept. She wanted to avoid her roommate, avoid a little longer the decision she must make. She went to the library, confirmed that the card file held no references to spells for invoking Dire Lords, and checked the table of contents in several spell books. Nothing. Yet such spells existed and were surely included in many reference works. The school was exercising censorship in keeping those books out of the hands of students. The thought made Tria angry. If she could read a summoning spell, see what it involved, it would help her make her decision. And it would not hurt simply to know how such a spell was cast. That information should be part of their education.

She'd go along with Lina to the extent of learning how to do the summoning. When she knew the process, she would decide whether to dare the attempt.

That resolved, she found Rehanne and went with her to breakfast. Several of the students who had left for the holidays had returned. Nubba was back, and Tria and Rehanne joined her rather than Lina. She treated them to a full account of her holiday, complete with inopportune appearances of the dreaded Shalreg, and thus spared them the need to discuss their problems. Tria was amazed that the ever-curious Nubba did not pepper them with questions about their activities. She could not have forgotten what had transpired on the eve of her vacation.

*Rehanne must be using her talent to suppress Nubba's curiosity. She swore she never used that talent on her friends.*

Tria did not get the chance to ask Rehanne about it. As they were finishing breakfast, Veronica approached and handed Tria a folded paper. Tria opened and read the note.

It was from Aletheia. The Transdimensional Studies instructor had returned, found Tria's request for an appointment, and would meet with her in the parlor of the faculty residence hall when Tria finished breakfast.

Tria showed the note to Rehanne and Nubba, telling Nubba that she intended to ask permission to enroll in one of Aletheia's classes. It was not a lie; she did plan to make that request, though that was not her main purpose. She asked to be excused and hurried from the dining hall, crossed the quadrangle at a run, and rushed breathlessly into the faculty residence hall.

The parlor was dimly lit and filled with overstuffed furniture upholstered in dark, unattractive colors. Seated in a heavy, high-backed armchair, Aletheia reminded Tria of a life-sized rag doll made of white cotton with white yarn hair. Her plain blue housecoat only added to the impression. A limp wave of one pale hand directed Tria to an adjoining chair.

Alarmed by the woman's pallor and apparent weakness, Tria murmured a greeting and said, "I hope you had a pleasant vacation."

With a wan smile, Aletheia said, "I haven't been on vacation. I've been in the Dire Realms trying to trace the evil creatures that invaded our Midwinter Ball and stole away our two students. I left on their heels, but the dark Dire Realm is a place of tortuous and perilous paths. I did not know I had been gone so long. When I returned last night, your note was waiting, and Headmistress told me of Mr. Brew's challenge and your acceptance. I supposed it was *that* you wanted to discuss with me."

Tria leaned forward eagerly. "Did you find them?"

Aletheia shook her head and let it fall back as though exhausted from the effort. "The evil ones were powerful and cunning and easily evaded me. I lost my way and had to

A SCHOOL FOR SORCERY

admit defeat." She paused and closed her eyes as if gathering strength to continue. Tria waited in an agony of impatience.

Finally, the pale woman spoke again. "I did find this." She reached into the pocket of her housecoat, drew out a small package wrapped in white paper and tied with gold-foil ribbon. A tag on it bore Tria's name.

Her date gift! Wilce had been snatched away without having given it to her. She'd forgotten about it.

With trembling hands she tore off the tissue paper and opened the velvet-covered box.

Resting on a bed of white satin was a gold chain with a sparkling crystal globe, about the size of a walnut. With a cry of wonder she lifted the chain from the box and cradled the crystal in the palm of her hand. Tears filled her eyes as she thought how she'd been cheated of the delight of opening this gift in Wilce's presence, of seeing his pleasure at her joy.

It occurred to her with a sudden thrill that he might have deliberately dropped the package for Aletheia to find and take to her, perhaps as a clue to help them find him.

"You must have been close to them," Tria said.

"Not close enough," the woman answered sadly. "I crossed their path many times, but I could not reach them."

The sorrow in Aletheia's voice brought an answering rush of grief to Tria. Tears spilled down her face, splashed onto her hands, onto the crystal.

The crystal warmed, reddened. Tria lifted it closer to her face, stared into it. Within it, white against the surrounding crimson glow, a parchment unrolled and tiny words appeared in smoking black letters.

*Tria,* the message said, *don't try to find me. It is too late. It will lead only to destruction.*

The words faded; the crystal cleared and cooled. Tria rubbed the tears from her eyes and looked at Aletheia.

The woman had fainted.

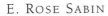E. ROSE SABIN

# 15

## VISION AND DECISION

Tria trudged to her first class of the new session, hardly believing that the normal school routine was continuing and she was following it as if nothing were amiss. The only concession to her quest was that she had been permitted to enroll in a course taught by Aletheia, usually restricted to second- or third-year students. That class would not meet during the first week; it would begin a week late because of the instructor's ill health.

Always Tria encountered delay! The whole world seemed to be throwing roadblocks in her path. She should be doing something more important than carrying an armload of books to Intermediate Ethics to endure another maddening session with Master San Marté.

"Good morning, scholars," the Ethics master greeted them with a bow. "Not many of you. Hmmm. Well, the school's enrollment has dropped a bit, you know." He twisted the ends of his mustache. "The small class will allow us to be a bit more informal and will, I'm sure, produce stimulating discussions."

To Tria's dismay, she was one of only four students. All too often it would fall her turn to be the focus of Master San Marté's attention.

She resented having been assigned to another Ethics class. Oryon and Kress were the ones who should have been placed on its roll. Of the five boys who had assisted Oryon and Kress the night of the ball, only Jerrol and Davy were consigned to share this particular purgatory. She'd heard Britnor and Fenton complaining that they'd been "stuck into" another of Old Tumbles's classes, and Reece had withdrawn from school.

Norietta, a shy second-year student Tria scarcely knew, was the fourth member of the Ethics class. She had the misfortune to be the selected target for this first lecture. While Master San Marté pranced back and forth, emphasizing points with affected gestures, pausing to reposition his sliding toupee or adjust the knot in his silk neck scarf, he directed his remarks to and kept his gaze focused on the hapless Norietta.

Tria's sympathy for the girl was diluted by her own private preoccupations. Her hand strayed to the globe hanging on its chain around her neck. As her fingers closed around it, she thought again of Wilce's message. It had not lessened her determination to push forward with her search; it only increased her impatience.

Although Lina claimed to be making progress with Kress, Tria was not certain she believed her. She resolved not to rely on the catgirl.

Tria had discovered where the books were kept that would have spells for invoking denizens of the Dire Realms. Yesterday evening she had accused the third-year student on duty in the library of having allowed Oryon to read forbidden material. Wide-eyed, the girl, Rozelle, asked Tria what she meant. "Wasn't it you," Tria asked innocently, "who let him see the special reference work on summoning spells?"

Horrified, Rozelle vehemently denied the charge.

E. ROSE SABIN

"I'm sorry," Tria said. "It must have been the other assistant."

"Nan? Impossible!" Rozelle shook her head. Her long straight hair whipped around her face. "We don't even have those books in the library. They're kept locked and under wards in Headmistress's office."

So Tria's ruse had won the information she was after, but it was of no use. She couldn't ask Headmistress for the book; Headmistress would not give it. And she certainly dare not try to steal it.

But where had Oryon found the spell? In some other source, surely. He probably had the strength now to dissolve the wards and violate the sanctity of Headmistress's office, but he got that power as a result of calling up the Dire Women. He hadn't had it before.

When the hour ended, Tria realized that she had listened to none of the lecture and didn't know the assignment. Unwilling to ask Master San Marté to repeat it, she hurried after Norietta. But the girl darted off before Tria could catch up with her, embarrassed perhaps by having been the focus of the lecture. Tria gave up her pursuit. The assignment held little importance anyway; she wondered why she was bothering to attend class. She should go back to her room and work on finding the spell book.

"I'm only saying that because next hour I have to face Mistress Dova," she confessed to herself. "Techniques of Divination is a course I need."

She had done nothing about the stolen *Breyadon* except hope that its owner had not yet missed it. She could not shake her dread that Mistress Dova would decide to use the book in her lecture, though she told herself the fear was irrational since the mage's untranslated lore had no relevance to this subject.

She regretted her decision not to skip class when Oryon

came into the room. What mistake in scheduling had put the two of them together? He took a seat and opened his notebook. Then he turned and gave Tria an arrogant wink. Her cheeks flamed. If he had not been seated between her and the exit, she would have left. She considered doing so anyway.

Too late. Mistress Dova entered and walked to the lectern. Tria avoided her gaze. Mistress Dova greeted the pupils and launched into her lecture. Tria heard it only because she was listening for any mention of the *Breyadon*, any indication of whether the instructor had discovered the theft. She took no notes; her pencil covered her paper with elaborate doodles produced with no conscious effort.

Her covert glances at Oryon showed him writing diligently, though the mocking smile that lurked at the corners of his mouth belied his apparent seriousness. Her fingers strayed often to her pendant. Stroking the faceted coolness of the globe calmed the rage that threatened to erupt when, like a model pupil, Oryon volunteered answers to Mistress Dova's questions about methods of divination in common use today, and the instructor nodded her approval.

The crystal got her through that hour and through her third class, Symbolism in Magic, taught by Master Hawke. Another course she judged unlikely to be of help in her contest with Oryon. Lina was also enrolled. Her roommate appeared to find the class interesting. To Tria it was only another hour to be endured, another useless lecture to be borne with the help of the crystal.

During the days that followed, the pendant served to keep Wilce's plight in the forefront of Tria's mind, to prevent her from lapsing into the deadly routine of classes and homework, of studying sandwiched in around work detail, of meals and breaks and petty gossip, of group study projects and Freedays with nothing to do.

These days of inactivity tortured Tria with guilt. She should be doing something, if only she knew what. On an evening when Lina was off somewhere and Tria was alone in their room, she sat at her desk, pushed her textbooks and notes aside, and divided a clean sheet of notebook paper into two columns. In column one she listed all the talents she was aware of—those of other students, of faculty members, those she had read or heard about even in wild rumors. The column stretched to the end of the page and had to be continued on the back.

In column two she listed her own talents, weighing the value of each one in her contest with Oryon. *Gathering and shaping light.* That *might* be of some use. *Making flowers bloom out of season.* No practical value in that. *Calling fish to the surface of the water.* She hesitated on that one and squeezed in beneath it, *and calling animals to me(?).* She'd remembered that once their old sow had broken through the fence and wandered onto their neighbor's property. Tria had sent out a mental call, and the animal had ambled home. It could have been a coincidence; Tria had never repeated the experiment.

*Locating buried metal.* She couldn't use that. *Causing objects to fly through the air.* That one had already proved itself. *Altering time.* She dared not use that talent. *Altering the shape of physical objects.* Helpful, but it gave her no advantage over Oryon. And that was the full list. It seemed pitifully short.

*But it isn't, really*, she thought. *Look how many students have only a single talent.* She thought of poor Gray and his wonderful, whimsical, useless art. She thought of Nubba, of whom she'd first written *sees a Shalreg*, then, remembering how Nubba alone had seen through the spell of invisibility cast by Oryon and Kress, crossed through her first notation and amended it to *special sight.*

*Invisibility!* Had that been the result of a spell or was it a talent? If a talent, it would be a valuable one. Suppose Oryon had it and was using it to spy on her?

Did she have it? How would one go about making oneself invisible? She closed her eyes and concentrated on minimizing herself. But she didn't want to shrink herself as she had Lina's trunk. She revised her mental image, visualizing the room and editing herself out of the picture. She got up and looked into the mirror.

Her image frowned back at her, mocking her failure.

She sat down at the desk and marked an **X** in column one by *invisibility*.

She looked at other items on the list. *Healing*. She had no way of testing for that talent, but surely she would know if she had it.

Many of the other talents in column one, such as Rehanne's gift of thought transfer and coercion, and Rehanne's roommate Elspeth's closely related gift of thought-reading, could not be tested without the aid of a willing partner. If necessary, she could ask Rehanne for help, but first she'd do all she could on her own.

Several items she could mark with an **X** without testing. She knew she wasn't an empath like Coral, nor could she read the future like Irel or truth-read like Wilce. And she certainly didn't have the gift of peace-bringing. Quite the opposite: she always seemed to be in the middle of conflict. If that was a gift, it was one she'd gladly lose.

And of course she could put an **X** by *windriding*. She'd put that on the list mostly in jest. No one could do it anymore, if anyone ever really could outside of her mother's tales.

*Weather-changing*. Taner had the ability to divert storms. And Tria had heard of those who could shift weather patterns to bring about any sort of change they wanted, though she herself knew no one with that power.

E. Rose Sabin

She went to the window, threw it open, and looked out. Stars played hide-and-seek through a fretwork of lacy clouds. A pleasant evening with only a light breeze and no sign of rain. She gazed at the clouds and thought, *Rain. Storm.*

Was it her imagination, or did the clouds begin to clump together and darken? She watched intently, heart pounding, repeating, "Storm. Rainstorm."

But the cold breeze held no hint of moisture, and after a while she concluded that the clouds were only drifting normally, coming together and gliding apart with no interest in bringing rain. Sighing, she shut the window, went back to the desk, and marked another **X**.

*Spellcasting.* Maybe it was true that any gifted could learn to cast spells, but Tria didn't think so. Rehanne had the talent, certainly, and probably Lina did. But Tria suspected that her own aversion to spells meant she didn't have that talent. She marked it with an **X** followed by a question mark.

*Shapechanging.* Dare she try it? Suppose she did change and couldn't change back? But that never happened to Lina. Still, Tria was afraid to attempt it alone. She left the item unmarked.

The next item, *place-shifting,* intrigued her. Davy claimed it as his gift, though she'd never seen him do it. It was the ability to change, in the blink of an eye, from one location to another within a reasonable distance. As Davy explained it, he couldn't go across the country or even across town, but he could go from one room to another or from one building to the next.

On an impulse, Tria visualized Oryon's room and pictured herself standing by his dresser where she had stood examining his wand. She concentrated, felt her power building, spreading. Her own room faded around her.

She heard a loud gasp, saw Oryon thrust back his desk chair and leap to his feet. He grabbed his wand, his expression changing from startlement to anger. But Tria could not hold her position. As Oryon lunged toward her, he vanished and her own desk reappeared in front of her. Dizzy and shaken, she sank into her chair, picked up her pencil, and in a quivering hand added *place-shifting* to column two.

Before she could use the ability again, she'd have to learn to control it. She only hoped she had frightened Oryon as much as she had scared herself.

The door opened and Lina came in. Hastily Tria thrust her paper into her desk drawer. She'd done enough experimenting for one evening.

The hope that Tria had pinned on the Paths to Other Worlds course withered after the class got under way. There were only two other members: Irel and Petra. Disregarding Tria's special need, Aletheia concentrated her attention on Irel, encouraging the withdrawn, frightened girl to speak, praising her contributions, exploring the questions she timidly raised for discussion. Ordinarily Tria would have approved of this nurturing, but desperate as Irel's need was, it did not exceed Tria's. It seemed to Tria that she and Petra might as well not attend, for all the notice Aletheia took of them. Tria began to suspect that the Transdimensional Studies mistress was deliberately ignoring her to avoid involving herself in Tria's quest.

Was no one willing to help her? Winter was dragging itself toward spring, yet she was becoming more and more frozen into a snowy waste of hopelessness, isolation, frustration, and defeat. She had no interest in her studies; her grades were mediocre at best. Her former friends avoided her, and even her conferences with Rehanne were becoming less frequent.

She plodded upstairs after supper. She'd choked down only a bite of leathery meat and a swallow or two of lumpy potatoes. The food had reverted to its former unappetizing appearance, taste, and smell; she could no longer dispel the illusion. She didn't really try; it wasn't worth the effort. Rehanne scolded her for not eating. She was becoming too thin, but her personal appearance no longer mattered. She entered her room, dreading another evening of ignoring Lina and pretending to study.

Lina wasn't in the room. Good. She settled at her desk, opened her Ethics book, tried to read. The words swam in a meaningless jumble. Her fingers toyed with the crystal. She found herself staring at it instead of at the book. It glittered in the lamplight; fire sparkled in its depths.

Something was taking form in it. Another message from Wilce? It was no parchment that became visible to her intent gaze but a small silver-clad figure. She recognized the scandalous gown, the voluptuous shape: the Dire Woman who had stolen Wilce.

Could the thing see her? Leering, the death's-head beckoned to something behind it, something that crept forward on all fours. It moved clumsily, its hind legs much longer than its forelegs. The Dire Woman rested her hand on the creature's back. Patches of pale, diseased-looking skin showed through a coat of thin brown fur. It raised its head.

Tria screamed. The beast wore Wilce's face.

The brown eyes held no recognition, only pain. A slovenly growth of whiskers failed to form a beard. The nostrils were pinched as though reacting to a foul odor. The lips parted in a grimace that exposed gnashing teeth. A trickle of saliva moistened the chin.

"Wilce!"

At her agonized cry the creature hung its head. Had he heard? He looked ashamed of his hideous transformation. *If he is, he still has human feelings. That means there's still hope.*

The vision faded. She let the crystal fall back against her breast and sat stunned, uncertain that what she'd seen was real. It could have been a cruel trick of Oryon's or a product of her own distressed imagination. As she tried to decide, the door flew open and Lina burst into the room.

"I've got it!" she announced. She whirled round to slam the door shut and lock it, then ran to Tria's side. "I know where Oryon got the summoning spell. Kress finally let it slip. I— What's wrong?"

"Never mind." Tria clutched Lina's arm. "Tell me."

Lina frowned. "I will, but . . . You look sick. Didn't eat again, I'll bet."

Tria dismissed Lina's concern with an impatient wave. "Tell me," she insisted.

"He found the spell in a book he borrowed from Master Hawke last term when he took Summoning and Expelling. And Master Hawke is scared to death somebody'll find out and blame him for everything that happened. Oryon gave it back, but Kress remembers the title. And he described the book—oversized, leather-bound, title imprinted in ornate gold script. It's called *The Perilous Art of Consorting with the Shadow Powers.*"

Tria rubbed her forehead to drive out the pain needling her head. "How will that help us? We can't ask Master Hawke for the book. He'd guess why we wanted it, and he'd never let us have it."

"Leave that to me," Lina said with a secretive smile. "I won't use Rehanne's spell, I'll tell you that much. What I want to know is, when I get it, will you dare to use it?"

Tria hesitated, thought of what she'd seen in the crystal, and was gripped by a cold fury. Why not? Oryon had dared. And all those who should be helping her defeat him had distanced themselves from her. The high moral principles they claimed had not translated into concern for Wilce and Gray. Even Rehanne seemed to have lost her zeal for the quest. Only

E. ROSE SABIN

Lina remained steadfast. And that though Tria had doubted her, questioned her methods, and impugned her motivation.

"Yes," Tria said with sudden decisiveness. "I'm with you. Get the book."

# 16

## The Summoning

Tria refrained from asking Lina about her progress in getting the book. She noted, however, that Lina had become much more animated in Master Hawke's Symbolism in Magic class, volunteering answers, taking detailed notes, asking probing questions, and often staying after class to discuss a crucial point that the rest of the class had overlooked. Once or twice Tria saw her accompany Master Hawke from the classroom wing across the quadrangle to the entrance of the faculty residence hall.

Late one evening, Lina walked into their room, announced, "I have it," and drew from beneath her jacket a large, leather-bound volume.

The book was over one hundred years old. It was not a replica like the stolen *Breyadon*. "He *loaned* you this?" Tria asked, running a cautious finger along the spine.

"Of course not. He invited me in to use his library. I'd asked him about reference works for a paper I planned to write on how water symbolism is used differently in the rituals of male and female workers of magic. It's a subject I knew would pique his interest. I told him I'd already reviewed all the material the school library had. His books aren't arranged in any particular order, so he had to go shelf by shelf looking for what I needed, and I tagged along behind while he did that. When I spotted this book, I waited until he was busy rummaging through stuff on another shelf, snitched this, and hid it under my coat."

She made it sound so easy. "He didn't have it warded or anything?"

"He probably did. I have a talisman that cancels wards." She pulled from her pocket a circlet of twisted gold wires into which five different gemstones were set, and tossed it onto the bed.

Her casual manner irritated Tria. "Why didn't you tell us you had a thing like that? We could have been using it."

Lina picked it up, held it in the palm of her hand, and regarded it with as much embarrassment as Tria had ever seen her show. "I, uh, didn't have it. I loaned it to Kress a long time ago so he could come up to this floor. That's how he got into the room the night you and Oryon had your big power duel. I didn't want to tell you that, especially since I couldn't get it back. Kress wouldn't return it. Then a couple of days ago he did."

"Kress and Oryon didn't come upstairs together that night," Tria recalled, thinking aloud, trying to make sense of this new revelation.

"Oryon didn't need it. He had his own . . . way of overcoming wards."

Lina had been about to say something else when she hesitated, Tria was sure of it. What more did she know that she had kept to herself? She glared at her roommate.

Lina pouted. "I knew if I told you about the talisman, you'd blame me more than you already did for everything that happened. I planned to tell you as soon as I got it back."

"And you got it back a couple of days ago."

E. ROSE SABIN

"We didn't need it for anything right then. You know about it now. Are we going to look at this spell book or aren't we?"

Tria regarded the book with distaste. More than ever she regretted having agreed to the summoning. If she wished to be released from her promise, this fresh evidence of Lina's untrustworthiness provided an excuse.

But if she backed out, Lina could justifiably accuse her again of doing nothing to rescue Wilce and Gray. Unsavory though her methods were, Lina had accomplished more than either Tria or Rehanne, and with Wilce's condition so critical, this was no time to quarrel with an ally.

"Let's see the book," she said.

Moving to Tria's bed, Lina opened the large tome, rested it across both their laps, and together they pored over its soft, clothlike pages. To Tria the paper had the feel of leprous skin; it smelled of dust and pestilence. Her nose wrinkled in disgust. She withdrew her hand and let Lina turn the pages.

The writing was in the common tongue, but the print was an archaic style and had faded to a dull brown, making it laborious to read. Tria felt defiled by her contact with the book; she wanted to scrub her hands, wash her clothes, and soak in the bath. She forced herself to read the spells and incantations, shuddering as she did so, feeling a revulsion that threatened to bring up the little supper she'd eaten. She was ready to slam the book shut and thrust it away from her, when Lina's forefinger stabbed the page resting on Tria's knee.

"That's it! We'll copy this, I'll return the book in the morning, and Master Hawke will never know." She lifted the volume, carried it to her desk, and got out pen and paper.

Relieved of the loathsome weight, Tria wondered whether she had only imagined the air of evil about it. Lina seemed oblivious to it. The catgirl's confidence made Tria set aside her doubts and resolve to carry out their plan.

A SCHOOL FOR SORCERY

They needed two or three days to gather the materials for the spell. Anxious to get the thing done, Tria complained about the wait, and Lina cheerfully reminded her that the weekend would be a better time than a school night when they needed to be studying. That bit of sarcasm drove Tria from the room.

Although it made her uncomfortable to talk to Rehanne and conceal the plans for the summoning, Tria sought out her friend. Rehanne needed to know what Tria had seen in her crystal. They met after lunch in Rehanne's room where they could be alone; Elspeth, Rehanne's roommate, had kitchen duty. They sat on Rehanne's bed, and as Tria described her vision, she plucked at a loose thread on the hand-embroidered coverlet.

Face pale, Rehanne stared at the crystal as though trying to glimpse a vision of her own. "It's only a piece of jewelry," she said. "How could it show you something from another plane? It had to have been some trick of Oryon's."

"It could have been," Tria admitted. "I hope it was. I don't want to think what I saw was real."

She wrapped the loose thread around her little finger. Too late she saw the widening gap in the floral pattern. "I'm sorry," she said, stripping the thread from her finger and clasping her hands tightly in her lap.

"I'm sorry," she repeated. "I *do* think it was real. If it had been a trick, wouldn't Oryon have shown me Gray as well as Wilce?"

"Why? He knows you cared about Wilce."

"But Gray was a friend. Besides, Oryon knows I'd tell you what I saw, and *you* care about Gray. I think I saw only Wilce because the crystal was his gift to me and forms a link between us."

"Have you tried to find him again in it?"

"No. I—I haven't wanted to see him like that."

Rehanne frowned. "But you should try. Maybe you could communicate with him. Let him know we're trying to help."

"I can't report much success," Tria said bitterly. "But all right, I'll try."

She held the crystal in the palm of her hand and peered into its depths. She tried to forget her surroundings, block out her awareness of Rehanne's intent gaze, and think only of Wilce, picturing him as she had seen him at the ball, not as he had been in her vision.

The crystal reddened, became like a drop of blood in her hand. No shapes appeared in that crimson sphere, but a feeling of terror mixed with unbearable grief shook Tria. She dropped the crystal and fell trembling and sobbing into Rehanne's arms. Rehanne wept, too. When their deep, sudden sorrow ebbed enough to let them draw apart and press handkerchiefs to their ravaged faces, they discovered they had missed their afternoon classes.

"What did you see?" Rehanne's voice quavered on the verge of further tears.

"Nothing," Tria said, her own voice far from steady. "But I felt—I felt what *he* must feel. Rehanne, we have to get them free. They can't wait any longer."

Rehanne nodded, and Tria nearly told her what she and Lina planned. But the words stuck in her throat as she thought of what the spell required. She would do it—she had to. But she could not confess it, even to Rehanne.

Tria's nervousness increased as the week's final day of classes wore on. Master San Marté chose that day to direct his lecture to her. She found herself arguing with him, disputing his claim that one could always determine the most ethical response to any situation. "Life is filled with ambiguities," she insisted, thinking of the unethical spell she had agreed to attempt.

"A situation seems ambiguous only because we do not perceive it clearly," he said, teetering on his tiptoes. "Ambiguities are the result of taking a limited view, of failing to see an action in its full context."

"A limited view is all a mortal *can* have," Tria objected. "Who but the gods know the full context of an action?"

At which Master San Marté harrumphed, adjusted his toupee, and moved to the next point in his lecture. And when the hour ended and the students filed out, he bestowed on Tria a final cold and hostile stare.

It was agony to sit through Mistress Dova's class, see Oryon, and try to conceal her agitation. His face wore its usual smirk. She kept asking herself, *Does he know what Lina and I are planning? Does his power let him spy on us and overhear everything we say? If it does, what will he do?*

Jittery and tense, she entered the Paths to Other Worlds class ill-prepared for the day's lecture and wondering how she would manage to sit still and look attentive for the interminable hour.

She greeted Aletheia, gave Petra a brief nod, and opened her notebook, though she knew she would take no notes.

Irel came in and walked toward her seat by the far wall. As she passed Tria, she paused and a spasm contorted her rabbity features. Aletheia greeted the girl, but Irel gave no indication of having heard. Trembling violently, she sank into her seat and put her head on her desk.

Aletheia hurried to her, rested a comforting hand on her shoulder, and bent to whisper something in her ear. Irel shook her head, shrugged off the sympathetic hand, and jumped up. She ran to Tria and shook a finger in her face. "No, no, no!" she cried in a shrill voice. With a final shrieked "No!" she turned and bolted from the room.

E. ROSE SABIN

Aletheia started after her, stopped at the door, and turned her head to call over her shoulder to her two remaining students, "I think it would be best to dismiss class today." Then she raced after Irel.

Too stunned to move, Tria stared at the empty doorway until beside her Petra asked, "Do you know what that was all about?"

Tria looked into Petra's anxious face. "I . . . maybe . . . I'm not sure."

Petra continued to hover. Unable to endure the girl's curiosity and concern, Tria jumped up and, like Irel, dashed from the room.

Badly shaken, she went upstairs and lay on her bed. Irel must have foreseen the summoning—and its results. And plainly she foresaw a disaster. She might tell Aletheia. Or Headmistress. Tria secretly hoped that she would and that someone would intervene and prevent them from performing the spell.

She could not force herself to rise from the bed and go to Master Hawke's class. Lina would wonder where she was. Also, she would face a stiff penalty for missing the class a second time in one week, but grades no longer held any importance for her.

She resolved to tell Lina about Irel and persuade her that they should abandon the attempted summoning. But Lina came bouncing in, flourishing a human skull. "Here it is," she announced, bubbling with triumph. "The last thing except for the dove. Master Hawke had it in a cabinet in his classroom. He opened the cabinet to get something else, and the skull was sitting on the shelf, grinning at me. After class I waited until everyone else left the room, picked the lock, and—behold! We're meant to do this, Tria. Look how easily we've found all the materials."

Tria said nothing.

A School for Sorcery

*　　　*　　　*

Lina had found most of what they needed for the spell, but Tria had to snare the dove. Bundled in her fleece-lined woolen jacket, hands in her pockets, she walked along the road leading away from the school. It was a clear, cold, crisp day. Sunshine glinted off patches of snow scattered over the fields. Green sprigs poked through the barren ground. Tria wished she could keep walking—away from the school, away from the responsibility thrust on her.

A dove cooed. The familiar, soothing sound froze Tria's heart. She stopped; her eyes searched the field. A brown head bobbed up and down, finding seeds hidden beneath the snow. Watching it, Tria hoped she was wrong about having this talent. But she had to try.

She gave an answering coo. Her power stretched forth, touching the dove, calming it, calling it to her. With a musical whir of its wings, it took to the air. Trustingly it landed on her outstretched hand.

She eased it beneath her jacket and hurried back to the school. She climbed the steps to the second floor, cast a guilt-laden glance at the closed door of Headmistress's office, and turned to go on to the third floor.

Veronica stood at the foot of the steps. Holding tightly to the dove through the fabric of her coat, willing it to be silent, Tria nodded a greeting and tried to go around the little maid. Veronica edged over and blocked the way.

"Excuse me, please," Tria said.

"Some things can't be excused," the maid said. "Have you forgotten the stairs?"

"I'm trying to climb them, but you're in my way."

"But you are not in mine. And I do not refer to these stairs." With that enigmatic comment, Veronica stepped aside and Tria hurried past her.

E. ROSE SABIN

*Has Veronica lost her mind? Or does she know what Lina and I are about to do?* Fear gripped her at the possibility that the maid might know what hid beneath her jacket, its small heart fluttering in terror.

Tria shivered. She and Lina wore sleeveless white smocks of light cotton, and the cold air flowing in through the open window raised chill bumps along her bare arms. As with the spell they'd done before, they sat on the wood floor, the carpet rolled up in the front of the room. This time they had spread no earth over the floor; they sat within the outline of a chalk-drawn pentagram. In the center of the pentagram, the skull rested on the round mirror taken from the back of their door. The candle set within it provided the room's only illumination, doubled by the reflection in the mirror. The light glared balefully through the empty eye sockets.

Trussed in scarlet yarn, the dove lay in front of the skull. From time to time its body twitched in a feeble attempt to escape. Its reproachful gaze burned Tria's soul. This was wrong. She should never have agreed to it, should never have gotten involved.

Lina chanted. The words were in no arcane language. Tria wished they were. She would have preferred not to understand the accursed phrases by which the Shadow Powers were invoked.

The chant grew louder. Lina's voice rose to a crescendo, dropped to an enticing whisper, fell silent. Tria sat as if paralyzed.

"Now!" Lina urged in a strident whisper.

Tria plunged her hands into the bowl of water mixed with bitter herbs. Numbed by the cold, her shaking fingers grasped the hilt of the silver knife but could not hold it. It clattered to the floor.

With an impatient grunt, Lina dipped her hands in the bowl and picked up the knife. She cut through the dove's neck with a single slash. Holding the headless corpse by the feet, she unwound the scarlet thread and let the body jerk about, spraying blood. The hot liquid splashed against Tria's icy arms. It spattered the skull, hissed in the candle flame, darkened the mirror, rained into the herb water, and pooled on the floor.

Fighting nausea and faintness, Tria gazed at the severed head, its beak open, its sightless eyes glazed over. If only she could rejoin head to body and restore the stolen life. But that was beyond her power.

The candle flame flared. A woman with a skull face took form within the circle. Her gown was as red as the blood of the dove. "I come to your bidding," she said.

"Where is he whom you stole away?" Lina demanded imperiously. "Bring him."

The death's-head bowed. Long-nailed fingers snapped.

A creature bounded out of the darkness and crouched like a dog at the woman's feet. Its hair was long and shaggy, its skin scaled, its nails taloned. Its pale blue eyes were bloodshot and unfocused. Its nose dripped, its fanged mouth slavered.

"Gray," Tria moaned and scooted back in revulsion.

"Don't move," Lina warned.

Too late. Tria's reflexive retreat erased a portion of the chalked pentagram.

The Dire Woman rose into the air and flew across that gap toward the door. The thing that had been Gray loped after her. Tria screamed and tried to grab it. Its claws raked her shoulder as it shoved past. Blood welled from the scratches and mingled with the blood of the dove.

The Dire Woman hesitated only an instant before the locked and warded door. She lifted her hands, spoke a single word, and the door swung open. She swept out into the hall.

E. Rose Sabin

Tria scrambled to her feet. "We've got to stop them."

Lina leaped past her, metamorphosing into a panther as she ran. Tria started after her, remembered the blood that spattered her thin smock, and turned back for her robe, which lay across her bed. She snatched it up, pulled it on, and yanked the sash tight, knotting it as she ran into the corridor.

Doors slammed. Girls screamed and darted in and out of rooms. The Dire Woman strode down the hall, skull head turning this way and that as though searching for something. Gray shuffled along behind her, walking on his knuckles like an ape. In panther form, belly low to the ground, emitting low snarls, Lina stalked them.

Rehanne opened her door and stepped into the hall as Gray passed. He paused and looked at her. She screamed and sagged against the wall. Lina pounced.

Yowling, hissing, scratching, biting, panther and Gray-thing rolled together on a floor soon slick with blood. Tria reached Rehanne and held her.

"Stop them! Stopthemstopthemstopthem!" Rehanne shrieked.

The Dire Woman turned and loomed over the battling creatures. She thrust her hand between them, and Tria thought she would separate them. Instead, she pulled her hand free, covered with blood, and raised it to her mouth.

"Stopthemstopthemstopthem!"

"Help!" Nubba's voice. "I need help for Irel."

"Get Headmistress!"

"DO something! Somebody DO something!"

Taner hurled herself at the Dire Woman and drove her dagger into the woman's shoulder.

The dagger shattered like glass. A flip of the creature's wing flung Taner backwards. She crashed to the floor and lay stiff and pale as a corpse. Verin crept fearfully to her side.

A SCHOOL FOR SORCERY

All this Tria heard and saw as though in a dream, a nightmare from which she could not wake. Her limbs were heavy; her strength drained. She could not summon her power.

And Lina and Gray fought on, flesh torn, bleeding heavily from gouges that exposed the bone. Again the Dire Woman touched them, smeared their blood on her hands.

"Cease!"

Oryon stood in the hallway. At his sharp command the combatants froze. The Dire Woman's hands stopped near her face. Sudden silence replaced the shrieks and pleas.

Oryon stepped forward, black wand in hand. "Take them!" The tip of his wand pointed in turn to the panther and to Gray.

The Dire Woman stooped, caught up the panther, tucked it under her arm, and caught hold of Gray with her other hand, lifted him easily, and pinned him under that arm.

The panther's face shifted to Lina's, but only for an instant. One paw became a hand, extended as if in a plea. The fingers curled, reverted to claws. Lina couldn't change. She was trapped in her panther form!

"Return from whence you came, and henceforth answer no one's call but mine," Oryon ordered.

The death's-head bowed assent. The creature turned and vanished, carrying Gray and Lina with her.

"And you, fool!" Oryon aimed his wand toward Tria. "You see how futile are your puny, ignorant attempts at thaumaturgy. Of what use was your furtive visit to my room? Your quest is doomed. Renounce it or be doomed yourself."

Tria spat at his feet.

# 17

## CLEANSING

Oryon whirled and strode to the stairs. Too shaken to speak, Tria glared at his retreating back until his descent carried him out of her sight. When she turned to the clustered onlookers, she saw several gazing after Oryon with awe and admiration. Her search for a friendly face met only pitying looks or hostile stares. Even Nubba averted her gaze when Tria tried to catch her eye.

Clearly, they all blamed her for the appearance of the Dire Woman. And Oryon's remark about her "furtive visit" to his room could only have aroused their suspicions even further. This was no time to explain her experiment with space-shifting. No one would listen.

Tria walked to where Verin knelt over Taner. "Is she? . . ." Tria couldn't finish.

Verin shook her head. "She's alive, no physical injury that I can find, but I can't bring her around. Whatever that thing did to her is beyond my power to heal."

"Maybe you can help Coral," Kathyn said, stepping in front of Tria as though she weren't there. "She's moaning and holding her head, and I can't get her to say anything."

"And Irel!" Nubba shouted. "She's having convulsions. Help her, please."

"We need another healer," Verin said as she brushed past Tria. "Somebody get Salor up here."

"What have you done?" Rehanne's horrified whisper pierced Tria's heart.

She couldn't answer. Shoulders slumped, she turned, walked to her room, and closed the door behind her. She nearly tripped over the rolled carpet. Leaning against her desk, she surveyed the bloody mess left from the spell. At the sight of the decapitated dove, she doubled over and vomited into the wastebasket.

She worked through the night cleaning the room. What else could she do? She had no way of rescuing Lina; she was powerless to confront Oryon; and she had no one to turn to for help. She expected a summons to Headmistress's office, but no message came.

Headmistress must know what happened. If her power had not shown her the events as they unfolded, by now someone would have reported the whole sordid story. Tria dreaded being reminded of Headmistress's warning that the battle could only be won by keeping to the moral high road. How many rules had she and Lina violated in performing the spell? Those infractions paled beside the enormity of having failed to save Gray and Wilce, having lost Lina, and having been indirectly responsible for Taner's injury and the mental traumas suffered by Irel, Coral, and who knew how many other sensitives.

She rubbed harder at the floor, scouring the boards to remove the stains. It was not enough, could not be enough, to spread the carpet out and hide the telltale splotches. She had to scrape away every trace of blood.

Dawn found her still at work, still unsatisfied, though no

speck of dirt or fleck of blood remained anywhere on the floor, walls, or furniture.

Soon the other students would be stirring. Knowing that the room was as clean as she could get it, she carried the bucket, mop, and scouring powder to the shower room, put them away, and spent the next hour scrubbing herself.

Forced from the shower by the shouts and complaints of those waiting their turn, she put on her robe, wrapped a towel around her sopping hair, and hurried from the washroom. No one spoke as she walked through the hall; she avoided eye contact with those she passed. One or two stepped back into their rooms as she approached.

She dressed but did not go to breakfast. When everyone else had gone, she bundled Lina's and her bed linens and her robe and carried them to the laundry room, washed them, and hung them to dry. They were not visibly soiled, but she needed everything cleansed.

She had already rinsed out her bloody smock and cut it into small strips. Rather than putting the scraps into the trash, Tria took them to the incinerator herself.

When she finished that chore, she slipped out the side door carrying a small package and hurried down the road to the field where she had caught the dove. Satisfied that no one was watching, she dug a hole with the trowel she'd brought and buried the body and head of the dove, wrapped in her best scarf.

"Forgive me," she said, and tears streamed down her cheeks as she smoothed the earth over the tiny grave.

By the time she returned to her room, the floor had dried. She spread the carpet over it and made both beds with clean sheets. She took her old pink blanket from her trunk and spread it on her bed in place of the fancier blanket and coverlet of Lina's she'd been using at her roommate's insistence. For the fourth or fifth time, she polished the round mirror, returned to its place on the back of the door.

Tria did not go to lunch. Although she was restless, she did not leave her room. She felt neither hungry nor tired. A dull ache filled her body and brain. Her ears buzzed. Her eyes were dry and scratchy. She wanted to cry but the tears no longer came.

She tried to think, to plan, but her thoughts were sluggish, freighted with defeat. She could conceive of no action that could possibly succeed. Oryon's power was growing; hers had waned. What talent did she possess that would help in this struggle? She took her list from the desk drawer and stared at it. Her ability to shape light and fire had served her well enough in her original power duel with Oryon, but what good was it in this duel of nerves and wits? She erased the question mark she'd placed after "calling animals." She'd proved she had that talent by calling the dove, an act she bitterly regretted.

Her abilities to find buried metal, to hurl small objects through the air, to alter the size and shape of larger inanimate objects all had no more value than parlor tricks. What else could she do?

She could shift time.

She recalled her discovery of that unknown talent and its disagreeable results. After Headmistress's stern lecture, Tria had vowed never to call on that power again, a vow that had been reinforced by Master San Marté's warnings in several of his lectures.

She got out her course notes from the first semester and reread the words: *Let those who have the ability to twist the dimension of time beware. The slightest manipulation can have far-*

*reaching consequences. The greater the displacement, the greater the certainty of disaster. An irresponsible time-shift could create anomalies impossible to reverse or correct. Every small adjustment, every tiny tuck in the fabric of time, must eventually be compensated for in order to maintain the stable balance of the universe. This effect must always be taken into careful account by the manipulator. I hold the firm opinion that time-twisting is a talent that should never be used.*

"But in that case," Tria wondered aloud, "why is it given to us? As a test? Or a temptation?"

If she could turn time back to the fateful night of the Midwinter Ball, she might be able to stop Oryon from carrying out his vile plot. But she couldn't be certain, and the probability of a catastrophe brought on by a time displacement of eleven weeks was too great to risk.

However, if she went back only twenty hours, to a time before the working of the spell, she could set the dove free, save Lina, reverse the injuries to Taner, Irel, and Coral, and prevent the further hurt done to Gray.

How dangerous was a time displacement of twenty hours? Would she be able to contain the damage? She needed to think, to consider carefully, but every moment's delay increased the time and therefore the danger.

If only there were someone she could go to for advice. But everyone she had turned to thus far had failed her. It was useless to waste time trying to seek out someone else. The responsibility had been thrust on her; she must make her own decision and abide by the consequences.

She cleared everything from her desk but her clock, even removed the lamp and placed it on the floor. She sat down and stared at the clock, visualizing its hands set at the time she wanted to return to. They had begun the spell at eight o'clock; she'd try for an hour before that. She took careful note of the present time: one forty-eight. Eighteen hours and forty-eight minutes to displace.

Tria concentrated on the clock face, let her eyes shift out of focus as she imagined the hands moving slowly backward. The clock face grew larger, brighter. Like a sun, it swam before her. The hands swept around it like swift, dark clouds, dizzying her. Her chair reeled, the room plunged into darkness, the world spun. She could no longer see the clock and her efforts to hold a mental image of the hands faltered.

With a thunderous crash the room righted itself.

Not her room.

A dim, diffuse light allowed her to do little more than distinguish vague shapes. She seemed to be among massive columns, some upright, some toppled and broken. In front of her, poised between two standing columns, her arms outstretched to rest a hand on each pillar, was Veronica.

"Restore the time," Veronica said. "You may not do this thing."

Tria noted the straining of the woman's arms, the perspiration studding her forehead, as though she was supporting the columns to prevent them from falling.

"Hurry!" Veronica cried.

Tria blinked. The scene vanished. Immersed in darkness, Tria tried to recapture the image of the clock. Again she experienced the sensation of floating, spinning, falling.

It grew light. The clock face took shape before her eyes, its numbers too blurred to read. She felt the chair supporting her, felt the floor beneath her feet.

The room steadied, the clock came into focus. The time read one forty-nine. She was back.

She had accomplished nothing, might have done more

harm. She had to find Veronica, talk to her, ask her how she had chanced to be in that place—wherever it was. But before she could move, someone knocked on her door.

She pushed back her chair, rose, and went on shaky legs to the door. She pulled it open. Her breath caught in her throat at the sight of Headmistress.

"May I come in?"

Tria stepped aside to let the tall woman pass.

Headmistress walked into the center of the room between the beds and looked around. Her long nose wrinkled, as if despite all the scrubbing she could smell the blood.

"Will you . . . will you sit down?" Tria scarcely knew what she was saying.

Headmistress nodded and lowered her long form onto Lina's desk chair. Tria dropped into her own chair, glad her weak knees were spared the effort of supporting her.

"You haven't been going to meals. You missed breakfast and lunch today and supper last night," Headmistress observed.

It was not the accusation Tria had expected. "I wasn't hungry," was all she could think of to say.

"And you've missed several classes recently."

"It seems pointless to go." Suddenly weary, Tria did not feel like sparring. She waited for Headmistress to speak of the true purpose of her visit.

"It is not pointless. You have already made at least one tragic mistake. You nearly made a worse one. The classes offer instruction that might prevent such mistakes."

Tria slammed her palm against the desk. "I've made mistakes because no one has given me any *practical* instruction. I've had theory up to here." Her hand drew a line across her nostrils. "Ethics, logic, symbolism, history, philosophy. What good have they done? No one teaches me how to counter

Oryon's power. No one teaches me how to deal with Dire Women. I thought Aletheia's class would help, but it's been nothing but theory. It's all a waste of time."

"I'm sorry you feel that way," Headmistress answered stiffly. "You are only a first-year student; you have been assigned to classes designed to give beginning students the foundation on which an ethical practice may be built. If practice is not undergirded by theory—"

"I know that," Tria interrupted. "Last term I understood why I was assigned those courses. But this term I'd accepted Oryon's challenge, and everyone knew it. Why wasn't I placed in classes that would help me?"

Headmistress sighed. "Your situation is, as you say, unique. No class we could offer would give you the kind of help you are asking for. You must find the resources within yourself; no one can give them to you. And, as I have pointed out before, your only advantage over Oryon is a moral one. He is motivated by selfish ambition, while you are trying to save your friends. Still, you are doomed to failure if you do not go about it in the right way. That is why the Ethics class is important. If you do not see the relevance of Mistress Dova's and Master Hawke's classes to your quest, it is because you are taking too narrow a view of the—"

Tria jumped up from her chair and shouted, "I've had all the theory I can stand! I want to get Wilce and Gray back. And Lina. You know about Lina, you must. And Oryon struts around like he already owns the place, and nobody lectures *him*. Do you think I'm not sorry for the mistakes I've made? I'm distraught about them. But how can I avoid mistakes when I know so little? How am I supposed to learn?"

Headmistress remained seated while Tria's outburst ran its course. Trembling, fists clenched, Tria waited for an answer.

Headmistress rose and moved quietly to the door. Her hand

on the knob, she paused and gazed into the mirror. Her reflection turned its eyes on Tria and said quietly, "Attend classes and listen to your instructors. Pay heed to your own inner voice. Study your opponent and discover his weaknesses. Do not accept the possibility of defeat. Cultivate patience. Do not compromise your integrity."

She turned the knob, opened the door, and glided into the hall, leaving Tria choking on the string of platitudes she'd been given instead of the help she'd begged for.

Tria dragged herself out of bed after a night of restless sleep punctuated with nightmares and dreams of ill omen. She resented Headmistress's order to attend classes, but what else could she do? She could not continue to hide in her room as she'd done yesterday. She had to confront her fellow students, had to find out how Taner, Coral, and Irel were, and whether Rehanne would continue the quest.

Tria could not renounce it. She could not turn her back on Oryon's helpless victims. She resolved to follow Headmistress's advice until she found better. She would try to find better. She intended to talk to Veronica and to request an appointment with Mistress Blake. Perhaps one of them would prove of greater help than Headmistress had.

She dressed in a dark brown wool skirt and a tan lumberjack blouse—plain clothes and dull colors to match her dark mood. When the breakfast bell rang, she waited until the hall cleared, sneaked into the dining room as Master Tumberlis was invoking the Power-Giver's blessing, and slipped into a seat at an empty table. A quick survey of the assembled students brought some relief. She caught sight first of Coral and then of Irel. So they were all right. But she couldn't find Taner, about whom she was most worried.

This breakfast was like her first at the school: the same

sense of isolation, of surrounding hostility. The same sickening effort to choke down weak, watery porridge and hard brown bread. The same haste to escape to her room. Only this time Nubba did not come to rescue her from her isolation. Alone and lonely, she trudged to her first class.

Her return was not auspicious. Master San Marté directed his lecture to her, and the students gave her no sympathy but continued to ostracize her. She tried to look attentive while her mind was elsewhere. Fortunately, the master's questions were rhetorical; he expected no answer.

A single phrase snared her wandering thoughts and snapped her attention back to the lecture: ". . . the ethical considerations to which all methods of doubling power give rise."

He paused, cleared his throat, smoothed his mustache, and launched into a new topic.

*Doubling power. What did he say about it? If only I'd listened.* She looked around, but no one was sitting near enough to permit her to read their notes.

*Doubling power. Did Master San Marté suggest how it could be done? If it was common enough to warrant a place in his lecture . . .*

Oryon had found a way, she was sure of it. His power had doubled—more than doubled—after their duel. *Maybe after class I could ask Master San Marté about power doubling. I'll have to confess I didn't listen to the lecture. He'll feel insulted, but what do I care?*

When class ended, she waited while the other students filed out, approached the master as he was gathering up his lecture notes. "Master San Marté," she began diffidently, "I wonder if you could—"

"Ah, Miss Tesserell, I wanted to talk to you. You have missed several classes lately, and that work must be made up if you are to pass the course. I've prepared a list of the assignments you missed. Please have these done by the end of the week." He pressed into her hand a sheet of paper covered with his crabbed script. "Excuse me. I have an appointment with Headmistress."

He turned and hurried from the room. Dispirited, she trailed out after him.

Dreading the confrontation with Oryon, she forced herself to enter Mistress Dova's class and take her usual seat. Again the other students shunned her, some switching desks to avoid sitting near her. Oryon, though, swaggered in and sat beside her. Her stomach lurched, and she hoped she would not disgrace herself by becoming ill. Staring straight ahead, she clasped her hands on her desk, her interlocked fingers straining not to tremble.

Mistress Dova stalked into the room and slammed her books down on her desk, making Tria jump. She glared at the students. "I have discovered a theft," she announced in a voice taut with rage.

Tria's stomach twisted. Acid filled her throat, making her cough and choke. The noise drew Mistress Dova's attention.

She fixed her angry gaze on Tria. "Many of you have seen my copy of the *Breyadon*, written by the mage Alair. It is one of only six replicas and is extremely valuable. It is also dangerous and must not be misused." Her gaze shifted back and forth between Tria and Oryon.

Oryon's response was a snort of disgust. Tria sat up straight and scarcely suppressed an exclamation of excitement. She *had* used the *Breyadon*, and it had led her to the crystal place. Perhaps the mysterious inhabitant of that place was the mage Alair. If so, he had seemed to look on her with favor.

But he had also warned her against following the wrong path. And she had done that since her visit.

She knew what she must do. Impatiently she waited for

A SCHOOL FOR SORCERY

class to end. When it did, Oryon sauntered past her, whistling. He almost seemed to be daring her to tell what she knew. She turned away from him, waited until the other students left, and went to Mistress Dova.

"I must talk to you, Mistress," she said. "I know what happened to the *Breyadon*."

Holding nothing back, she confessed all she had done.

# 18

## Doors

Tria ate her lunch alone though all the other tables were filled. She told herself she didn't mind; the isolation gave her time to think about the conversation she'd had with Mistress Dova. The Arcane Studies mistress had been more sad and hurt than angry at what Tria had done, and had charged her with the responsibility of recovering the *Breyadon*, as Tria had more or less expected. But she had been shocked to hear Mistress Dova admit she had never considered the possibility of Oryon's using magic to break the code in which the book was written. Because the mistress had devoted several years of arduous scholarship to the task of translation, it had not occurred to her that the task could be accomplished in days or weeks by someone untroubled by scruples. To Mistress Dova the illicit use of power required for a magical assault against the secrets of an ancient mage was unthinkable. When Tria convinced her that Oryon would make the attempt, she had questioned Tria about her progress and plans in her struggle with Oryon.

"Headmistress has forbidden any of the faculty to assist you in any way, you know," Mistress Dova said when Tria finished. "I can't advise you about your quest, but I can remind you that *Breyadon* means 'doors.' I have always believed that fact to be of key importance to the unraveling of its secrets. You have tried to force open doors that must remain shut. It is wiser to go through doors which are open, though you may not know what lies beyond them."

Tria had been unable to pry more than that enigmatic counsel from Mistress Dova; nevertheless, she felt great relief at having unburdened herself. Now, puzzling over what doors the instructor could have been referring to, she chewed and swallowed her food mechanically, neither tasting it nor noticing what she was eating, wanting only to empty her plate and leave.

As she exited the dining hall, Kress rose from his table and walked past her. Outside the entrance he slowed, and as she passed him, he whispered, "I have to talk to you. Don't lock your door tonight."

He hurried on, and she knew better than to pursue or call to him, but her head whirled with questions: *What does Kress want? Is it a trap, a scheme of Oryon's? Or have I been offered one of Mistress Dova's mysterious "open doors"?*

She went upstairs, intending to rest until time for her afternoon classes. But Taner's door was open, and as she passed she saw Taner kneeling beside her footlocker. So Taner, too, had recovered. On an impulse Tria stepped inside. Taner looked up.

"I'm glad to see you feeling better." Tria spoke hesitantly, uncertain how she would be received. "I—I wanted to tell you how sorry I am for bringing so much trouble on everyone. I've been terribly worried about you."

Taner sat back on her heels and lifted an unsmiling face toward Tria. "The evil from the Dire Woman burned deep within me. Because I am strong, I live. But I am not whole. I have lost the use of my power."

E. ROSE SABIN

Tria gasped. "Your power is gone?"

"Not gone. Dormant. I sense it hiding within me, but I cannot call it forth. So I am returning to my people."

Tria saw that Taner had been packing clothes into her footlocker. "You're leaving? You won't finish the year?"

Taner shook her head. "How could it benefit me? At home among my clan, I may recover what I have lost. I will go before the elders of my people and ask the right to earn a new dagger in an ordeal that may bring the healing of my power if it does not bring death. If I succeed, I may return and complete my studies. I can bring no honor upon my people by staying now."

Not knowing how to respond, Tria stood in awkward silence until Taner spoke again.

"I do not blame you, Tria. I cannot say that in your place I would not have made the same attempt. Perhaps, had you had a better partner than Lina, you might have succeeded in controlling the Dire Woman. Lina betrayed you. You should never have trusted her."

The accusation shocked Tria. "Why do you say Lina betrayed me?" She hesitated only a moment before confessing, "It was my carelessness that allowed the Dire Woman to get free. I accidentally erased part of the pentagram that would have confined her."

Taner's thick eyebrows met in a fierce frown. "Such a foolish thing, to try to bind a Dire Woman. But Lina attacked Gray, not the Dire Woman. Why?"

The question startled Tria. "Why, because he was between her and the Dire Woman. He would have defended the Dire Woman."

Taner shook her head. "I think you are wrong. You do not comprehend the ways of evil. I had just come out of the washroom, and I had a clear view of the Dire Woman and Gray and the panther. When Gray passed Rehanne and she

A SCHOOL FOR SORCERY

screamed, I think it jogged his memory. I am sure he was about to attack his keeper when the panther sprang on him. By subduing Gray, Lina may have hoped to win favor with the Dire Woman. She was hungry for power and would take it any way and anywhere she could. You are well rid of her."

"I don't think so. But even if you're right, I intend to try to rescue her as well as Gray and Wilce."

Taner set a last pile of clothes into the footlocker and slammed the lid shut. "It is too late. Forget the foolish quest. One thing you must do: kill Oryon."

"Taner, I can't kill!"

"It is the only solution."

"You cared for him once—or said you did."

"I did." Taner jumped to her feet, waving her fists. The scar on her cheek gleamed white. "He betrayed me. For that alone he deserves death."

Frightened, Tria muttered that she needed to get ready for her next class and backed into the hall.

She'd gone only a few steps when someone called her. Down the hall she saw Rehanne beckoning her. She hurried toward her friend.

Rehanne stood in the doorway of her room; she did not invite Tria inside. "I just wanted to tell you," she said in a strained voice, "after seeing what Gray has become, I won't go on with the quest. You should give it up, too. Gray and Wilce are lost, and you've only made matters worse."

The cold words stabbed Tria's heart. "What about Oryon?" The words came out in a strangled whisper. "What about his threat to take over the school? He's got to be stopped."

"Headmistress will stop him when the time comes. If she doesn't, the school isn't worth saving."

"But, Rehanne—"

"My mind is made up, Tria. I won't discuss it further." Rehanne stepped into her room and shut the door in Tria's face.

Tria walked numbly to her room.

*They are both wrong,* she told herself. *Both Taner and Re-hanne. I do have to stop Oryon, but not by killing him. And I can't give up on Wilce and Gray. I'll find a way to restore them. And Lina.*

Tria could not be sure Lina hadn't betrayed her as Taner said. But she must be rescued. No matter what she had done, she didn't deserve to be left in the hands of the Dire Women.

Tria closed the door and stood facing it, regarding her reflection in the round mirror. The face that gazed back at her she hardly recognized as her own. Pale and thin, its shadowed eyes gave evidence of the strain she'd been under. New worry lines marred the high forehead; they deepened as she frowned, remembering another image in another mirror.

Oryon's image had appeared in his mirror to mock her and Rehanne when they had searched his room. An image. A reflection. A double.

Doubled power.

Tria stared at her reflection, visualizing it as a second living self. She summoned her power, cast it outward, willed her mirrored self to absorb it. Something sucked the power from her, and at the same time her image acquired a glow, an impression of strength. The glass between them seemed to disappear, and Tria felt that if she put out her hand, she could clasp the hand of her flesh and blood double, drawn to her, perhaps, from some other dimension.

She did not test that theory. She said to her mirrored self, "Now give me *your* power." What she had sent forth she drew back. Her image paled. Power flowed into her, more than she had sent out. She took deep breaths, let the strength fill her. Whether her power had doubled she could not tell, but it had increased. It coursed through her, infusing her with energy.

A SCHOOL FOR SORCERY

Even her dull brown and tan clothes looked brighter. She smiled at her image. "Thanks, sister," she said.

She thought of the list in her desk drawer, wondering whether she could add a new talent to the second column. Not yet, she decided. She did not yet know what she had accomplished. She needed to test the strength she'd gathered, but her clock told her she had only a few minutes to reach her Paths to Other Worlds class. She could miss it again, but an inner voice urged her to attend and defer the experimenting.

"I'm sorry," she spoke to her reflection. "I wanted to try to send you to spy on Oryon. We'll do it later. Stay with me for now and lend me power."

With a new bounce in her step, she walked to class.

Aletheia looked up from the papers spread out on her lectern. "Good afternoon." She delivered the brief greeting with unusual animation. Tria returned it with answering enthusiasm.

Petra came in right after Tria and, disarmed perhaps by Tria's welcoming smile, returned the smile and sat beside her. Irel tottered in three or four minutes late and collapsed into the seat nearest the door. Alarmed by her frail appearance, Tria went to her and touched her hand. "Courage, Irel," she said.

Aletheia came and stood beside Tria. "Yes, courage, indeed. I have planned a special class today."

Irel lifted her head and gazed at Tria and at Aletheia. Her lips achieved a weak upward curve.

"That's better." Aletheia returned to the lectern.

Tria slipped back to her seat and waited with growing impatience while Aletheia riffled through papers, glanced up at the clock hanging on the wall above the blackboard, interlaced her thin fingers, and bestowed a solemn gaze on each of her three students in turn.

"I have decided that today we shall attempt a cross-dimensional excursion. How far we go and what you experience will be determined by your receptivity. And I warn you, we must all stay together, which means that we may go only where the weakest of you is capable of going. None of you must wander off on her own. Is that understood?"

Tria nodded and the others likewise gave assent. Aletheia came from behind the lectern and stretched out her hands. "Come, join hands and form a circle."

Tria rose and clasped Petra's hand; Petra took hold of Aletheia's. Irel stood, but kept her hands to her side.

"Come on, Irel." Tria stepped closer and caught hold of Irel's hand. It was cold and limp, and the fingers lay inert in hers.

Aletheia took Irel's other hand. "I will have to turn around in a moment so that I can lead you," she said. "I will release you only long enough to turn and take your hands again. Keep a firm hold and don't let go.

"Now I want you to focus on this spot." A round, dark hole the size of an eyeball formed in the air in the center of their circle. "That is the keyhole about which I have taught you. Let your power flow to it, surround it, sense it. When your powers converge, close your eyes and use your inner sight to follow the path that opens before us. But remember, stay together."

Tria concentrated on the dark spot floating at eye level between them. Aletheia's power was creating that focal point, the point of entry, but Tria understood that the instructor was leaving to her students the task of transforming that point into a door. Tria urged her power toward it, imagining a key inserting itself into a lock. The image strengthened as power poured into it from a second source. A third source joined in,

A SCHOOL FOR SORCERY

and the key began to turn, but slowly, ponderously.

With a jolt, a fourth source surrounded and infused the other three. The dark spot widened, lengthened, and became a door.

Tria closed her eyes.

At first she saw nothing. Tugs on her hands drew her forward. She sensed she was walking through that dark door, but she walked blindly, drawn along by her companions. She resisted the temptation to open her eyes, visualized a spark, and sent it flying along the line of power. It ignited in a starburst of white light as blinding as the darkness had been. Gradually it dimmed to a comfortable level, and she could see her companions, not at first in recognizable form but like stick figures made of light brighter than the illumination around them. They moved through a round tunnel, with pearlescent walls that resembled a kind of membrane, pulsating slightly, like the vessels of a living creature. As Tria's inner vision grew clearer, the tunnel walls acquired translucency, and through them she saw mysterious, shifting shapes that gave her the impression of huge beasts lumbering about.

They continued, passing areas where the walls became transparent, giving Tria glimpses of weird and indescribable vistas: the first, a golden ocean hanging upside down over carnelian latticework through which and over which clambered an assortment of many-limbed creatures like nothing Tria had ever seen. Some were furred, some scaled, some winged. Some had long, twisting necks with heads like snakes; others were balls with legs sticking out all over them but with no head that Tria could see. Waves lapped the surface of the overhead ocean, and silver shapes erupted from these, flew in graceful curves, and returned with a plop that sent a shower of golden spray raining down on the creatures in the lattice. The ocean dwellers were not fish; they were two-dimensional geometrical figures: triangles, squares, rectangles, circles, and trapezoids. Fascinated, Tria stared until the wall-membrane thickened and became opaque.

Another area of transparency showed a view of what she took to be forested mountains beneath a rosy sky, until the mountains straightened their humped backs and hobbled about like crippled old men, changing places, winding in and out among each other before settling down into a new configuration, while the sky changed hue from rose to orange to beige to bright yellow.

With a pulsing motion, the tunnel wall became opaque.

The next time the walls cleared, Tria gasped at the sight of a large crystal sphere rising from a barren plain. The sphere sparkled and shimmered; rainbows danced over its sides. Tria felt drawn to it, sure it was the place she had visited by the power of the *Breyadon.* But she could spot no way to get out to it and no door or other opening was visible in its faceted surface. Aletheia hurried onward, pulling Tria away from the tantalizing sight.

The tunnel branched. Aletheia led them to the right, but as Tria glanced into the left-hand tunnel, a black panther streaked across it. A moment later she heard the cry of a large cat.

Lina! Could it be?

She had to know. Swiftly she pulled her hands together and clasped Petra's hand around Irel's, freeing herself from the circle. The others marched on. Turning, she raced back to the fork and started into the other tunnel.

The light was much dimmer here, the walls completely opaque. As she ran forward, she became aware of sounds, soft at first but growing louder as she moved farther into the tunnel. Some might have come from human throats; others assuredly did not. Mingled with wails, sighs, sobs, shrieks, moans, and hisses, she distinguished the yowl of the panther.

A SCHOOL FOR SORCERY

She must be nearing the region from which the Dire Women had come. If she found Lina, she would also find Wilce and Gray. Excited, she sped faster.

The shimmer across the path in front of her seemed insubstantial until she crashed into it and was hurled backward by the force of the unexpected collision. She picked herself up and limped to the shimmer. She could see through it as through a faint haze. She probed it with her hand. It seemed a mere trick of light, yet to the touch it was as solid as a brick wall. Her careful exploration found no way around it.

While she looked for a way to breach it, a panther bounded into view on the other side of the barrier and loped toward her. Sleek and shiny-coated, it rose on its hind legs and clawed at the impregnable curtain of light.

"Lina?"

At Tria's question, the animal showed its sharp teeth; its tail twitched. It lunged at Tria with a ferocity that made her glad for the protection of the mysterious wall. Its attack frustrated, the cat sat back on its haunches, ears cocked, tail swishing back and forth.

"Lina?" Tria asked again. "Is it you? Do you remember who you are?"

The ears flattened. The animal crouched as if for a spring. Its slitted eyes radiated rage.

"You do remember. I'm sure you do," Tria persisted. "You must change back. Try. Try now."

The panther rose, flicked its tail at Tria, and stalked away. Uselessly she called after it until it disappeared around a bend in the tunnel.

Tria became aware of an ominous stillness; the hideous noises had ceased. A charnel stench poured over her, making her gag. She whirled around.

The thing that stood behind her had the appearance of a

E. Rose Sabin

ravaged corpse wrapped in a decaying shroud. Its eyes were sunken deep within their sockets, its face half eaten away; its blackened flesh hung loose in places, revealing diseased bone. But it lived. It moved. It groped for her.

Her back pressed against the barrier that cut off her only means of escape.

The living corpse's lipless mouth was a jagged hole. Within the hole a swollen tongue moved. A croaking sound issued forth, repeated. With difficulty, Tria recognized the sound as human speech. "Help me," the thing said.

"Who—who are you?" Scarcely able to breathe, Tria gasped the words.

"Oryon," the thing croaked. "I was Oryon."

A skeletal hand plucked at her sleeve. She tore free, shoved the thing away, and vaulted past it. She heard it blundering behind her, moaning piteously. She raced away until she could no longer smell the odor of putrefaction. Slowing, stopping, she looked around her.

She was alone in the tunnel. Unless she could find Aletheia and the others, she would never find her way out of this dreadful place.

# 19

## REFLECTIONS

Turning and seeing the passageway empty, Tria slowly started to retrace her steps along the first tunnel. She had to find the door Aletheia had made, had to get out.

But without Aletheia the door might not be there. She hesitated, trying to think. It might be better to go back to the window through which she'd seen the crystal sphere and try to find a way out to it.

No. She turned again. She'd go in the direction she'd last seen Aletheia, Petra, and Irel, and hope she could catch up to them.

But that would require traveling an unfamiliar path, and if it branched she would have no idea which direction to take. She stood still, hugging herself, trying to tell herself that her trembling was from the chill of these tunnels.

Was that a step behind her?

She whirled around, saw nothing, heard nothing but the drumming of her own heart.

Finally she walked forward. Better to hunt for an exit in the tunnel she knew than to chance unknown ways alone.

Aletheia and the others must be searching for her. They'd

find her any minute. They had to—before that nauseous thing that had named itself Oryon found her again.

Casting frequent glances behind her, she hurried along the way she thought the four of them had come. The tunnel was the same everywhere; the only identifying features were the scenes visible through the transparent sections. To Tria's dismay she recognized none of those she passed.

One "window" revealed a field of unblemished snow spreading outward from a blue-white glacier so bright with reflected sunlight that it hurt her eyes to look at it. She *knew* she had not seen it before. Other scenes were equally unfamiliar. She must have taken a wrong turn, but how? She had separated from her companions at the only fork they had passed.

She stopped at the next transparent section and stared at water that poured from an unseen sky, but did not fall straight down. Instead, its separate streams twisted, braided, looped around each other, and finally splashed onto a shiny flat surface resembling steel. On striking that surface, it fountained upward again in even more intricate patterns. Tria stared in fascination.

Several minutes passed. The scene blurred and disappeared, a different section of wall cleared, and a new scene appeared in it a short distance beyond where she stood. *No wonder none of the scenes look familiar,* she thought. *These windows shift around all the time. I'll never find the crystal sphere.*

The new window revealed a pit filled with a fleet of huge machines moving on treads and equipped with giant jaws that bit into the earth and devoured dirt and rock, so that as she watched, the pit deepened and widened beyond the limits of her viewing space.

With a shudder she turned away, feeling that machines like those in the pit were digging at her brain.

E. Rose Sabin

Aletheia *had* to come back for her! She squeezed her eyes more tightly shut and sent her power questing for them. It found nothing, but the attempt reminded her that all this time she'd been using her inner vision; her eyes had been closed since she'd passed through Aletheia's door. Aletheia had insisted on the necessity of relying on inner vision in traversing the paths to other worlds, but Tria could not recall being told what would happen if she tried using normal sight. Maybe if she opened them, this whole nightmare scene would vanish, and she'd be back in the classroom.

Her eyelids resisted her attempt to raise them; she used her fingers to pry them up. Her opened eyes refused to focus and take over their normal task. They provided no sight beyond a vague gray blur. Of only one thing was she certain—she was not in Aletheia's classroom.

After trying in vain to clear her vision, she closed her eyes again. The inner vision was gone; she saw only darkness. With neither inner nor normal vision, she was blinded and helpless.

*Mustn't panic. Think! Got to think!*

She thought of her earlier success at using her mirror image to increase her power. She wasn't sure now whether her power had truly increased or her active imagination had only made it seem so. But not knowing what else to do, she tried once more to call up the reflected power.

Eyes closed, she visualized the mirror hanging on the back of her door. When she could see it before her, she bade her reflection appear in it.

Wavery and indistinct at first, the reflection grew clearer. She saw herself positioned before the mirror, behind her the two desks, hers and Lina's, and behind the desks, the beds. The window was open, as she had left it, the green curtain blowing in the breeze. The wind riffled the pages of the book she'd left lying on her trunk beneath the window. It was so vivid, so real that Tria's eyes popped open. The scene remained before her. Her reflected self faced her with a wide-eyed stare and lifted her arms as Tria raised *hers*. They reached toward each other.

Tria's outstretched hands encountered cold glass. She let her arms fall to her side. Her mirror image duplicated the gesture. Tria turned her head. From the corner of her eye she saw her image do the same.

But unlike the reflection in the mirror, Tria saw no familiar room around her. Her wandering gaze met only darkness. The mirror alone held light. With a jolt the terrifying realization hit her: *she* was the reflection within the mirror. The room she saw through the glass was not reflection but reality.

But the girl in that room couldn't be real. *She* was the real Tria—wasn't she?

Footsteps behind her sent her whirling around. The other Tria had been alone in her room.

The putrid smell more than the dimly seen form identified the shrouded specter that called itself Oryon. "Now," the ghastly voice croaked, "now you begin to understand."

Tria turned away from the mirror feeling oddly diminished. Again she wished she'd heard all of Master San Marté's lecture. Gazing at her reflection this time might have returned the power she'd taken before. Aletheia had warned them that the trek through the interdimensional pathways could leave them tired and weak. Probably that was all that was wrong.

She slipped out of her skirt and blouse, hung them in the chifforobe, and put on her old blue robe. Sitting on her bed, she massaged her temples, recalling how the strength gained from her mirror image had drained away in the tunnels between the worlds.

The drain had not been gradual; it had occurred without

warning. They had passed a fork in the tunnel, and Tria had wondered how Aletheia knew which way to take. Suddenly she found herself drawing her hands together and leaning forward onto the clasped hands of Petra and Irel. They kept moving, though at a slower pace, and gradually Tria was able to let her arms relax and walk on without the support of the others. The weakness eased, and Tria again took note of her surroundings, fascinated by the scenes revealed through the transparent wall sections. When Aletheia stopped at one of these, the incident passed from Tria's mind.

She lay back on the bed and wrapped her blanket around her to ward off the chill in the room. Her thoughts turned to Irel. Had the girl known what Aletheia planned? Tria had certainly never suspected, and she was sure that Petra hadn't, either.

Compared to the other scenes they'd passed, the one at which they stopped looked surprisingly ordinary. They looked at a garden filled with familiar plants and flowers, with graveled paths winding through it and red-tiled roofs visible beyond it. An older man and woman strolled down a path and paused by a small fountain.

Aletheia released Petra's hand and, reaching forward, drew the tunnel wall aside as if it were a curtain. Tria heard birdsong and the tinkle of the fountain; she smelled the fragrance of the flowers.

"Petra and Tria, wait here," Aletheia said and drew Irel with her into the garden. The "curtain" closed behind them, shutting off the sounds and smells.

The man and woman looked up as Aletheia and Irel approached and greeted them with welcoming smiles. Tria wished she could hear their conversation. After a few minutes, Aletheia placed Irel's hand into the woman's. The man and woman walked away, taking Irel with them. Aletheia watched them go, then stepped backward to the window and passed through it, rejoining Petra and Tria.

"We must go back," she said. "Irel will stay here. She could not endure our world. Where I've left her she can be happy. Time moves in the opposite direction in that world: our past is its future and our future its past. Irel's foreseeing will be nothing more than remembering, and memories, even sad ones, cannot cause the pain that foreknowledge brings."

Taking their hands, she led them away from the pleasant garden and back the way they had come. The return seemed to take much less time; in only three or four minutes they stepped through the gate into their familiar classroom.

But perhaps it had taken longer than Tria had thought. The bell rang to end the class period at the same moment that Aletheia dissolved the door. Aletheia dismissed them with the warning that they would feel tired and shaky and should rest until time for supper. She promised to devote tomorrow's class to a discussion of their experiences.

Thinking about all the questions she wanted to ask Aletheia in that discussion, Tria drifted off to sleep.

A soft but insistent tapping on her door awakened her. The room was dark; she rose, found her way to her desk, and fumbled for the light, turned it on, and looked at her clock.

She blinked and looked again. It was ten at night. She had slept through supper and most of the evening. No one should be knocking at such a late hour.

She shrugged out of her robe and grabbed the first thing she saw in the chifforobe, a dark red dress that was too large for her, with the weight she'd lost. She slipped it on anyway and went to the door. She barely had it open when Kress slipped inside and slammed it shut behind him.

"What took you so long?" he asked, clasping a paper-wrapped bundle in front of him. "If Oryon catches me . . ."

He shuddered and thrust the bundle at her. "Take this."

She guessed what it was before she tore it open and saw the *Breyadon*.

"How did you—?"

"Stole it." He was breathing hard; his face was pale, his hands shaking. He walked to Lina's desk and sat on its edge. "He's got too much power already. He doesn't need what he says this will give him. He's ready to use it. I couldn't let him. He's not—he's not sane anymore."

Tria frowned. She didn't trust Kress, though his fear seemed genuine. "Why bring it to me? Why not take it back to Mistress Dova?"

"I'll need protection when Oryon finds out what I've done. I'm not sure Mistress Dova would—or could—protect me from him."

"And you think I can?"

"If anybody can. Lina said you had more power than anybody she'd ever known, but you were afraid to use it. She said you'd find a way to defeat Oryon. She was willing to bet her life on it."

Tria stared at Kress in stunned disbelief. He *had* to be lying. Lina would not have said such a thing.

Would she?

"You can't believe that," she stammered when she'd found her voice. "Not after what happened to Lina. If she really did bet on me, she lost."

Kress rubbed his chin, drawing Tria's attention to its covering of blond stubble. He might be trying to grow a beard, but his haggard face and haunted eyes suggested that he was merely too frightened and dispirited to attend to his personal grooming.

"You're trying to get her back." It was a statement, not a question.

A SCHOOL FOR SORCERY

She'd done absolutely nothing to merit his confidence. More than ever, she distrusted him.

"How did you get past the wards on the stairs?" she asked. "You gave Lina's talisman back to her."

He shrugged. "There are other ways." But he couldn't meet her eyes.

Oryon could break the wards without the talisman, Lina had said. Kress couldn't.

Oryon must have sent Kress here with the *Breyadon*. That could only mean that he had all he wanted from it. And was using it to set a trap for her. A trap that required her to be holding the book when it was sprung.

She tossed the book past Kress onto Lina's bed. As it landed, a yellow light burst from it and spread out, forming a large amber globe. Tria shrank back against the door. Kress let out a yelp of terror and tried to push away from the desk. The globe engulfed all but his left arm and left leg from the knee down before its expansion stopped and it solidified into an opaque resinous substance. Kress's hand clenched, opened, clenched again. His foot twitched.

It wouldn't take Oryon long to discover that his trap had caught the wrong victim. She had only seconds, surely, before he came to check. She had to be ready.

She turned toward the door, saw her frightened face reflected in the mirror. Doubled power.

But she'd need it more than doubled. She swung the vanity around so its mirror caught and repeated the reflection in the door mirror. She tugged at Lina's heavy chifforobe but couldn't budge it; she'd have to do without its mirror. Two would have to be enough.

Positioning herself between the two mirrors so that her image was repeated in each, she summoned her power, spread it outward, drew it back, hurled it forth again, farther, deeper, sharing power with her imaged twins, drawing their power back into herself until she was bursting with it, and the reflected Trias were pale, wavering phantoms.

The mirror in front of her moved, dispelling the clearest remaining image. The door opened. Like a black shadow, Oryon stepped into the room.

"Here's the real one," he said, holding up the *Breyadon*. "I assume you still want it."

# 20

## ALLIANCE

Oryon's dark presence eclipsed the mirrors. Tria faced him alone. His haughty gaze took in the angled vanity mirror, the amber globe with its hapless victim. If he was surprised or disappointed to see his trap closed on his fellow conspirator instead of on Tria, he concealed the emotions well. Although the globe took up much of the room and Kress's limbs dangled pitiably from it, Oryon dismissed it with a casual glance.

He nodded at the mirrors. "I see you finally discovered the first of my little secrets. Far too late, of course, to do you any good."

Tria did not answer. She kept a wary eye on the *Breyadon*, fearing another trap. But Oryon clasped the book against his black shirt. He was not carrying his wand.

"Still," he continued, "it was clever of you to work it out. Clever of you to evade that, too." With a nod of his head he indicated the amber globe.

Tria's anger mounted, pushing her fear into the background. "What about Kress?" she snapped. "He wasn't clever. Aren't you going to get him out of that thing before it kills him?"

A nonchalant shrug showed his lack of concern for his erstwhile partner. "He was careless. Stupid. He knew the danger. I can't get him out."

"That's all? 'I can't get him out'? All your vaunted power, and you can't get your friend out of the trap *you* created?"

"Not a friend, really. An ally, while I needed him."

"And now you don't need him anymore, so you toss him away like a piece of garbage! Oryon, you are despicable."

"Oh, it's not that bad. He isn't dead. Let's see, maybe there *is* something I can do." He walked to the globe and, holding the *Breyadon* with one arm, used a finger of his other hand to probe the surface near Kress's leg. "Hmmm. Solid, but . . ." He pushed against the border between globe and flesh and mumbled a few words in a mage tongue.

Cautiously Tria moved closer to watch. She was alarmed to see that Kress's hand had grown blue. Abruptly both arm and leg slid into the globe, and the amber surface closed over them.

"That should make him more comfortable," Oryon announced, turning back to Tria.

She stared at the smooth surface. "Can he breathe? Or do you care?"

"I don't know. Forget about him. Or get him out yourself." He sat on Lina's desk chair and settled back comfortably, resting the *Breyadon* on his lap.

Tria curled tendrils of power around the globe and tried first to squeeze it then to pry it apart, while Oryon watched the useless efforts with amusement. She increased the power, knowing that by doing so she was making herself vulnerable.

She suspected that Oryon's plan was to goad her into expending her power and attack when she became weak. But she could not ignore Kress's plight. He had brought it on himself, but he did not deserve to die because of his own foolishness and Oryon's cruelty. She redoubled her efforts.

With a loud crack the globe shattered and crumbled into tiny fragments that fell as a rain of yellow dust. Nothing else. Kress was gone, along with Lina's bed and desk, transformed into motes of dust or transported to another place. Oryon threw back his head and laughed.

She whirled on him. "Where is he? What have you done?"

"Whoa!" Still laughing, Oryon held up his hands as though to ward her off. "Merely a small conjuring trick. Nothing to get excited over."

"Bring him back. The furniture, too." She raised her own hands curved into claws, ready to hurl herself on him and tear at his face.

A snap of his fingers sent her flying backward to land with a painful thump in the other desk chair. "I don't take orders, I give them," he thundered. "Listen to me."

Pinned to the chair, she could do nothing but glare at him. She'd guessed right; she had squandered her energy on the globe and left herself helpless.

"I've decoded the *Breyadon*." He held the book upright so that she could read its title. "The scholars were either fools or pitifully lacking in power."

"You know the reason. They're too ethical to use your methods."

Oryon shrugged. "As I said, fools. Their stupid ethics brought them only wasted years. But I shouldn't complain. The book's secrets have opened to me, and I intend to use them in ways those weak-livered professors wouldn't dare."

*Keep him talking*, Tria told herself. *Stall him while you try to recover some power.*

"Have you forgotten Mistress Dova's warning?"

"That skittish old maid." Oryon spat. "She's had this treasure for years, and what has she done with it? Let it gather dust. I owe you thanks for leading me to it and inspiring me to liberate it."

He grinned. "In fact, I'm so grateful, I'm going to offer you a deal. I'm willing to let you form an alliance with me."

Tria choked back a cry of rage and indignation. She could feel her power seeping back, sluggish and slow like cold syrup. If she could let him talk, keep him distracted, she might recover enough to launch an unexpected blow. "What kind of alliance?" she asked.

He patted the book. "When I use this, it will unleash tremendous force. That force will need to be contained, shaped, directed. I'd intended to have Kress help, but I concluded he lacked the strength. You, though—you could do it. But you'd have to follow instructions, do exactly what I tell you."

"Why should I do that?" Sitting quietly, Tria asked it in a reasonable tone, as though she really wanted to know. Let him think she was interested while her power continued to build. It was coming faster. Soon . . .

"For what I'm willing to give you in return." His eyes played over her, measuring, testing. "You could be the new Headmistress here. This could be a school that really teaches the use of power; no more of the ridiculous Logic and Ethics courses. The emphasis would be on practice, not endless theory."

"What about Wilce and Gray? Will you restore them?"

"I'll bring them back, if you really want them. You can keep them as pets."

"Why don't you bring them now? If you really want my help, it would be evidence of your good faith."

He shook his head. "Not until we have an agreement. Not until after you've done what I ask."

E. ROSE SABIN

"Show them to me, at least. Prove that you can do what you say."

He frowned. "It's not necessary. You've seen them. You know what they've become. Maybe, after we unleash the *Breyadon's* power, they can be restored. Now . . . no."

"Then bring Lina back. If you do that, I'll consider your offer." She held her breath, aware of the chance she was taking.

He rubbed his hands over the *Breyadon's* leather cover. "I don't think you appreciate the opportunity I'm offering you. If you did, you wouldn't try to bargain."

"I know what power the *Breyadon* holds," Tria said. "What I *don't* know is whether I can trust you to keep your word after I've helped you gain that power. I'm asking you to give me a token of your good faith."

*Good faith!* Could he possibly think she meant those words? But he seemed unaware of her sarcasm.

"Token," he mused, stroking his chin. "Token, hmm?"

He stood, tucked the *Breyadon* under his arm, and walked to the center of the room. Facing the empty space where the bed and desk had been, he threw his head back and gazed upward, traced a mystic symbol in the air, and spoke a word of power.

With a loud crash the bed materialized amid a cloud of yellow dust. A second pass of his hand and the speaking of another word brought the desk jolting back into its place. "There!" he said. "Those are tokens enough."

Tria jumped to her feet. "No," she cried. "The furniture means nothing. Bring Lina if you want me to trust you."

His eyes narrowed; he regarded her speculatively. Too late she realized that by leaving her seat she had revealed her returning power.

But Oryon nodded. "All right. Remember, you've given your word."

A SCHOOL FOR SORCERY

He adjusted his grip on the *Breyadon* and with his other hand again drew symbols in the air. This time a fiery glow outlined their twisted configurations. In a low voice he spoke several words unintelligible to Tria. Finally, he clapped his hand against the hand that held the book.

A panther fell snarling and spitting onto the floor in front of him. It jumped up, looked around, and with a terrified yowl leaped through the open window.

Horrified, Tria dashed to the window and looked out. Barely visible on the ground three floors below, a dark form staggered to its four feet, shook its head as if dazed, and limped off into the darkness.

Tria spun toward Oryon. "What have you done?"

"Exactly what you asked me to do," he said. "Now it's time for you to do what I asked."

"Never!" Tria drove her power at him, flinging him back against the bed, knocking the *Breyadon* from his grasp. She caught up the book and bounded past him, yanked open the door, and dashed into the hall. He raged after her.

In her panic she turned toward the washroom instead of the stairs. Hugging the book to her breast, she strove to outdistance the footsteps pounding behind her. As close as he was, she had no hope of escaping. He'd see her duck into any of the rooms.

*Use the stairs.* The thought came to her as distinct as a voice—Veronica's voice.

It rose before her, a wide stairway illuminated by glowing silver risers. Without hesitation she surged up the steps. The footsteps did not follow. She heard them clatter on down the hall and stop. As she ascended, she heard as from a great distance Oryon's puzzled outcry.

She reached the top of the stairs. A long hall stretched before her, lit by candles flickering in wall receptacles. No doors opened off it. In wonder and fear she started down it.

The hubbub that had arisen in the hall after Oryon's abrupt exit faded away. Doors that had opened closed again. The late night quiet returned.

Oryon must have used his power to slip away unnoticed. If he had remained anywhere on the girls' floor, Tria could have sensed his presence. She was sure of it. Relieved, she slipped from the shadows and shut the door. She crossed to the window and looked out. No sign of Lina. She hadn't expected to see any. A black panther would find it easy to hide in the night. She would have to search for her, but she'd wait for daylight.

She pulled the window closed and shuffled over to her bed, sneezing as she scuffed through the yellow dust. Tomorrow she'd clean; tonight she could do nothing. She felt tired, weak, a shadow of herself. Maybe a good night's sleep would restore her energy. She took off the dusty red dress, put on her nightgown, and climbed into bed.

The way between the worlds was a desolate, lonely place. The tantalizing views of other worlds no longer fascinated but rather tormented Tria because she could find no way to reach them. She stopped looking at them, and it seemed that they appeared less often and for briefer periods. The tunnel walls remained mostly opaque with only a rare, quick glimpse of the worlds beyond. Needing more color than those brief flashes provided, she wished she'd worn something bright and colorful to Aletheia's class. The gloom was oppressive, and her brown clothing offered no respite.

When again she heard steps behind her, she was not so

quick to run. She turned, looked, and backed away so slowly that the hideous apparition came closer.

"I am Oryon," it said. "Or at least, I am a part of him, a fragment of reality. And you are only a part of Tria, fashioned from her reflection and given a modicum of life by her power."

"No!" she screamed at it, and then she did run away.

But in her subsequent wanderings she caught an occasional glimpse of a gleam as of light reflecting off glass and beyond it a distant figure moving away. She could not be sure in the dim light—did not want to be sure—but the figure seemed to be her own.

She wanted to reject the possibility it was her real self she saw, but the unreality of her present existence forced her to consider that she might be only a flawed duplicate. Lost in this complex of tunnels, suspended in timelessness—what could this be but a dream state, an illusion? And she was no more than a part of that illusion.

She ran from the thought, tore at the tunnel walls with her nails, kicked at them, shouted, screamed. She pinched and poked herself to wake herself from the dream. Useless, all of it. The walls were impervious to her attacks, no one responded to her screams, and there was no waking from the nightmare in which she was caught.

She was going mad. Had gone mad. That was it! She was lost in some quirk of her own disordered mind. She had to find her way back to sanity.

What she needed was contact with another human being. But the only other inhabitant of this nonworld was the thing that called itself Oryon, and he could be nothing more than a figment of her fevered imagination. Still, the company of another being, even one of such ghastly appearance and noxious odor, was better than the terrible isolation. She even sus-

E. ROSE SABIN

pected that she might be degenerating into a similar creature herself.

If she talked to him—at a safe distance, of course—she might learn more about him and thus about herself. She sat cross-legged on the tunnel floor, hugged the brown wool skirt close around her knees for the warmth it offered, and waited until he found her.

He hunkered down beside her. She scooted away and held up a hand to keep him back.

He did not move closer. "You're bearing up better than I have," he said. "There's more of you left."

Tria shuddered and looked away. "This isn't real," she whispered.

"Real enough for us," he answered. "Although in a sense you're right. Reflections only hover between reality and unreality."

"I have flesh. So do you. How can we have any substance if we're only reflections?" She had to argue, though she was contradicting her own denial of his reality.

"We perceive ourselves as having flesh." He held out his bony arms with their rotting skin and added ruefully, "Though I seem to be losing mine."

"Why is that happening to you? Will it happen to me?"

He turned up his palms and stared at the gaping wounds in them. "I don't know," he said. "I think the reality I left behind has no more need of me. He's found other ways of compounding his power, and he's left me here to rot. Unless he calls me back and gives me a new infusion of life, I'll slowly decompose into dust."

Tria examined her hands and arms. They were thin and the marks left by her pinches and prods were painfully evident. But she found no open wounds. The skin's gray color could be an effect of the inadequate light.

She recalled seeing herself in her room. She had thought she had used her power to obtain that vision. Now she wondered whether it had instead been a summons from her other, her original, self. And those other Trias she had glimpsed, or thought she glimpsed, retreating into the distance—could they be other versions of herself?

"Do you ever see yourself, or reflections of yourself?" she asked him.

He scraped a skeletal finger over the floor. "I did at first," he said slowly. "I wasn't confined here. I could enter my room, walk around the school, talk to people. But I grew weaker, and one day I found myself in here. In my wanderings I saw my own face staring at me once or twice. The last time, I fought giving it the power it wanted. I knew it intended evil."

"And that bothered you?" Tria shifted, looked him in the eye.

He nodded. "I always liked to test my limits, and often I did things I knew I shouldn't. But I didn't mean to hurt people. I was greedy for power, I admit that, but I wasn't deliberately cruel. Well, I got the power—or, part of me did. *I* don't have it. My other self took it all and gave none back, as far as I can tell. He also took all the evil and left me with the conscience."

"So if we could find a way to get back, to reunite you with the other Oryon, and I could go back into the other Tria, we could resolve our differences and persuade Oryon—*that* Oryon—to undo the things he's done." Excitement gave Tria renewed strength. She jumped to her feet and extended her hands toward him.

He shook his head. "Not that simple. We're locked here, outside our world—outside all the worlds. And without power we have no hope of getting back."

E. ROSE SABIN

238

Her hands fell to her sides. He was right; they were merely powerless shadows. What could they do?

But she couldn't give up. Maybe if she knew more . . . "How did Oryon—you—learn about using reflections to gain power?"

"Taner told me. She was teaching me her tribal lore. She spoke of it casually, not as a thing she'd tried herself but as something she'd heard from the clan elders. She is not a curious person, and I don't think it occurred to her that I might experiment with the idea."

Tria's hopes fell even lower. "Taner has left school and returned to her home. We have no way of contacting her and learning how to reverse the process."

"Taner left school?" Oryon lurched to his feet and clutched his rags about him. "Why? When?"

As Tria started to answer, he shook his head. "It doesn't matter. We aren't in the school. If it is possible to contact her at all, it's possible wherever she is. I don't think we have any hope of succeeding, but if you want to try, I'll help."

This time he reached toward her, and without flinching she clasped his filthy hand with its open sores. "We'll try," she said. "Between us we may have a bit of power left."

# 21

## $\int$EARCHES

Tria's footsteps echoed in the long, empty corridor. She tried walking more softly and heard her pounding heart echoing louder than her steps. Its beat drummed in her ears, urging caution, urging retreat. But she couldn't go back where Oryon waited. And Veronica had told her to use the stairs, implying that they led to a place of safety.

Where was she? The hall stretched on and on, making her feel small, insignificant. She had walked too far to be still within the school. Anyway, the school building had only three floors, and the stairs had led upward from its third floor. This must be another dimension, but it was unlike anything she had studied in Aletheia's class, and nothing like the paths through which Aletheia had led her. If this was not the school building, it *was* a building of some kind. She trod on a highly polished parquet floor of natural woods in a wide range of colors. No harsh electric light robbed the corridor of its mystery. In their reflective bronze sconces tapers burned slowly with a sweet floral scent. The walls gleamed in the candlelight in a way the school walls never could. The rich paneling's deep sheen revealed meticulous care. It was the kind of hall Tria imagined in a governor's mansion, even in the Palace of the Triumvirate in Tirbat.

She had walked a great distance, and the *Breyadon* had grown heavy in her arms when at last the hall ended in beautiful oak doors covered with elaborate carvings. She halted before those massive double doors and stared at the scenes consummately executed in high relief. They were—she was sure they were—the same scenes that were barely visible on the school's battered front doors. She had polished those doors when she and Lina were assigned to work with Veronica. Her efforts to make the neglected carvings visible had not been entirely successful, but she *had* dug out enough dust and grime to recover vestiges of the original form.

Reluctantly she tore her gaze from the panels, gathered her courage, and knocked on the doors. They swung open, revealing a large room lit by candles set in a magnificent crystal chandelier. Under the enormous chandelier, at the head of a large rectangular table, sat Headmistress. The six faculty members sat three on each side of the table. The foot of the table was unoccupied, and no chair was placed there.

"Come in," Headmistress called as Tria stood gawking at the unexpected scene. "We've been waiting for you."

Tria stepped forward, hugging the *Breyadon*. She was suddenly aware of her disheveled appearance, her dusty and ill-fitting red dress. In a state of shock, she stumbled over the fringe of the lovely tapestry rug. When she recovered her balance, Headmistress beckoned her onward until Tria stood at the foot of the table, the focus of seven pairs of eyes.

Unable to endure that silent scrutiny, Tria settled her own gaze on Mistress Dova. Holding out the *Breyadon*, she said, "I've brought back your book."

Mistress Dova, seated in the middle on Tria's left, merely nodded. It was Master Hawke who reached out to take the book from Tria's shaking hands and place it on the table in front of Mistress Dova. A low cough drew Tria's attention to Aletheia on her immediate right. The Transdimensional Studies instructor gave her a curt nod, turned toward Headmistress, and nodded again.

Headmistress folded her hands on the table in front of her. Her ring sparkled in the light of the chandelier's array of candles. "Miss Tesserell," she broke the silence at last, "congratulations. You have attained the third level."

When the unexpected announcement penetrated Tria's consciousness, she leaned heavily on the table and wished for a chair she could sink into before her quivering knees betrayed her.

Master Tumberlis beamed nearsightedly in her direction from his place at Headmistress's immediate right. "It has been most gratifying to watch your rapid ascent through the first two levels," he said. "I had feared that your difficulty in mastering Logic would prove an insurmountable barrier, but you seem to have been guided by a certain innate logic of your own."

Master San Marté cleared his throat and adjusted his cravat before addressing Tria as though delivering a lecture. "You made several wrong turns in your journey along the ethical way before selecting the way of the wise. You caused us grave concern, most grave indeed. But aided, I trust, by my instruction, you found the way at last. Not, of course, that you have arrived. Oh, no. The hardest part of your journey lies ahead, and the danger of diverging from the right path will increase as you push onward. You must fortify yourself with the lessons I have taught. You must never lose sight of the principles which I—"

"Come, man," Master Hawke interrupted. "Save all that for your classes. Miss Tesserell will have the benefit of at least two

A SCHOOL FOR SORCERY

more terms of instruction; you'll have better opportunities to review the principles of Ethics."

Master San Marté glared at his colleague but did not speak again.

"I am grateful for the return of the *Breyadon*," Mistress Dova said, patting the book's leather cover. "I understand, however, that Mr. Brew claims to have broken the code and intends to use the book's magic despite my warning."

Tria nodded. The speeches had given her time to calm herself and gather her courage. "He was chasing me. I ran up the stairs to escape him." She paused, wondering how much of what had transpired in her room was already known to the faculty.

"Please tell us about it." Mistress Blake's request, delivered in a soft, musical voice, ended Tria's hesitation. She launched into a description of the evening's events while her audience of seven listened intently but asked no questions. Perhaps they *did* know all that had happened but wanted to hear it from Tria's point of view.

When she finished, Headmistress rose from her seat. "So," she said, "Mr. Klemmer must be added to the list of those to be recovered. And Miss Mueller, trapped in panther form, is wandering lost in the night. She must be found, Mr. Brew must be stopped from using the illicit knowledge he has gained, and the missing ones must be restored. It appears you have gained the third level none too soon."

Headmistress spoke as if reaching level three solved everything. But Tria felt no different. She had no more wisdom, no more power than before. "What level has Oryon reached?" she dared to ask.

"He, too, has achieved third level," Headmistress acknowledged. "He seems to have gone beyond that level only because he is drawing on power not his own."

E. Rose Sabin

"That still gives him the advantage over me." Tria's complaint sounded whiny to her own ears. Her conflict with Oryon had left her weary, and she dreaded the prospect of having to go back and face him again. It was unfair for them to force her to struggle on alone.

"You are not alone," Aletheia answered Tria's thought. Tria waited, but the wraithlike woman said no more.

Headmistress, however, walked around the table to Tria. "You willingly accepted the challenge," she reminded her. "You must carry on to the conclusion of the contest."

"But Rehanne and Lina were to help me." More whining. She couldn't help herself.

"So they were, and so they have. Nor, I think, is their part finished. That is why your immediate task must be to find Lina. After so long a time in the dark Dire Realm, she will not be able to resume her own shape. It would not do for a farmer or a hunter to spot her in her animal form."

"No," Tria agreed with a shudder, recalling how her father had once lain in wait with a shotgun for a bobcat he suspected of killing their chickens. He'd spied the animal running away from the henhouse with a chicken in its mouth and blasted it to bits.

Headmistress removed her ring and held it out to Tria. "I can give you little help, but I can lend you this. Wear it; it will provide a measure of protection."

Startled by the unexpected generosity, Tria took the ring and slipped it on her finger. It fit perfectly.

"I will show you a way that leads directly to the garden," Headmistress said. "It would not be wise to return to your room before beginning the search for Miss Mueller."

"But what of Oryon? If he can use what he learned in the *Breyadon* even though he's lost the book—"

"He can, and you must try to stop him. But not before you

A SCHOOL FOR SORCERY

find Miss Mueller. Come." While the rest of the faculty remained seated, Headmistress led her to a door at the rear of the room. The door opened onto a landing from which a stairway spiraled downward into darkness.

"Good luck, Miss Tesserell," Headmistress said. "I commend you for your courage." With that she retreated into the room where the faculty waited, closing the door behind her and thereby cutting off the illumination that had shown Tria the landing and stairway.

She groped for the banister, found it, and clung to it as she felt her way down the stairs. She shivered in a chill wind and glanced upward at a starry sky. So the stairway itself was outside. As her eyes became adjusted to the night, she could see the outline of the stairs and beyond it the shapes of plants and trees. No building was visible; the stairway seemed to come from nowhere.

Tria reached the ground, stepped away from the stairs, and looked around, trying to get her bearings. She recognized her location: the far end of the vegetable garden. In the distance she saw the school buildings, mostly dark, with lights shining in two or three windows where students were studying late or had fallen asleep over their books.

The stairway she had descended had disappeared.

Shivering, she hugged herself and wished she'd been allowed to go by her room for a jacket. But such practical matters would not occur to Headmistress. At least the red dress, though it fit poorly, was of all-wool homespun material that provided some warmth.

She had no idea how to find Lina. They should have sent out a search party. Nor did she understand why she had been sent on this errand when at any time Oryon might carry out his threat to make use of the *Breyadon*'s magic. Possibly he would, as Mistress Dova seemed to believe, destroy himself by that act, but he might also destroy the school and its students. The entire Community of the Gifted might be at risk. And she had been sent on a panther hunt.

If only she had a lantern! She stumbled in the dark through the row of poplars that formed a windbreak at the rear of the school's garden, then struck out across the fields. She had to pick her way over ground that was plowed and furrowed, prepared for spring planting. Except for the windbreaks, there were no woods in the area. Where would a panther hide?

She could not escape the nagging thought that she'd been sent on a fool's errand. She had little chance, alone, of finding the black cat hiding in the night. Nor of capturing her if she did find her. She lacked the power to restore Lina to human form, and in her panther form Lina was less rational and would be less open to persuasion.

She tripped over a rock and sprawled facedown in the dirt. Not trying to rise, Tria fought back tears of frustration and defeat. Third level! It meant nothing if it brought no added power. Never had she felt more helpless.

She pulled herself to a sitting position and brushed dirt from her face and hands. Maybe she should go back to the school—except that she wouldn't be able to get in. The doors would be locked and warded. Again she wondered why she'd been set this task instead of being sent to keep Oryon from using the *Breyadon*.

Oryon had said he needed help in containing the power that would be unleashed. Tria had told Headmistress how Oryon had urged her to help him. Perhaps Headmistress had sent her out here to remove her from that temptation. Knowing that Tria was weak, her power drained, Headmistress might have wanted her well away from Oryon.

It made sense. Tria hauled herself to her feet and shook dirt off her dress. Headmistress's large gem snagged her skirt; she

A SCHOOL FOR SORCERY

had forgotten she was wearing the ring. "For protection," Headmistress had said. If only it would protect her from the cold.

Somewhere off in the distance a dog barked, a deep baying magnified by the quiet night. A second dog joined in with a high-pitched, furious yipping. The cacophony jolted Tria out of her haze of exhaustion. The dogs could merely be barking at each other, but it sounded more like they had spotted an intruder. Perhaps had it cornered. Or treed.

She had to have light. She risked enough of her depleted power to gather starlight and form a small light sphere. With the aid of that dim illumination, Tria set off at a run toward the source of the barking.

Oryon backed away from the mirror, allowing Tria to step into the room. She looked all around first to be sure they were alone. "What have you done with Jerrol?" she asked.

"He's studying with Davy. They have papers due tomorrow in Mistress Blake's class, and I planted the suggestion in their minds that they needed to work late into the night if they expected to pass the course." He chuckled. "In Jerrol's case that's probably true. I may have saved his neck by making him worry about his grade. Have a seat." With the wand in his hand he pointed at a desk chair.

The room was as Tria remembered it from the time she and Rehanne had sneaked in to hunt for the *Breyadon*. It surprised her that the two young men kept it so neat. Both desk lamps and the overhead light were lit. In black shirt and trousers, Oryon stood like a dark shadow in the midst of the bright room. She went to the desk chair but did not sit in it; she did not care to be at a disadvantage while he stood.

"I've invited you here to give you another chance to consider my offer," he said.

E. ROSE SABIN

The statement puzzled her. "What offer do you mean?"

"You don't remember?"

She frowned. "No. Should I?"

"Apparently not." He smiled as though she had passed some sort of test. "Please, sit down."

This time she did so, though she sat stiffly on the edge of the chair, her hands clenched in her blue skirt.

He dropped into the other desk chair. "Did you know," he asked, "that I have succeeded in deciphering the *Breyadon*?"

"I suspected as much." Again she scanned the room. "Where is it?"

"I don't need to have it at hand to work its spells." He leaned forward, his face eager. "But I do need an assistant."

"Why ask me? What makes you think I would ever be willing to help you?"

"You want your boyfriend back. Wilce. And Gray, too, I suppose. I could arrange for that as your reward."

She shook her head. "I've seen what you've turned them into, and what your magic did to Kress. I want no part of any spells of yours."

"But I'm asking you to help me shape and contain the power the *Breyadon* can bring. If you work with me, you'll get some of that power for yourself. Think about it. Think what you could do."

He meant to trick her, she was sure of it. He'd never willingly share power. But by pretending to help him, she could learn the *Breyadon*'s secrets for herself. She could wrest power from him, free Wilce and Gray, and set everything to rights. Of course, she'd be taking a terrible chance, but it was time to take chances. She'd dithered about long enough. This was what she had gathered power for.

She did not want to seem too eager. She hesitated a while longer, asking questions, arguing, obtaining Oryon's solemn promise, sworn on his wand, that he would not betray her.

The promise was meaningless, she knew. Nevertheless, when he had given it, she agreed to help him.

"Good. Excellent." Rising, he rubbed his hands together. "We'll get busy right away. I'll explain what we need, and we'll search out the right time and place."

The tunnel grew colder. Tria sat hugging her knees to her chest, trying to get what warmth she could from the brown wool skirt. Oryon, too, clutched his pathetic rags more tightly around him. The light was growing dimmer as well, Tria noted anxiously. As though everything was shutting down, fading out. She did not understand what this path was, whether it possessed independent reality or was a creation of Aletheia's mind, an extension of her power. If it winked out, she and Oryon would wink out with it, shadow beings that they were.

Her existence, ephemeral though it might be, felt real enough to her, and she did not relish the thought of being snuffed out like the flame of a candle. It helped to have a goal to strive for, though she doubted their ability to achieve it. Mere reflections with faint traces of power could hardly expect to contact a dweller in the real world.

"What *is* reality?" Oryon asked. "How do you know Taner is more real than we are?"

She had no answer and did not think he expected one. She admired his determination, his refusal to yield to hopelessness. She pushed aside the smothering curtain of her own doubts and centered her inner vision on her careful recreation of Taner's physical appearance. She wished she could supply more knowledge of Taner's character, but for that she had to rely on Oryon. She'd never tried to get close to the strange girl from the far northern islands. Taner's alien accent and rough ways had put her off; she'd been wary of Taner's quick temper and everpresent dagger.

"Taner is an idealist," Oryon said, picking up her thoughts in that uncanny way he had. "She wants to right all the world's wrongs. It makes her angry when she can't. In fact, I'm not sure that she ever really admits she can't; she only concedes that it won't be easy. She admires strength, despises weakness in any form—moral as well as physical. She has little patience, no empathy at all, but she is intensely loyal, and she expects loyalty in return. That was why, when I became fascinated with Lina . . ." He shrugged, not needing to say more.

But there was more, Tria knew. Taner was a husky, raw-boned, plain-looking girl, yet Oryon had seen beauty in her. She was blunt of speech and stubborn in her ways, yet he had found tenderness and constancy. She guessed that *this* Oryon had truly cared for Taner, though the Oryon in the world they'd left behind cared for no one but himself.

Tria joined her power to Oryon's, weaving its strands with his to form a mental net to snare Taner's awareness. The net was weak and tenuous, though she poured all her feeble strength into the casting of it, knowing Oryon was doing the same. The tunnel grew colder, dimmer, more constricted. And their net snared nothing.

# 22

## Multiple Woes

The frantic barking was more distant than Tria had thought. She stumbled on, holding the gathered light, though it did little to dispel the darkness. By the time she neared the source of the sound, she was breathless and sweating despite the cold, and a sharp pain lanced her side.

She located the dogs in a small grove near a farmhouse. They were hunting hounds, and that was bad enough, but praise the Power-Giver, they weren't the big mastiffs so often used as guard dogs. However, their baying had already alerted their owner. The trees, stark in winter bareness, did not block her view of the burly farmer approaching from the other side, a rifle in his hands. The dogs pawed at one tree trunk and leaped toward its lower branches. On one of those branches a black shape crouched, one leg dangling down toward the dogs.

The smaller and more agile dog leaped for the leg, yelped, and fell back to the ground yipping and whining. Its distress drove its larger companion into a greater frenzy of howling and scratching at the trunk.

"Back, Towser, back, Essie," the farmer shouted. "I'll get it for you. Back, I say!" He aimed the gun at the dark form.

"No!" Tria's scream was drowned in the blast of the gun. As she sprinted forward, the large cat toppled from its perch.

The dogs charged. Hissing and snarling, the panther tried to pull itself to its feet though one leg was shattered and blood gushed from a wound in its belly. Tria hurled her light sphere at the dogs. Startled, they backed off, but rushed back when the light vanished. With her summoning gift she ordered the hounds off their prey, but their blood-lust blocked her call. She ran forward and aimed kicks and blows at the maddened dogs.

"Get away, girl," the farmer bellowed. "You crazy?"

"Get the dogs," Tria pleaded. "Stop them."

The larger dog sank its fangs into her leg.

"Let her go, Towser. Heel!" When Towser ignored his shouted commands, the farmer knocked the dog aside with the stock of his gun. The hound yelped and retreated. The man grasped Tria by the wrist and jerked her away from the bleeding cat.

"Got to finish that thing off afore it mauls my dogs." He pushed Tria aside and took aim.

"Stop!" Tria hurled herself at him, threw him off balance. She felt the recoil when the rifle fired. The bullet smashed into the tree trunk.

The farmer whirled and swung the butt of the rifle at Tria. Automatically she shielded and hurled her power at man and weapon. He staggered and fell; the rifle flew from his hand. Tria leaped to defend the panther from the circling hounds.

The cat had fallen still. The small dog leaped for its throat. Tria grabbed the animal by the scruff of its neck and tossed it aside. She bent over the injured panther. It lay in a pool of blood, sides heaving, tongue lolling from its mouth.

"I won't let you die, Lina," Tria sobbed. She gathered the

animal into her arms and lurched to her feet. Behind her she heard the snick of the rifle bolt.

"Witchwoman, are ye?" the farmer growled. "I s'pose that's your familiar. Neither of ye'll leave here alive."

He jabbed the barrel of the gun between Tria's shoulder blades. Good. She knew without turning where the rifle was. Her power flowed around the barrel, twisted it upward. With a cry of terror the man dropped the gun and ran.

The hounds were more persistent. Wanting their prey, they circled her. One nipped at her heels, while the other lunged at her, trying to tear the panther from her.

Burdened as she was, leg aching where she'd been bitten, she could not outrun them. Nor could she waste her waning power; she needed it to help her carry the heavy panther. She had to fell both dogs with a single swift blow. Her eyes searched out a low, heavy limb. She darted beneath it and used her power to wrench it free and crash it down onto the pursuing hounds.

Not sure whether she had stunned them, killed them, or merely frightened them off, she ran until she was certain they no longer followed and her aching lungs and weary legs could keep the pace no longer. She stopped and caught her breath, her arms straining despite the power that eased much of the weight.

Her dress was soaked with the panther's blood. She strained to see in the darkness whether Lina still lived. A healer could close the gaping stomach wound. If only she had that ability. She focused her power, willed it to staunch the flow of blood. The wound did not close as she had seen Jerrol's ripped throat close beneath Headmistress's hand on the night of the ball. Blood no longer poured from the open cavity, but that could be an indication of death rather than of healing. She had to get Lina to a real healer.

A SCHOOL FOR SORCERY

She could see the school, but her flagging steps would never cover the remaining distance before Lina's feeble thread of life ran out. Unless she had the power to space-shift.

*I'm third level now. That* has *to count for something.* She pictured the third-floor corridor, pictured herself standing at the door to Verin's room. A wave of dizziness staggered her, and the panther shuddered in her arms. But she did not move.

She tried again, this time building the mental image of the second-floor landing outside Headmistress's office. Her mind created every detail of that spot she knew so well. But her body went nowhere.

*Maybe I'm trying too great a distance. If I could just get to the front entrance . . .*

Although she couldn't distinguish them in the darkness, she stared at the point where she knew the front doors to be and pictured the worn wood and damaged carvings, adjusted her grip on Lina, and willed herself to stand at the doors.

A jolt drove her to her knees. The world spun around her. When the dizzying motion slowed and she could see, the building loomed in front of her. Not the doors, but the side near the front corner. She was close.

She was also utterly exhausted, unable to lift the dying panther, unable to rise to her feet. She had to get someone's attention. Her fingers scrabbled in the loose soil until they turned up a stone. With the last vestige of her power she sent it soaring toward a lighted second-floor window. The window opened and a figure leaned out, silhouetted against the light. It might have been Fenton; she couldn't tell. It didn't matter. At the top of her voice she shouted for help.

The figure retreated. Tria sank to the ground, dragged Lina onto her lap, and prayed the help would come in time.

Blind. Cold. Alone.

Tria floated in a void. All sensation was gone. Her thoughts were dim, confused. Fragments of memories surfaced briefly, then sank back into nothingness.

Her mother standing at the kitchen door dreamily watching a flock of birds fly south. Her father delivering their old cow of a stillborn calf, cursing his "witch daughter" as though Tria were to blame for the misfortune. Headmistress's long, thin fingers riffling through a stack of papers on her desk. Mistress Dova reading meaningless syllables from the *Breyadon*. Wilce, hands in his pockets, standing by the patio fountain. A crystal sphere glimpsed through a transparent section of the tunnel between worlds. A stick figure in rags and rotting flesh saying, "I am Oryon."

"Taner." Oryon's voice. He'd reached her. "Taner, I must know how to reverse the process of creating mirror-image duplicates."

For no more than a second Taner's face, disembodied, ghostly, floated before them, lips parted, moving.

"Death," the barely audible voice said. "The secret is death."

The link broke, and with the breaking Tria felt final darkness close over her.

"Death. The secret is death."

Oryon's head jerked up from the papers he was studying. He glared at Tria. "What are you talking about?"

"I . . . I don't know." She rubbed her forehead. "I didn't mean to say that. It was just a . . . a thought that jumped into my mind."

"You're not losing your nerve, are you?" His voice was knife sharp.

She shook her head. "I want to get it over with, that's all. When will you be ready?"

A SCHOOL FOR SORCERY

"Soon. I can't rush it. The timing has to be right." His gaze dropped back to the papers he was studying. With his index finger, he underscored a line of writing. "The calculations are tricky. I've almost got it."

He fell silent and Tria watched him uneasily. That intrusive thought could have been an omen, a warning surfacing from her subconscious mind to tell her she didn't have the power for what she intended to attempt.

"Ah!" Oryon jumped up and stretched, clutching his paper in one hand. "I have it. We can get to work. It will take several hours."

Tria rose, straightened the pleats of her blue skirt, and tugged at the cuffs of her white middy blouse. She glanced anxiously at the door. "Won't Jerrol be back soon?"

Oryon nodded. "We can't stay here. A few hours ago I found the perfect place. Did you know this building has an attic?"

"Attic? No."

"It does. I found it while I was looking for—while I was doing some exploring. It will be the perfect place from which to cast our nets over the whole school."

He picked up his wand and led her from the room and through the silent hall. At the stairs to the third floor Oryon paused and traced symbols with his wand. "That takes care of the wards," he whispered.

She followed him up the stairs. They tiptoed down the girls' hall. Tria cast a longing glance at the door of her room. If she could only go in, shut the door, and leave all this behind her. The room she had found so ugly and inhospitable on her arrival now seemed an oasis of comfort, a warm refuge.

Toward the end of the hall, near the washroom, Oryon led her to a door she had never noticed before. She could not possibly have passed it every day without seeing it.

Nevertheless, it was there. Oryon opened it, and beyond it narrow stairs led upward into darkness.

Oryon kindled a pale-blue mage light, balanced it in the palm of one hand, and ascended the steps. After pulling the door closed behind her, Tria followed.

They emerged through a trapdoor into a low-ceilinged area that was little more than a crawl space. Boxes and crates were stored along the sides; Tria recognized some of Lina's hatboxes. Dust and cobwebs covered everything.

Oryon dragged a crate into the open space, blew the dust off, sat, and motioned Tria to do the same. Coughing from the dust, Tria selected a large box and pulled it opposite his.

When both were seated, with the mage light bobbing eerily in the space between them, Oryon grinned. "Wasn't this a lucky find? Not a fancy hiding place, I'll grant you, but the location is ideal. Why, it could have been designed for my use. From here I can stretch the lines of power over the entire school. No one will escape my net."

Tria sat up and drew her blanket around her, clasping it tightly beneath her chin. "Death," she said aloud. "The secret is death."

She listened to the night's stillness and heard nothing out of the ordinary. Strange that those words had popped into her head as she woke.

She must have had a dream. A nightmare, more like it. But she couldn't remember any part of it.

She got out of bed, padded to the door, and in her night-gown stepped out into the hall. She looked up and down; it was empty and quiet, and the lights, left burning all night, revealed nothing that could have startled her. Shrugging, she relocked the door and turned on her room light to see the clock.

Two hours until time to get up and get ready for class. She turned off the light and returned to her bed. No point in worrying about an unremembered dream. Better to sleep while she could.

"Death," Tria mumbled to the hands that unfolded her from around the panther and lifted the animal out of her arms. "The secret is death."

"So it is, but life is a great secret as well."

The firm response focused Tria's scattered wits. Her bleary gaze fixed on the speaker. Veronica.

The little maid helped Tria stand and supported her as they walked toward the school. Davy and Jerrol walked ahead of them, bearing the panther on a litter between them.

"Is she—is she alive?" Tria managed to form the words.

"Barely. It'll take a powerful healer to save her."

Tria groaned.

"Don't give up hope," Veronica admonished. "We're blessed with healers here at Simonton School. Verin and Salor have the gift to a high degree, and healing is Headmistress's greatest talent. They've all been sent for. If she hangs on till we get her into the building, she'll have a chance."

Tria wondered why the healers hadn't come out here but couldn't muster the energy to ask. She stumbled along until they reached the building. Tria was dismayed to see Davy and Jerrol waiting for them at the front doors. They should have carried Lina inside.

As she and Veronica approached the entrance, she fell against an invisible barrier, reeled back, and would have fallen if Veronica had not caught her. A power net surrounded the school and would not let them pass. Those inside must be trapped within, while they were barred from entering. Despair staggered Tria. When Veronica released her, she crumpled to the ground.

Veronica stepped over her and bustled forward. Her small hands grasped unseen threads, pulled, tugged, and spread apart. With her arms stretched wide, she called Davy and Jerrol. "Come, lads, I've made a way through. Hurry."

Carrying Lina, they ducked under Veronica's arms and snaked through the barrier, opened the front doors, and went inside.

"Your turn, Tria. Get up and get a move on."

Tria stood, swaying, and somehow forced her feet to take those few steps past Veronica, gather in her loose red dress, and squeeze through the opening. She halted just inside the doors, unable to go farther until Veronica popped in beside her and took her arm.

The boys had set the litter down in the middle of the foyer. Headmistress bent over the panther, with Verin and Salor both hovering beside her. Tria stared anxiously and was annoyed when Veronica tugged her arm and pushed her around the healers and their patient.

"They'll be at it for some time," Veronica said. "They don't need gawkers. And you have work to do."

"Work!" Tria gasped. Surely the woman could see how weary and drained she was.

Veronica nodded. "That net outside is Oryon's doing. He's drawing his power around the school, getting ready to make his big move. And you'll have to stop him."

"Me? I've used up all my power. I haven't had any sleep. I can't—"

"We'll all perish if you don't," Veronica declared. "You'll have to try. You have time for a cup of tea first. That'll refresh you a bit."

A SCHOOL FOR SORCERY

Too weak to protest, Tria limped after Veronica all the way to the faculty residence hall. She had never before been in Veronica's small ground-floor apartment; she had not known it was there. Ensconced in a soft armchair in the small, comfortable sitting room, she sipped the tea the little maid served and thought of home.

Her family's farmhouse had a parlor like this one, with old-fashioned wingback chairs in front of a cheery fireplace. On wintry evenings, she had often sat cocooned in the chair's soft cushions, listening to her mother's tales. It was a place of warmth and safety, and now, as then, she relaxed and her eyelids drifted shut. Dimly she was aware of Veronica's taking the teacup from her hand.

# 23

## ſHADES OF CRYSTAL

His long legs stretched out in front of him, Oryon placed his hands behind his head and grinned at Tria, excitement sparkling in his eyes. "Best shield I've ever spun. Nothing less than a seventh-level Adept will break through."

With his hair mussed and a smudge of dirt across one cheek, he looked like a mere schoolboy bent on some harmless bit of mischief. She had to remind herself of his earlier attempts on her life, of what he had done to Wilce and Gray, to Lina, to Kress. And of what he intended now.

He'd spent the last hours of the night weaving a net of power and setting it in place around the school's three buildings, testing it, muttering that it had to hold against anything and anyone, even Headmistress and the other sixth-level masters, could do to counteract it. At his insistence, Tria had reluctantly let him draw on her power to supplement his. She knew she couldn't spare it, but neither could she let him suspect the treachery she planned.

By the time Oryon announced his satisfaction, the night had passed. Not that any sunlight penetrated their attic hiding place; only the mage light relieved the darkness. But the sounds of activity—hurried footsteps, calling voices, running water, slamming doors—rose from the floor below. The clang of the breakfast bell reminded Tria of her hunger. A good breakfast would replenish her lost strength, but Oryon refused to let her leave the attic.

"We'll eat when we've finished. In fact, we'll feast. It won't be long; you can wait."

"Suppose I don't have the power to do what you want?"

"You'll have enough. I don't want you too strong." He chuckled. "Wouldn't want you to think you were strong enough to double-cross me."

So she hadn't fooled him. He was on his guard against her. She had little hope of foiling his plot, but she had to try.

He had decreed that they should relax for a time, letting their power build back up. Not too long, however, because when the power net was discovered, the faculty and students would undoubtedly mount a defense. But before their efforts could have any effect, Oryon would act. Another hour, maybe two, and the school would be at his mercy.

Tria felt drowsy but dared not fall asleep. Although a nap would strengthen her, her distrust of Oryon was too great to let her sleep in his presence. To keep herself awake, she said, "Why have you decided not to wait until the end of the year as you promised?"

"I offered a full year because my bargain with the Dire Women required it. They supply me with daily infusions of power in exchange for Wilce and Gray and anyone else I send them. By the end of a year their victims would be used up, and I'd have a surplus of power stored up for my takeover. But why should I wait? What I learned from the *Breyadon* will let me unleash more power than I could gather in a year's time. I don't need the Dire Women anymore. They're nasty creatures; I'll be well rid of them."

E. ROSE SABIN

Tria wondered how the Dire Women would accept the abrupt cancellation of their bargain. Despite his confidence, Oryon might not be able to recover Wilce and Gray. And if he did, it might be too late—they might have no humanity left.

She did not voice her thoughts, but they gnawed at her brain, so that she could not relax, could not open the channels and let power flow back into her.

Too soon Oryon stood, stretched, and announced, "It's time."

Tria wasn't ready. She had no chance of overcoming Oryon. She had been fooling herself all along; she had never really had a chance.

It was appropriate that the blue skirt and white middy blouse she'd worn the day she arrived at the school was the outfit she wore now, the day she'd witness the school's and her own destruction. She was glad she'd thought to put it on before going to her meeting with Oryon.

"Stand here," he said, calling her to a place in front of a stack of boxes leaning against the wall. "Don't move from this spot. What I do will create an immense surge of force. When it comes, extend your own power to meet it and channel it into the net I've placed around the school."

"Suppose I can't do that?"

"You can. It shouldn't be that difficult. The net will attract it to some extent anyway."

Tria took up her assigned position. "What happens when all that added power flows into the net?" she asked.

"You'll see." He moved away from her to stand near the door, his back to it, facing her. "I promise you a spectacle you'll never forget."

*   *   *

Tria woke, yawned, indulged in a luxurious stretch, then bolted upright as the full sunlight streaming through the window penetrated the haze of her sleep. She jumped out of bed and checked her clock. She'd slept through breakfast and had fifteen minutes to make it to her first class.

She tore off her nightgown and looked for something to wear. There was almost nothing on the rack; most of her things must be in the pile to be washed. She hadn't had much time to do laundry lately. The only blouse hanging there was a dressy green charmeuse. She put it on along with an old black tweed skirt—no time to worry about the mismatch. She pulled on her high stockings and jammed her feet into a pair of work shoes when she couldn't find her good ones. After racing to the washroom to splash water on her face and run her toothbrush over her teeth, she ran back to the room, pulled her brush through her hair, grabbed her books, and dashed down the stairs. As the final bell rang, she skidded into the classroom and flopped into her seat, too breathless to reply to Master San Marté's exaggerated greeting.

It was inevitable after her spectacular entrance that Master San Marté should fix his gaze on her as he launched into the day's lecture. "Today we shall consider the ethics of using power to acquire power. Those gifted with the ability to draw power from others have, of course, a clearly defined moral choice. They may ethically draw only from those who give free consent to the process, who in effect enter into willing partnership with the one to whom they lend power. The drawing of power from an unwitting victim or the coercing of a donor is manifestly illicit. But other means of using power to beget power are more problematic." He stroked his mustache. "Miss Tesserell, can you describe for the class an ethically ambiguous means of gaining power?"

Not yet recovered from her frantic rush and embarrassed

by being thrust into the spotlight, Tria blurted out the first answer that entered her mind: "Accepting a gift of power you know the giver cannot spare."

"Hmmmm. An interesting problem." Master San Marté scratched his head, skewing his toupee to a rakish angle. "Yes, indeed. A question worthy of debate." He pressed his fingertips together at his waist. "Let us see who can suggest a specific example for our analysis."

Tria awoke to Veronica shaking her shoulder, rousing her out of deep slumber. She blinked and looked around, not remembering at first where she was. Gradually the night's events seeped back into her awareness. She recalled her battle with the farmer and his hounds, her running and space-shifting, carrying the injured panther, the memory reinforced by the look and smell of her blood-stained dress. At least the stains didn't show up badly on the red wool.

"It's morning," Veronica said. "I let you sleep long. Oryon will make his move soon. You'd best get ready."

Tria cast off the lingering tendrils of sleep. "How do I do that?"

Veronica shook her head, sending her gray curls wriggling about her face. "That's something none can tell you; you'll have to discover it for yourself. Your rest has built up your strength."

"But what will he do? Do you know?"

"I only know that the power net around our buildings bears his signature, and that means he has decided to make his move. A tension's been building since the net was cast. Can you feel it?"

Tria sat quietly, testing all her senses. A certain indefinable dread pressed in on her. She felt threads of power woven around the building, forming a barrier that was tightening,

A SCHOOL FOR SORCERY

not only closing them in but growing stronger, more deadly as it drew on the power of those it enclosed.

Yet nothing was visible. Perhaps she felt nothing more than her own inner fear.

"Trust your senses, miss," Veronica said.

"What are you, Veronica?" Tria dared ask. "You're no maid, that's certain."

Veronica turned away. "Come, no time for puzzles." She walked to the door and opened it. "If you survive this challenge, you may know what I am."

Tria nodded and got to her feet. At the door she paused. "What about Lina?" she asked. "Is she alive?"

"The panther lives. The healers were able to seal the wound. Whether Lina survived with it, I cannot say." As she spoke, Veronica pushed Tria through the door and closed it behind her, leaving Tria standing uncertainly in the corridor of the faculty residence hall with no idea where to go or what to do.

She headed for the foyer and passed from it into the quadrangle. The fountain had been turned on in recognition of winter's passing. She lingered beside it a moment, thinking of Wilce and how he had chosen this spot to invite her to the Midwinter Ball. The memory strengthened her resolve. "I have to free you," she whispered. "I don't know how I'll defeat Oryon, but I must find the way."

She entered the main building. Classes were already in session. She hurried through the halls, noting with relief that the door to Master San Marté's classroom was shut, so no one would notice her passing and report her truancy. Although surely the instructors all knew what she was about and would not expect her to attend class. In fact, she marveled that classes were being held despite the threat of doom that hung over the school.

The sense of dread, of imminent disaster, hung more heavily in this building. Twisting Headmistress's ring on her finger, she fought down an urge to run. The net, she knew, made escape impossible. And how could she flee when the fate of the school rested in her hands?

Hardly knowing what she did, she climbed the stairs to the second floor and on to the third. She walked to her room, opened the door, and went inside. Drawn perhaps by the strong memory of Wilce she had experienced by the fountain, she went to the dressing table and from a drawer took the crystal pendant he had given her. She had not worn it since that day in Rehanne's room when it had communicated such terror. Now, though, she clasped it around her neck. The reflected red of her dress gave it the color of blood.

Lina's talisman lay on the dressing table. Tria snatched it up; she might encounter wards she'd need to break.

Turning away from the dressing table, she glanced at the bed and was startled to see it unmade, the covers thrown off as if someone had arisen in haste. The bed had been made yesterday when she'd last seen it. Someone had slept here last night, someone who had rushed out, leaving the room in disarray.

She moved to the bed, stooped, picked up the pink blanket from the floor. She dropped it again, paralyzed by the sensation of horror that crept up her spine and spidered over her scalp. While she dithered and dallied, Oryon marshaled his strength. The air crackled with menace. The time of doom had come, and she was not ready.

Her skin crawled; her hair rose. A thousand needles stabbed her flesh. She stepped to the center of the room and clasped her hand over the pendant. "Wilce!" she cried as a force like a giant hand shoved her to her knees.

The crystal warmed against her breast. Strength flowed from it into her. She staggered to her feet. As if heading into a strong wind, she struggled toward the door, got it open, and forced her way into the corridor.

The stairs! She had to reach the stairs. Pummeled by that gale of power, she pushed toward the steps she'd climbed to safety the night before.

She couldn't find them. As hard as she tried to visualize them, as much as she willed them to appear, she saw only the beige walls and the washroom door.

"Oryon!" she yelled toward the ceiling. "Oryon, show yourself, you coward!" At her shout, a narrow doorway became visible in the wall in front of her. Without stopping to wonder at its appearance, she hurled herself through it.

The bell finally signaled the end of Ethics class, and Tria escaped into the hallway. She might have found the discussion interesting had Master San Marté not kept her at the center of his persistent questioning. In need of fresh air, she hurried into the courtyard.

The spring sunlight transformed the splashing fountain into a marvel of shimmering crystal. Tria stood close enough to let the cold spray sting her face. She thrust a hand into the falling water, scattering beads of light. A tap on her shoulder startled her, spun her around.

Kathyn and Rehanne had come up behind her without her hearing them. "Sorry, didn't mean to scare you," Rehanne said.

"We've been looking for you," Kathyn said. "Ever since we heard the news."

"What news?"

"Davy and Jerrol told everyone how you spent the whole night outside hunting for Lina and found her after she'd been shot by a farmer, and you fought off the farmer's dogs and brought her back." Rehanne paused and gazed curiously at Tria. "I don't know how you did it. And without getting hurt.

You look like you've done nothing but sleep all night."

Tria opened her mouth to protest that she *had* done nothing but sleep all night and had not the slightest idea what Rehanne was talking about. But before she could speak, Kathyn clutched her arm.

"Kress and Oryon are missing," she said, her face pinched with fear and anger. "The school's enspelled so nobody can go in or out, and Verin and Salor and Headmistress worked together to heal the panther but none of them, not even Headmistress, can make it change back to Lina. Terrible things are happening, and I didn't expect to find you out here playing in the fountain." Tears rolled down her cheeks as she finished.

Rehanne handed Kathyn a handkerchief and said to Tria, "I came to say I was wrong in abandoning you to face Oryon alone. I've been feeling guilty about going back on my promise to help you fight him. When I heard what you'd done all by yourself, I felt so ashamed that I knew I had to do whatever I could. But—you didn't go to class, did you?" The question held incredulity and reproof.

Tria nodded, not knowing what to say. She understood none of this, though she did remember that she had planned to search for Lina this morning. She was horrified to think that the panther's plight had slipped her mind. But they said that she *had* rescued it. Something very strange was going on.

And now they wanted her to find and confront Oryon and Kress. She realized with a sudden shock that they didn't know what had happened to Kress. Kathyn assumed that her brother was with Oryon. When Tria told them the truth, they'd think her foolish for going off to class as if this were a normal school day. She'd have to tell them, though, and together the three of them would find a way to stop Oryon. It was good to have allies. She'd fought the battle alone too long.

*        *        *

A SCHOOL FOR SORCERY

With his wand, Oryon traced a series of symbols on the attic floor. They left no mark, and Tria could not visualize the results of the complex strokes. The marks seemed visible to Oryon; he stared intently at the floor, lifted his wand, and waved it about like an orchestra conductor engaged in a triumphant production. The mage light dimmed to near darkness. From the floor below, someone shouted Oryon's name. The girl's voice sounded hauntingly familiar.

Oryon seemed not to hear the shouts. He spoke a sentence he must have taken from the *Breyadon*: "*Calyor margra felefor, tisitiya mura calyor na.*"

The building shook. The mage light went out. A shout of "Oryon, stop!" was followed by steps scrambling up the stairs in defiance of the wards Oryon had set.

"*Tisit felefor mu ragana lo!*" Oryon cried.

In the blackness, steps pelted toward the sound of that cry. Tria tried in vain to rekindle the mage light. A crash and a curse told her Oryon had been tackled. Forgetting his warning against moving from her position while he worked the spell, she leaped to aid her unknown ally.

A pillar of flame spouted in front of her. Unable to check her speed, she plunged into its intense heat. Her gasp filled her lungs with searing fire.

Lina's ward-breaking talisman clamped between her teeth, Tria climbed the stairs into the darkness above. Oryon's voice guided her, chanting words that could only come from the *Breyadon*. At the top she spat the talisman from her mouth and heard it clatter to the bottom of the stairwell. The chanting voice persisted; she shouted again for it to stop. She could see nothing in the utter blackness. Although she had left the door open below, no light penetrated this place of evil.

*How different this dark and musty place from the bright and*

*opulent hall the stairway led me to last night;* the thought flitted through her mind as she groped for solid footing. When she found it, she sprang toward the chanting voice.

Oryon was closer than she'd thought. She crashed into him, knocked him backwards, fell on top of him. With a curse, he grabbed at her and tried to throw her off. She clung to him and summoned her power.

But it was no power of hers that ignited the sudden conflagration swirling around them. They were at the vortex of a cyclone of fire. She caught a glimpse of something white amid the flames and heard a scream; it might have been her own. A terrible stench choked Tria, made her gag. She could hardly breathe. The light of the flames showed her Oryon's face peering into hers.

"You're too late," he gloated. "I've done it!"

The scorching heat receded. The walls of flame curved out, away from them, leaving them suspended in the center of a candescent sphere. The floor on which they'd fallen was gone. Oryon scrambled away from Tria and stood, though no solid surface rested beneath his feet. He pointed his wand at her. She tried to rise, struggling like a swimmer in deep water. Oryon laughed at her clumsy efforts.

"Fire is my element," he said. "It is the symbol of my power—all-consuming, invincible. Nothing will stand in my path."

"You betrayed me. I knew you would." The thought formed and spoke itself, though Tria did not understand why she said it.

"As you tried to betray me," he said. "But you lacked the strength. You've never been a match for me. Headmistress thought she was pitting me against my equal; that shows how foolish and impractical she is."

"I think you underestimate her."

"You are about to see how wrong you are. I brought you here to witness my triumph."

But he hadn't brought her here. She'd searched for him and found him; she'd broken through his wards to get to him.

Yet she had been here with him, as well. She remembered as though it were a dream waiting here with him through the night, trying vainly to summon the power to turn his spell back on him, to save the school. She recalled the certainty that her power was not great enough, recalled despair changing to hope when she heard—when she'd shouted—when someone—when *she* attacked Oryon. A vision of devouring flames brought a scream to her throat. She clutched her breast. Her fingers closed around her pendant.

The crystal in her hand brought to mind the crystal place to which the spell from the *Breyadon* had carried her. She remembered the crystal sphere she'd seen through the window in the tunnel wall when Aletheia had led her along the paths between the worlds.

Another alien memory surfaced: of wandering through those paths alone. Alone—and in the company of another. Oryon. Not the Oryon who stood regarding her with a contemptuous look. A second Oryon, tattered and decaying.

Where were these thoughts coming from? She must be going mad.

She gripped the pendant more tightly. It seemed to bring strength and stability. She righted herself, faced Oryon. "You will *not* win!" she told him. "The *Breyadon* cannot be used for evil."

She directed her thoughts to the one who dwelt in the crystal. *You said I could come again in time of direst peril. You also said I might not be able to leave. I'll take the chance. I can't let Oryon carry out his plan.*

Holding the pendant, she pictured the crystal place with its dancing rainbows, mentally re-created its beauty around her. The red light of the flames softened, the fiery sphere solidified.

Oryon looked around in bewilderment. "Where are we? What's happening?" His voice echoed profanely off the faceted crystal all around them.

And in Tria's mind a voice said, *Welcome back, daughter. Who is this you have brought?*

As Tria prepared her mental response, Oryon stalked around the delicate structure, a dark cloud menacing a rainbow. "What have you done?" he demanded again. "Where's the school?"

*An impatient and surly young man,* spoke the voice. *He reminds me of someone I once knew, long ago. His mind is closed to me. I could force it open, but I would prefer, if you will permit it, to see him through your eyes.*

Remembering her previous experience here, she understood what the voice asked of her. She gave her consent and steeled herself for the coming of the burning white light.

It filled her with a cauterizing pain. The intense heat and light cleansed and purified as it probed. She hid nothing from it, though she was aware that the light would touch only what she permitted.

The light receded; the voice spoke. *Thank you, daughter. You have learned much since our previous meeting. You have found your way through difficult paths, but tortuous ways lie yet before you. I shall think what is to be done with this young man. He will not be receptive to my voice, as you have been.*

Tria could see again. She found Oryon standing in front of her, staring curiously.

"You went into a trance," he said. "You're trying to work some kind of spell, but I won't let you." He pointed his wand at her. "I have not lost my power. Take us back to the school or I'll kill you."

She shook her head and would have explained that she was powerless to do as he asked, when his head jerked back and his arms flung out as if to ward off blows. "No!" he shouted. "Get out of my head! You can't do that!"

He spun around and with a cry of *"Felefor mura-na!"* he hurled his wand against the wall.

A single high note pealed out from the crystal. The rainbows quivered; the walls shattered. Stiletto-sharp slivers of crystal rained down. Oryon cried out and leaped over a jagged crystal barrier. Tria heard his footsteps recede as she crouched with her arms over her head.

She was rising to follow him when a loud crack heralded another crystal fall directly overhead. Like dozens of knives the shards sliced into her.

*Be comforted, daughter,* the voice in her mind soothed. *Another will complete what you cannot.*

There was nothing more.

E. ROSE SABIN

# 24

## WAR AND DEATH

Tria and Rehanne led a weeping Kathyn into the main building. Tria intended to hurry through the classroom section before the bell rang for the next class, find a secluded spot in the parlor, give Kathyn a chance to recover from the news of her twin's disappearance, and plot what to do about Oryon. But they'd barely got inside the door when the building shook as if struck by a powerful earthquake. Hurled against the wall, they struggled to keep their balance as the floor rocked like the deck of a ship in a storm. The electricity flickered out and an eerie red glow replaced the natural daylight.

"We're too late!" Rehanne screamed.

Students who had gone early into the classrooms spilled out into the hall along with the instructors. They stampeded toward the quadrangle, carrying Tria and her friends along with them.

On the quadrangle, students huddled in groups, crying and screaming. Over their heads, a dome of fire replaced the sky. Blood-red water spilled from the fountain and flooded the flagstones.

Coral, hysterical, stumbled into Tria, dug her fingers into

Tria's arms, and screeched, "Do something!" Rehanne embraced her and pulled her away. Coral quieted, and Tria guessed Rehanne was using her power to shield the empath from the panic around her.

Stung by Coral's plea, Tria cast about for something she could do. Only one thing came to mind. She launched her power upward at the mantle of flame and tried to blast a hole in it but failed. Desperate, she drew the flame toward her, brought it funneling down around her. Heat struck, and unbearable pain. She fell screaming into the consuming flames. She felt her flesh burning, melting, and at the same time a terrible, desolate cold filled her and darkness swallowed her.

Light returned. Her eyes opened. She gazed into Verin's worried face. The fire had not killed her; she had only fainted. She was lying where she had fallen, but the ground beneath her was solid and unmoving, and ordinary daylight shone around her. Hushed voices replaced the cries of panic.

Verin helped her sit up. Coral clasped her hand. "You did it!" Awe and admiration filled her voice.

All around, the muted murmurs gave way to shouts of thanks and wild applause. She heard the noise through a cloud of confusion, of conflicting memories swirling through her mind.

Rehanne knelt beside her. "Tria, you were wonderful! Drawing all that fire into yourself! I thought—we all thought—you'd be burned to a cinder, but the flames simply vanished. Your pretty green blouse isn't even scorched. How did you do it?"

"Such power!" Nubba loomed over her, her round face beaming. "It's like I always said, nobody can equal Tria for talent."

"The net's gone!" a triumphant voice shouted from the direction of the garden gate.

E. ROSE SABIN

Britnor stepped up beside Nubba, a broad smile transforming his usually somber face. "Wonder where old Oryon's hiding, now that you've defeated him so soundly?"

The words pierced Tria's lingering mental fog. She scrambled to her feet. Kathyn moved in to offer a supporting hand, but Tria shook it off. "Help," she gasped. "Got to help her."

Rehanne stood in front of her. "Help who? What are you talking about?"

No time to explain. Tria dodged aside. "Come on," she called to Rehanne as she sprinted toward the faculty residence hall.

"Petra," she shouted, catching sight of her classmate. "Where's Aletheia?"

"I haven't seen her," came the puzzled answer.

"Help me find her," Tria ordered. She dashed into the hall and headed toward Aletheia's apartment calling for the Transdimensional Studies mistress.

"She isn't here." Stopped by the soft voice, Tria saw Mistress Blake coming toward her. "May I help you?"

"I've got to find Aletheia. She has to open a door for me so I can get to . . . to . . ." She stopped in confusion. Why *did* she have to find Aletheia? What had put this sudden compulsion into her mind? She only knew that she was being given credit for something someone else had done, someone who was in terrible danger. Chills like daggers stabbed into her back.

Mistress Blake caught hold of Tria's hands, raised them, looked at her fingers, and nodded as though the examination had answered a question. "You are being summoned. You must go."

Tria pivoted at the sound of footsteps behind her, hoping to see Aletheia. But it was Petra, with Rehanne and Kathyn following her. "Aletheia's not outside," Petra said.

"We'll have to do it without her." Tria turned back to Mistress Blake. "Can you help us, Mistress?"

"I don't have Aletheia's gift," Mistress Blake said. "But I can lend strength to you and Petra. You've both studied under Aletheia; you have the knowledge and power to open a door."

Tria gazed at Petra. "We've got to get to the passage Aletheia took us through the day she left Irel in the world where time runs backward. We have to hurry. It's urgent. I can't explain."

Wide-eyed, Petra stared back at her. "I've never opened a door."

"But you have the talent. Come on. We've got to do it." Tria reached for Petra's hand.

Mistress Blake held Tria's other hand. "Everyone who's willing to help, form a circle," she ordered.

Rehanne joined hands with Mistress Blake. "You can count me in," Kathyn said. "Anything to save Kress." She took Rehanne's other hand and reached for Petra's.

Verin stepped up and took Kathyn's hand and Petra's. Tria was glad to see her; she had not known the healer had followed them in.

Tria concentrated as Aletheia had taught. A wave of weakness washed over her. Her mind faltered. Blackness closed in around her. She felt she was fading away, dissolving into nothingness.

From somewhere, a surge of power revived her. Her mind snapped back to its task.

A small black speck floated in the center of their circle. The keyhole! Tria aimed her power at the speck and felt other flows of power join hers. The speck grew, became a gaping black hole. Tria closed her eyes and stepped toward it, pulling the others with her.

She could see nothing. She stumbled blindly through an

intense cold that felt like death. "The wall!" someone said. "She's opened it!"

She didn't stop to wonder what was meant. The impulse that guided her tottering steps forced her onward, her flagging strength sustained by her companions' power. She moved as in a dream, hardly aware of those with her, hands grown too numb to feel their touch, ears only dimly receiving the sound of their voices.

She stopped. Someone cried out. The icy cold grew more intense. Her limbs stiffened. She could not move; she could do nothing more than lean on supporting arms.

"She's dead." Verin's voice spoke the first words Tria heard clearly. "That piece of crystal pierced her heart."

Gentle hands turned Tria around and led her away. "No one should have to see her own death," Mistress Blake spoke beside her. "Here, this is yours now." A chain was slipped over her head, and the familiar weight of the crystal pendant fell against her breast. "And you must wear this." A ring was slid onto her finger. Wonderingly she lifted her hand. An orange light shone through her darkness, the gem of Headmistress's ring became visible, and by its reflected gleams she saw her companions.

Kathyn's face was pale and streaked with tears. Petra looked stunned. Verin wore a grim expression, and her hands were stained with blood. Rehanne slumped against the tunnel wall, and Tria wondered if she was going to faint. Only Mistress Blake seemed unaffected.

"Rest a bit," she said to Tria. "Let your strength come back."

"*My* strength? Is it mine—or hers?" Tria did not need to ask what the others had seen. Memories flooded into her—from the original Tria and her other shadow selves.

*She* was only a reflection. How could she live, when the real Tria was dead?

A SCHOOL FOR SORCERY

"All that was hers is yours," Mistress Blake answered. "The reflection has become the reality."

"Then I. . . . I have to do what she . . . Oryon! Was he—"

"He was not there. We found only his wand, broken into three pieces."

"We've got to find him." Tria urged her feet into motion. "Come on," she called to the others. "He can't have gone far."

Tria had little doubt where Oryon would have gone. She remembered the mysterious barrier she had encountered in her previous foray through the tunnels, the barrier behind which she had seen the panther that could only have been Lina. And where Lina had been, it was likely that Wilce and Gray would be, and possibly Kress as well. And, of course, their keepers, the Dire Women. Oryon would seek help from those who had been supplying him with the power he needed to carry out his plans. He had broken faith with them because he thought he could get what he wanted from the *Breyadon's* secret knowledge, but since that plan had failed, he would attempt to reestablish his agreement with the Dire Women.

She could not tell where in the tunnel she was or in which direction the barrier lay. Nor did she know how to get through it if she found it. But she did not share these doubts with the others. They were already badly shaken; how far would they follow her if they knew she was lost?

The tunnel was cold, the light dim. Its walls remained opaque, giving no clue about whether she was in a section she had passed through before. With nothing to guide her, she could only march onward with a pretense of confidence and hope the others would not guess her true state of mind.

She wished she knew what had happened to her host in the crystal palace, whether its destruction had killed him or freed him. If only he were here to act as her guide . . . She sent out a mental call, but he did not answer. Again and again

E. ROSE SABIN

her mind broadcast the vain plea as the tunnel wound on and led them nowhere.

"What's that?"

Rehanne's question startled Tria, brought her to a stop. Rehanne stepped to her side and pointed to a black heap lying in shadow against the tunnel wall. It looked like a pile of rags. In her preoccupation, Tria would have passed by without noticing it. But any object in the otherwise empty corridor merited investigation. She and Rehanne approached it cautiously while the others hovered behind them.

At the fetid smell that rose from it, Rehanne stepped back, gagging. "Something dead," she said.

Tria gasped and knelt beside it. Gingerly she reached to touch it, turn it over. She flinched at the feel of rotting flesh on bony arm. He could not be alive.

A shallow, rasping breath told her he was. "It's Oryon," she said. "Not the Oryon we're looking for. A shadow Oryon. I met him when I—when one of me—was lost in here. In fact—" She looked around, knowing what she'd see close by. Before she could catch more than a glimpse of brown skirt, Mistress Blake interposed herself between the other crumpled figure and Tria.

"That one *is* dead," the woman said. "Don't look at it, Tria."

Tria shuddered and turned her gaze back to the piteous wreck at her feet. "I thought he'd died, too. I should have realized he hadn't. He's good. If he had gone back into Oryon, he would have drawn Oryon from his evil course. But how he can live in this condition, I don't understand."

Mistress Blake knelt beside her and looked on the ravaged figure. "Oryon won't *let* him die," she said. "He doesn't want him back. Verin," she motioned to the healer, "Can you relieve his suffering?"

Tria gave up her place to Verin. The healer eased the pitiable form into a more comfortable position and with no sign of repugnance ran her hands over the tortured body. "Not much I can do," she said, shaking her head. "By all rights he shouldn't be alive. This is no more than a breathing corpse. If we could find a way to release him, it would be a kindness."

"And it might stop the real Oryon," Petra said. "All of us together ought to be able to break whatever link Oryon is using to keep him alive."

"I don't like the idea of using power to kill, but in this case . . ." Rehanne's voice trailed off as she gazed with pity on the near-corpse.

"Let's do it and get on with our search for the real Oryon," Kathyn said, her impatience showing that she was less moved by this shadow Oryon's plight than she was concerned about her twin.

"No! Wait!" Tria grabbed Petra's arm. "What was that you said about a link?"

"Why, that if Oryon is keeping him alive as Mistress Blake said, he must have some kind of link to him. Isn't that right, Mistress Blake?"

"A tenuous one, but, yes, something through which he channels just enough vital force to prevent death."

"We've got to keep him alive," Tria said. "If we find and follow that link, it will lead us to Oryon."

Mistress Blake nodded slowly. "It's possible," she agreed.

"Good." Tria saw clearly what must be done. "Verin, you stay here with him and use every bit of skill you have to help him live. Petra, you stay with her so if anything happens to the rest of us, you can get her back. Everyone else, come with me."

No one questioned her orders. Even Mistress Blake seemed willing to let Tria take the lead.

E. ROSE SABIN

"Rehanne," she went on, "you can get into people's minds. Try to get into his and find that thread. Kathyn, lend her power if her own isn't enough."

Rehanne's brow furrowed in concentration. Without speaking, she reached for Kathyn's hand. The tunnel was silent except for the shadow Oryon's labored breathing. When Tria thought she could bear the wait no longer, Rehanne said, "I have it."

Hand in hand with Kathyn, she moved forward. Tria followed, relieved to be moving away from the near-dead Oryon and the corpse of her alternate self. Mistress Blake fell into step beside her.

The trek was maddeningly slow. Several times Rehanne halted to search again for that tenuous thread. "It's like trying to follow a single strand of spiderweb," she explained. "It's nearly impossible to see, and it's too fragile to touch."

Rehanne stopped again, and Tria groaned, thinking she'd lost the thread.

"I've hit some kind of obstacle," Rehanne said. "The thread goes through it, but I can't."

Tria hurried to her side and confirmed the barrier's presence with a touch. Concentrating her gaze, she saw its faint shimmer. "This is the place where I expected to find him," she said. "But I don't know how to get through this barrier."

"Let me feel it." Mistress Blake edged between Tria and Rehanne, placed her palms against the barrier, rubbed them up and down over it.

She stepped back. "This is Dire work," she said. "It's strong, but if everyone lends me power, I think I can breach it enough to let one person go through. Tria?"

"I'll go," Tria said. "Just open the way."

Mistress Blake worked quickly. Tria had no time to reconsider the folly of going in alone to face Oryon, the Dire Women, and the things Wilce and Gray had become. Plus Kress.

Mistress Blake spread her arms apart and motioned Tria to duck under them. She did so and found herself on the far side of the barrier. The corridor in which she stood was empty, but it curved a short distance ahead.

Resolutely she strode forward, all too aware that on rounding that curve she would pass from her companions' sight.

Beyond the curve the empty corridor continued, and another curve lay ahead. At least she passed no side tunnels; she had to be heading in the right direction.

Around that second curve lay a third. Discouraged, Tria fought the temptation to turn back. As she rounded the curve, a scream and a hideous, inhuman cry told her she was near her goal. The sound chilled her, but she kept going.

The tunnel ended in an open archway. Through it she saw a field strewn with dismembered and decaying corpses beneath a sky like molten iron. The stench of blood and excrement and putrefying flesh rolled out in heavy waves, choking her so that she could not breathe. Jagged boulders studded the field, and on many of these perched vultures with human faces. As she watched, two or three of these hideous birds fluttered down to feed on the dead. Harpies! She would have turned and run, but the screams prevented her. Something in that terrible place was not yet dead.

Clamping her hand over her nose and mouth, Tria passed beneath the arch and picked her way around the corpses. Her feet sank into a vile muck, and she had to pluck them out and set them down slowly and carefully. She gagged and her empty stomach heaved. She wanted to flee, but her other selves, having passed through death, fed into her thoughts the courage to continue.

E. Rose Sabin

She stumbled and nearly fell over a severed arm. Shuddering, stomach churning, Tria halted and listened. The screams had changed to wracking sobs. They were coming from a jumble of large boulders to her right. She made her way around them, careful not to approach too near in case she was being drawn into a trap.

As she came around the side of the boulders, she saw Kress. Long chains wrapped around him, securing him to a rocky spire. His head fell forward; spittle hung from his mouth and streaked his bare chest. She did not think he was dead, but it was not he who cried.

Oryon was spread-eagled against a rock. An iron collar around his neck was bolted to the rock. His black clothes hung in shreds. On one side of him a Dire Woman gripped his arm and tore flesh from it with her teeth. On the other side, the second Dire Woman used her long nails to rip the skin from his shoulder. At his feet, two beastly creatures gnawed his ankles. One looked up from its grisly feast, and Tria realized with heart-wrenching horror that she had found Wilce and Gray.

"Tria! Help me!" Kress had seen her. His calls alerted the Dire Women. They looked toward her.

Alone she didn't stand a chance against them. She glanced at Kress. He didn't seem badly injured. If she could free him in time . . .

She concentrated on the chain that bound him to the rock. Ignoring his cries and Oryon's mindless keening, she visualized the chain stretching, lengthening, so that it fell away. As Kress pulled free of its slack loops, the Dire Women shrieked and launched themselves at Tria.

Kress grabbed the chain and held it in both hands. Tria hoped she hadn't stretched it too thin and too long to make a usable weapon. She threw up her hands to ward off the Dire Women. *Hurry, Kress!* she thought.

Headmistress's ring glowed like fire in the weird red light of the molten sky. The Dire Women veered, unfurled their wings, and flew over her head, cursing and gibbering. The gem! It was protecting, as Headmistress had said. But it couldn't hold the women off for long.

Tria looked for Kress. He had run to Oryon, not to her. He raised the chain and with a sickening thud crashed it against Oryon's skull, stilling Oryon's cries forever.

He swung the bloody chain at the things that had been Wilce and Gray.

"No!" Holding her hand up to keep the ring visible to the Dire Women, Tria ran toward Kress. "Chain them, don't kill them."

Her words had no effect. She extended her power and wrenched the chain from his grasp. As the Gray-thing attacked him, she sent the chain looping around its neck and pulled it back. The Dire Women shrieked in rage. The Wilce-thing snarled and hurtled toward her.

"No, Wilce! Stop! It's Tria! I've come to take you home."

It skidded to a halt in front of her, its gaze fixed on the crystal pendant. A glimmer of intelligence flickered in the brown eyes. It hung its head.

"You do remember," she said softly. "Come with me. I won't chain you." To Kress she shouted, "Take the chain. Bring Gray."

This time he obeyed, grabbed the end of the chain, and headed toward Tria, pulling Gray along. The Dire Women dove at him, driving him back toward the boulders. He dropped the chain, and Gray scuttled out of reach, the chain trailing after him.

"Wilce," Tria said. "Get Gray. Bring him to me."

Wilce bounded off, leaped for the end of the chain, caught

it in his teeth, and dragged Gray, snarling and spitting, back to Tria. But the Dire Women had snatched Kress up and were flying off with him.

The ring was the only protection against them.

She yanked it off her finger, tossed it into the air, and used her power to send it speeding after them. She guided it into Kress's hand. If only he'd have the presence of mind to hold on to it.

He caught it. The Dire Women shrieked and released him. He plummeted to the ground. A heap of corpses broke his fall. Tria saw him stagger to his feet holding the ring and run toward her.

The Dire Women flew faster. Without the ring Tria was vulnerable. They swooped down on her.

Words popped into her head. Words she had heard Oryon use. What they meant, she had no idea. She shouted them anyway: "*Calyor margra felefor, tisitiya mura calyor na.*"

The Dire Women wavered in flight. Wings fanning her, they flew past, circled back around, and perched on the top of the boulders above Oryon's body.

"*Tisit felefor mu ragana lo!*" Tria shouted the words burned into her memory.

The ground shook. The boulders split apart, forcing the Dire Women to leap into the air. Fissures opened in the ground, swallowing corpses. Steaming gobs of liquid metal fell from the sky, burning whatever they touched. "Hurry, Kress," she shouted.

Dragging Gray on his chain, with Wilce bounding beside her, she dashed toward the arch. Harpies screeched. Rocks exploded. Boulders crumbled into dust. She hurtled through the arch and turned to look for Kress.

Bloody, covered with soot, like some hellish apparition he ran toward her out of the smoke and flames. He gained the arch, and without a word Tria turned and sped away with her charges. Behind her, wails and shrieks were swallowed up in one final cataclysmic blast. And as they ran, the tunnel closed behind them.

They crashed into the barrier. Behind it Tria saw the frightened faces of her friends. How were they to pass through? Mistress Blake had only been able to open it enough for a single person.

Wilce and Gray hurled themselves against it, their claws scrabbling against the invisible surface.

"Use this?" Kress handed Tria the ring. She held it against the barrier, but it did nothing. She slid the ring onto her finger.

Surely they hadn't come this far to be trapped here. She took a deep breath and called out the last words Oryon had used from the *Breyadon*: "*Felefor mura-na!*"

With a loud ripping sound, the barrier split open and they tumbled through.

Kress rushed to his sister's arms. Mistress Blake helped Tria hold Gray's chain. "Gray. Oh, Gray!" Rehanne mourned.

Wilce tried to stand upright and for a few seconds he succeeded. But Rehanne shouted, "The tunnel!"

It was rolling up behind them, and its sides were closing in on them. Wilce dropped onto all fours, and they ran for their lives.

They passed the place where the tunnel forked, and the branch they'd run from sealed shut as they escaped. They kept running until Tria was convinced the destruction had stopped. Breathless and panting, she called the others to a halt. They rested until they'd caught their breath, then went on to where Petra and Verin waited.

They found the shadow Oryon sitting up, his back supported by the tunnel wall. His flesh seemed to have acquired

E. Rose Sabin

290

more substance. The corpse was gone, to Tria's great relief. She didn't ask what they had done with it.

Kress hurled himself on Oryon, pummeling him. Kathyn, Petra, and Verin pulled him away and restrained him. "He did this!" he said. "He did this! Why is he alive?"

"The Oryon who did all the evil is dead, Kress," Tria said, not mentioning for Kathyn's sake that it was Kress who'd killed him. "This Oryon helped to save us."

Kress grumbled but ceased trying to attack. Later Tria would have time for long explanations. Now, she only wanted to get back to the school. "Petra," she asked, "can you find our door?"

Verin and Petra supported Oryon, who was conscious and clearly much stronger. He had not spoken since Tria and her group had arrived. Tria knew he had felt the original Oryon's agonized death.

Mistress Blake took over the burden of pulling and controlling the chained Gray. Rehanne walked beside Mistress Blake and talked quietly to Gray, trying desperately to reach that clouded mind. Hand in hand, Kathyn and Kress lagged behind the others, whispering together. Tria hoped Kress was telling his twin he was sorry for his part in Oryon's conspiracy and for all the things he had done, but she thought it more likely that he was trying to justify his actions.

Wilce stayed at Tria's side and from time to time was able to walk in human fashion for a short distance before dropping back to all fours.

They came to the door Tria and Petra had made and passed through. Although they had made the door in the corridor of the faculty residence hall, they exited into the long, candlelit corridor Tria had found at the top of the elusive and elegant stairway.

Mistress Blake placed Gray's chain in Rehanne's hand and spoke to the bedraggled group. "You are summoned to the faculty council. However, you need not all attend. Tria and Oryon must attend, and I know the faculty is concerned about Wilce and Gray and will want to see them. The rest of you may choose whether or not to go with them."

Tria alone had been before the council in this place and therefore had an idea of what she faced. Her companions looked puzzled by their unexpected location and more than a little frightened by the prospect of facing Headmistress and the rest of the faculty in their exhausted state.

But Verin said, "I'll stay with Oryon. He's still far from fully healed."

Kress looked around frantically as if hunting for a known exit. "I don't want to see anybody right now," he blurted.

"You need not attend, Mr. Klemmer," Mistress Blake told him. "You are free to return to your room and rest, though I'm sure Headmistress will want to speak with you later."

"If Kress doesn't go, I won't either," Kathyn said.

Mistress Blake nodded and pointed out the stairs at the end of the corridor. "That stairway will take you to the third floor. Mr. Klemmer, you have permission to go to your sister's room and rest there until the supper hour, since Verin, her roommate, will accompany us. I believe you and Kathyn need to be together a bit longer."

Gratefully, Kathyn linked arms with Kress, and the twins headed for the stairs.

"I'd like to leave, too," Petra said. "I'm too worn out to face anyone right now."

"Of course," Mistress Blake responded. "Most of the burden of opening the door to the paths between the worlds fell on you."

Petra moved off after Kathyn and Kress. Mistress Blake

looked at Rehanne, who had remained silent. "Do you wish to go with us?" she asked.

"Yes," Rehanne answered, gripping tightly the chain that held Gray. "Gray needs me."

Tria wished she had been given a choice. Her strength depleted, she felt near collapse.

But Mistress Blake said, "Come, then. They are waiting for us." She led them toward the doors to the mysterious conference room.

Tria followed, Wilce stumbling along beside her, attempting to walk upright and almost but not quite succeeding. Gray, head hanging down, padded along beside Rehanne. At the end of the procession, Oryon leaned heavily on Verin.

Mistress Blake threw open the double doors and ushered them into the plush chamber where the rest of the faculty sat around the long table. She stepped aside, so that Tria found herself in the forefront of the group.

Headmistress rose to greet them. "Welcome and well done," she addressed Tria. "You have won the challenge."

It was such an anticlimax that Tria nearly laughed. After all she'd gone through, Headmistress could say no more than, "You've won." It seemed that this had been, after all, only a game to her.

Turning to Mistress Blake, Headmistress said with a stern frown, "It was agreed that none of us should interfere or lend assistance."

"That is true," Mistress Blake replied. "And you were the first to break that agreement by lending Tria your ring. What I did was a small thing by comparison."

To Tria's surprise, Headmistress smiled. "I suppose you are right. I meant the ring to distinguish the original from the shadow Trias, but if its other properties proved useful, I am glad."

A SCHOOL FOR SORCERY

From his place at the table, Master San Marté cleared his throat. "It is, we must acknowledge, impossible to act in an entirely ethical manner one hundred percent of the time. Intentions must account for something."

Mistress Blake smiled, too, and took the seat waiting for her at the table.

Tria removed the ring and handed it to Headmistress. "It saved our lives," she said. But she did not add that the original Tria had perished and she, a shadow, had received the ring's protection.

Rehanne, who'd been staring about in wonder at the magnificent room, stepped up beside Tria. "What about Gray and Wilce? Look at them! Restore them, please!"

The smile vanished from Headmistress's face, and sadness filled her gaze. "Their condition lies beyond my healing ability," she said.

"But they can't remain like this," Rehanne cried out.

Headmistress turned to Oryon. "Mr. Brew, can you restore what you damaged?"

Still leaning on Verin's arm, Oryon hung his head. "No," he murmured. "My power is gone."

Headmistress confronted him, touched his shoulder, gazed into his eyes. "Not gone, I think," she said after a time. "Dormant as Miss Mayclan's was after her encounter with the Dire Woman. You were wounded more deeply than she, and your power may never be what it was, but you will in time regain some of it.

"Well, Miss Tesserell, it's up to you. Your labors have brought you to a higher level. You should have the power—"

"My strength is completely drained," Tria interrupted, unable to contain her anger. "Do you know what I've been through?"

"No one ever attains the higher levels without great pain,

my dear. And I think you have resources of which you are unaware."

Tria began an indignant denial, but a voice cut her off. Not an audible voice, but one that spoke in her mind alone. *She is right, daughter*, the voice said. *She has been right all along.*

*You—you're here? With me?* Excitement reverberated through Tria's mental query.

*I am here—and not here. The breaking of the crystal prison freed me to be many wheres, though you cannot at present understand that. However, I will tell you what you must do to heal these unfortunate young men.*

Following her mentor's instructions, Tria turned to Wilce. He stood upright, and she clasped his paws, willing them to become hands. She spoke words placed in her mind, and a power not her own flowed through her into Wilce. His body straightened, his features softened, claws became fingers and intertwined with hers. His voice, hoarse from disuse, said, "Thank you, Tria," and he leaned forward and kissed her cheek.

It was harder with Gray; he had farther to come. Wilce and Rehanne held him upright so that Tria could grasp his taloned paws. The power flowing through her was greater, too, and the words she spoke seemed to come from another dimension and roll through time to call their hearer back from a far place.

When Tria finished, Gray stood before them in his own form. He gazed bleakly at them for a moment, then swayed and might have fallen had not Rehanne rushed to support him. She helped him into the empty chair at the table's end. He buried his face in his hands.

"He is not yet whole," Headmistress observed to Tria. "He will need time to recover completely, but you have set him on that path. You see, you did have the resources." Headmistress beamed at her.

A SCHOOL FOR SORCERY

"But I didn't. It was—" Tria stopped in confusion. How could she explain? She didn't know her mentor's name. "The power wasn't mine," she finished lamely.

Headmistress nodded enthusiastic approval. "That, Miss Tesserell, is the most important lesson Simonton School strives to teach. Our power is never our own. We are only channels through which the Power-Giver sends his power."

Power-Giver? Could it be? . . .

It didn't matter. Headmistress was still talking as though this entire horrific ordeal had been no more than a training exercise.

It could not have been. She looked at Gray, whose hands still covered his face. He'd been hurt so deeply; Wilce, too, though he seemed to be handling it better.

Oryon—the original Oryon—was dead, as was the original Tria. Oryon's surviving shadow had much to recover from. She herself was no longer sure of her identity or of her reality.

Abruptly sickened, Tria whirled and fled the room.

She'd run only a short distance down the long hall when she collided with Veronica, nearly knocking the little maid off her feet. With a mumbled apology, she steadied the woman, then tried to edge around her.

Veronica caught her arm and held her. "Running away from your triumph, miss?"

"Running away from Headmistress's hypocrisy," Tria answered through sudden tears. "Tell me this wasn't just a cruel test," she begged.

"All of life is a test," Veronica said. "And it is often cruel."

"So this was planned? A training exercise? A game?" Tria was perilously close to hysteria.

"It was not planned in the sense you mean," Veronica said. "Oryon, you, the others, were all presented with choices. You chose freely, and the choices you made—each of you—set

 E. Rose Sabin

 296

other events in motion that then required the making of other choices."

"Like a game," Tria said, calmer but still bitter.

"The game of life," Veronica responded. "Some play it better than others. Some win and some lose. None has the option of not participating."

"But Headmistress—she implied that everything that happened was no more than a means of bringing me to a higher level. Doesn't she know what we all went through?"

"Oh, indeed, she knows," Veronica said sharply. "She did not cause your pain, and though you think she could have prevented it, she could not, except by taking away your freedom to choose. Would you have wanted that? Miryam—that is, Headmistress—suffered with you and grieved for you, though she conceals her sorrow, as she must. Had you failed, it would have caused her untold anguish."

"So we could have failed?"

"You need not ask that question. Look within yourself. You know all too well how close you came to failure."

Tria felt suddenly ashamed. But there was one more thing she had to ask.

"What of you, Veronica? What is your place in all of this?"

The little maid smiled. "My place, miss? I just came here to remind you that it's time for dinner. You'd best hurry downstairs."

A SCHOOL FOR SORCERY

# 25

## PANTHER

Tria looked at the clock and sighed. Time for her visit to Lina. These daily visits were becoming harder and harder to face, and today she was already depressed. Another failure to call Lina back to human form would depress her more. Yet she had to try.

The first time, fresh from her success at restoring Wilce and Gray, full of confidence, she had entered the cage where Lina was confined and called for help from her mysterious mentor. He had not answered. Nor had he spoken since in her mind, though at times she felt his presence. And nothing she had done on that day or on all the successive days to the end of the school year had brought Lina back; the panther remained unchanged.

She knew her unseen counselor had not deserted her. When during the time of spring rains a child on a nearby farm fell into a deep well, Tria had gone with a rescue party and had used her power to lift the tot from the narrow shaft in time to save him from drowning. She had sensed her mentor augmenting her strength. The grateful parents had insisted on paying her tuition for the coming term. Perhaps her mentor had had a hand in that decision.

During the two months' vacation between the spring and fall terms she had returned home, a glowing commendation in hand from Headmistress. Her mother had been overjoyed, but it was her father's unexpected reaction that pleased her most. He told her he was so proud of her that he would pay her for her summer's work on the farm. So her second year's tuition was taken care of, and she had fulfilled, at least in part, her promise to her mother.

At the beginning of the new school year she again felt the presence of her benefactor from the crystal sphere. It had to have been he who helped her break up a fight between Taner and a first-year student. Taner had returned with restored power but without a dagger to replace the one she'd lost. Often angry, quick to take offense, Taner might have killed her less-talented opponent had Tria not been led to use her power to deflect Taner's.

Yet her mentor still refused to make his presence known to her when she was with Lina. Nothing she or others did to try to restore Lina accomplished anything. Rehanne's mind-probe, Verin's healing touch, Taner's peremptory demand, Wilce's soft coaxing were all as futile as Tria's attempts. Oryon had tried to use the feeble power that had returned to him. His effort had failed like the rest. Only Kress had made no effort to help, and Kathyn confided the thing that Headmistress had told her when they'd all gotten into trouble after the power duel: Kress had almost no gift of his own beyond that of drawing power from others. Now that he was abstaining from stealing others' power, he could do almost nothing.

Tria thought of the list she'd made of her talents. It had grown longer; the items she'd added included mind-speaking. But not that one or any other had served to help Lina. Perhaps it had been as Veronica suggested the night Tria had rescued Lina: the panther had been healed but Lina had perished. Yet Tria refused to abandon hope. This day she'd try again to find the key to recall the catgirl to her human nature.

She looked around the room for something to take with her that might help. Her first selection was Lina's talisman for breaking wards, though she had tried it many times in the hope that its magic would have some effect. Nubba had found it lying in the hall near the washroom the day after Oryon's defeat, had shown it to Tria, and Tria had claimed it for Lina.

The green scarf spread over the two trunks caught her eye. Had she taken it before? She thought she had, but she'd try again. She swooped it off the trunks and folded it, thinking as she did so of the day she'd met Lina. The recollection of the contest they'd had evoked a sad smile. She hadn't known how easily she could shrink or enlarge objects when she'd reduced Lina's trunk to the size of a matchbox and kicked it under its owner's bed.

On sudden impulse she duplicated that feat, picked up the doll-sized trunk, and carried it with the other items.

She hurried downstairs and out through the patio to the faculty residence hall where Lina's cage occupied a spare room next to Veronica's apartment.

The large cage filled most of the room. The panther paced back and forth, head swaying, green eyes baleful. "You're edgy today," Tria said, leaning against the bars of the cage. "So am I."

The panther continued its prowling.

"Look, I've brought your talisman." Tria held the golden, jeweled circlet toward the cat, which ignored it.

"Take it. It's yours." Tria hurled the talisman at the panther. It struck the animal's flank. The panther whirled and charged toward Tria, snarling.

A SCHOOL FOR SORCERY

Tria jumped back from the bars. "Well, at least that got your attention. Look at this." She shook out the scarf. "You always said you liked green because it brought out the color of your eyes." Tria tossed it the scarf.

The panther caught the green silk in its jaws, shook it, dropped it, and shredded it with its claws.

"You *are* in a nasty mood today. Let's see what you do with this." She threw the miniaturized trunk past the panther.

It landed near the rear of the cage. The animal crouched and sprang toward it. As it pounced, Tria expanded the trunk to its original size. Thrown off balance, the panther toppled backward.

It twisted around, regained its feet, and turned its back on Tria. Tail twitching, it stalked to a corner of the cage, where it settled and licked its paws.

"Well, I wounded your dignity, anyway. Come on, Lina. Rescue your trunk." Tria shrank it again, picked it up with her power, and pitched it at Lina.

Wary, the cat backed away from it. Tria pushed it closer, expanded it again, this time to twice its correct size. The panther reared back, yowling, circled the trunk, vaulted onto it, and clawed at it. Tria reduced the trunk to fist size, sending the panther crashing to the ground.

"Enough of this!" Lina stood dressed in the short, white cotton smock she had been wearing when Tria last saw her, the night they'd summoned the Dire Woman. Green eyes flashing, she caught up the trunk and hurled it through the bars at Tria. "Leave me as I wish to be!" she shouted.

Tria dodged the flying trunk and stared in amazement as Lina reverted to panther form. The panther yawned, stretched, and lay on the floor, its back to Tria.

Tria gripped the bars of the cage. "So, you're choosing to be an animal, are you? To laze in a cage all day eating all you want, having people make a fuss over you. No books, no class- es, no tests to study for, no work detail." She frowned, think- ing of all she knew of Lina and recalling the night when the Dire Woman had abducted her.

"No, it's more than that. You're avoiding something. That night when you summoned the Dire Woman and we both chased her into the hall and you shapechanged. I thought you'd leap on the Dire Woman and try to stop her, but you leaped on Gray instead. I thought it was because he was pro- tecting his mistress, but it wasn't that, was it? You didn't want to attack the Dire Woman. You wanted power from her, the kind Oryon had. Your own greed made you a captive."

The panther lay unmoving but breathing too rapidly for sleep. One ear twitched. Lina was listening.

"No one will hold what you did against you. We all made mistakes, but the whole incident with Oryon is over and for- given. It's a new year, now. All anyone cares about is passing courses and discovering the way to the next level.

"Lina, I miss you. I haven't taken another roommate. I've waited for you to come back, and I've kept all your things in the room, but it seems empty without you. I get lonely; I even miss the arguments we used to have." Tria rested her forehead against the cool steel bars a moment, gathering courage to go on. "Lina, everyone's been standoffish since I won the chal- lenge. All of them—even Rehanne and Wilce—treat me like some kind of goddess. I know you wouldn't do that. I need a friend. I think you need one, too. Come back, please."

Tria's voice trailed off into silence. Tears leaked from her eyes and trailed down her cheeks; she didn't have the energy to wipe them away. Slowly she turned toward the door. Her hand touched the latch.

"Wait. Get me out of this cage. I'll come with you."

Tria whirled around. Lina stood at the front of the cage. "I

A SCHOOL FOR SORCERY

guess my power's not all gone," she said. "I could make the transformation. But I don't have enough left to bend these bars. That's the main reason I haven't changed: I couldn't face being helpless."

Tria called up a surge of power and spread the bars apart. Lina stepped through. Tria threw her arms around her and hugged her. "Your power will come back. Oryon's was stripped by the Dire Women, too, but he's gradually getting it back. I'll tell you about it, but first let me get your trunk." Her power brought the trunk through the bars and set it in front of Lina. "Better get something out of it to wear instead of that smock. You can't go through the school in just that. You've been a panther so long you've forgotten about wearing proper clothes."

Lina looked down at her scanty garment and laughed. She unlatched the trunk, opened it, and pulled out clothes. When she'd dressed, Tria reduced the trunk, picked it up in one hand, and slipped her other arm around Lina's waist. "Come on, roommate," she said. "I'll catch you up on all the news."

# 26

## The Gifting

It was time to go. Lina had left several minutes earlier to find a good seat in the audience; she would not graduate for another year. The assembly hall would be full for once, crowded with students, families, and friends come to watch the Gifting of the graduates. Tria's parents would not be there; the trip was too long and too expensive to permit them to come. They'd sent their regrets, their congratulations, and assurances of their love for her and their pride in her accomplishments.

Tria didn't have to worry about getting a good seat. She'd be in the procession of graduates. It was time for her to join that procession, but instead she stood in her long white gown and stared out the window.

The school had become her whole world. For the past two years she had not left it except to make short trips into town. She did not count the forays into the paths between the worlds and, in her second class with Aletheia, brief visits to two or three of those alternate worlds. She could never decide whether those journeys took her away from the school or whether the school encompassed the other worlds and the paths between them. She understood that the three buildings of yellow brick that she had seen on her arrival and explored during her first months in residence were mostly illusion. The real school was much larger, more beautiful, more complex than the fictitious representation in the brochure that had drawn her here. She could not yet guess its true extent or complexity.

She had expected to be here four or five years before satisfying the requirements and reaching third level. Instead, she had attained the mandatory level before the end of her first year, but courses remained to be taken and exams to be passed. She'd finished her second year and thought to go on to a third, but a week before the end of the current term, Headmistress had told her she was to be graduated. She had instructed Tria to attend the Gifting Ceremony along with the other graduates. The prospect of receiving from the hands of Mistress Blake the parting gift that would focus and define her talent excited her. But Tria couldn't get used to the idea of leaving the school.

Another glance at her clock made her gasp in horrified disbelief. An hour *couldn't* have passed since Lina left. The Gifting must already have started.

She dashed into the hall, bounded down the steps, and sped through empty corridors. Too many empty corridors.

Where the first floor hallway should have been, she faced another flight of stairs, a wide, curving cascade with gold runners and crystal risers. Her hand caressed the gleaming brass banister; here was a stairway begging to be descended slowly and gracefully. She pointed her toe, brought it to rest daintily on the first step, then paused. This was not a time for self-indulgence. She was late!

Dared she fold time? A mere tuck would supply the needed minutes. She pressed her fingertips against her closed eyelids and stretched her mind outward. The disorientation that preceded time-shifting was beginning when she remembered how she had accidentally moved time back an hour on her first day in the school. The stern prophecy of Headmistress rang out

E. ROSE SABIN

in her brain: "You will be required to return the hour you took." She was suddenly sure that time had come, and she was being required to return the hour at this critical point. She dared not upset time's balance even if it meant missing the Gifting.

Tria withdrew her concentration, opened her eyes, and charged down the stairway, hitting every other step.

At its end was a wide, carpeted hall she'd never seen before.

To steady her nerves, she recited the first theory lesson, spoken in the dry, pedantic tone of Master Tumberlis. "The worlds are born of dust and the tears of the gods. How many worlds we cannot comprehend. The dimensions of existence are infinite, yet most of our race experience no more than three or four."

Now, with the Gifting Ceremony under way, she was experiencing those other dimensions. Open doorways offered tantalizing glimpses of lavish parlors, winding stairways, and branching corridors, none of which she had time to explore. She had to find the quadrangle.

Maybe she could space-shift. She squeezed her eyes shut and concentrated, visualizing the solid oak door that opened onto the courtyard. She opened her eyes; the door loomed in front of her. She reached for the handle, jerked it open, and darted outside. Organ music drifted from the assembly hall. She gathered up her long, white graduation gown and raced across flagstones and flower beds.

A leap over a rose bush sent her sprawling, her gown snagged on a thorn. She picked herself up and ruefully disentangled the hem of her dress from the bush's grasp. Rearranging the folds of her skirt to conceal the jagged tear, she muttered, "Should have known shortcuts always turn out to be the longest way to where I'm going. Haven't I learned anything these past two years?"

She hurried to the fountain to wash the dirt smudges off her hands and dress. A tousled head popped up over the op-

A SCHOOL FOR SORCERY

posite side of the fountain. Dark gamin eyes peered at her. "See my boat, lady? It runned away."

This must be a visitor's child. Tria followed the direction indicated by a muddy finger. A roughly carved wooden boat bobbled perilously close to the fall of water from the fountain.

"Catch it for me, please?"

She leaned over the rough stone edge, soiling her dress again. The wind caught and billowed the paper sail on its twig mast, sweeping the tiny craft beyond her reach. The loud chords of the processional rang out, reminding her of the time. She straightened.

"Please, lady!" The anguish in the child's voice caught at her heart. She focused her attention again on the toy boat. Sunlight glinted off the fragile sail; for an instant, her vision blurred. She saw before her a great sea. Men rushed across the slippery deck of their wave-tossed vessel, shouting as they struggled to furl the mainsail.

She blinked. A jet of water deflected the wooden ship, spun it toward her. She reached out, grabbed it, placed it in its owner's eager hands, and ran toward the assembly hall.

Thudding up the wide marble steps, she stopped short at the sight of a figure huddled on the top step. She knelt beside the crumpled form and placed her hand on the brown hair. From within the hall the organ music continued to chart the progress of the service.

"Nubba?"

The head lifted, revealing a tear-streaked and swollen face.

"Nubba, what's wrong? Why aren't you inside?"

"The Shalreg," the girl whimpered. "It won't let me in."

"By the Seven Levels, Nubba," Tria snapped. "You let that thing keep you from the Gifting?"

Nubba's shoulders shook. "You wouldn't talk like that if you could see the vile ogre," she got out between sobs.

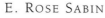 E. ROSE SABIN

"Never mind," Tria interrupted before Nubba could launch into the familiar description of the fanged, slobbering, scaled creature.

Resisting the impulse to leave Nubba blubbering on the steps, Tria helped her classmate to her feet. "Come on, we'll go in together."

She dragged the quaking Nubba toward the entrance.

"It's still there," Nubba wailed.

Drat the foolish girl! This was not the Shalreg's usual well-timed appearance. Nubba had no reason to invoke its presence now.

They reached the open door. Through it, Tria could see the double line of graduates filing toward the dais where the gifts were displayed. With a sinking heart, she measured the dwindling line. Over half the graduates had already selected their gifts.

Clutching Nubba's arm, she stepped through the entrance. A giant hand pressed against her chest, shoving her to the ground. The Shalreg? Tria's trembling hands traced warding signs in the air.

"See. I told you!" Nubba's dolorous cry brought Tria to her feet. She dusted off her gown.

"I'll find a way to get us both through," Tria vowed. She dragged Nubba back toward the unseen barrier and extended one hand, half expecting sharp talons to grab her.

Instead, her fingers slid along the weave of a net pulled taut across the entranceway. No monster but a warding field barred their way. A faculty member must have set it to prevent late entries from marring the Gifting Ceremony.

She stepped back while Nubba sniveled at her side. Dare she disturb the field? If she did not, she'd miss the Gifting. So would Nubba. Surely the net was to keep out tardy spectators, not participants.

A SCHOOL FOR SORCERY

"Stand in front of me, Nubba." Tria accompanied her order with a guiding shove and extended her arms on either side of her classmate. "Keep quiet."

Weaving hex signs with her fingers, Tria chanted a counterspell to break the warding. Her fingers burned; a tracery of sparks made the ward-net visible for a brief instant. She and Nubba moved forward but were brought short again; the net held.

Nubba groaned. From inside, Tria heard the murmur of voices. The Gifting continued; the last of the graduates approached the dais. Tria gritted her teeth.

"Don't make a sound," she again instructed Nubba. She screwed her face in concentration and recalled the glimpse of shimmering net. Her inner vision focused on a single minute opening between the tightly woven threads of force. Holding that eyelet in the center of her mind-vision, she pictured it expanding, slowly at first, then rapidly until it became a window large enough to step through. Tria pushed Nubba forward, felt for and found the opening, boosted Nubba through it, and jumped through after her.

Together they raced past startled spectators to the end of the procession. Tria smoothed her wrinkled gown and ran her fingers through her long hair, parrying with a smile the scandalized stares of the four classmates waiting to be gifted. Grateful that their presence shielded her and Nubba from Headmistress's sight, she nodded pleasantly to each.

The dour-faced Salor returned her nod without a smile. Tria wasn't surprised to see Salor so near the end of the procession. Quiet and shy, he always deferred to the others. Tria guessed that empathy with Salor's solitary nature as well as the fact that he was, like her, a healer had led Verin to position herself at his side.

Wilce smiled and bowed at both Tria and Nubba. His place

at line's end probably meant he had gallantly permitted all the others to go before him. Tria was glad he had been able to complete his studies this year despite the time he had lost. Gray had not been so fortunate; he'd remain another year.

Tria was surprised to see Taner at Wilce's side; it would have been more like the fiery-tempered girl to claim first place in the line.

Salor and Verin climbed the three steps to the dais, knelt before Headmistress, received her blessing, and walked to the table on which the gifts were spread. Tria and Nubba moved forward together.

Now Tria could see the gifts.

Regal in a wide-flowing azure gown, Mistress Blake in her role as Gifting Mistress greeted the graduates with a hand raised in benison and said, "Select your gift."

"There's hardly anything left." Nubba's dismayed whisper echoed Tria's thought.

Salor passed his hand above each article on the table. Like a bird, the hand hovered, soared on, hovered again, swooped down, and seized its prey.

The Gifting Mistress smiled. "Well chosen, Salor," she said when the hand lifted, clutching a small red book fitted with a silver clasp. "That gift will serve you well. The Book of Truth will complement your skill of physical healing. When you face someone in need of healing of the soul, read to that one a page from your book, and you will read into the patient's mind a mending and the strength to know and speak truth."

A rare smile illumined Salor's face. Clasping the book to his breast, he joined his fellow graduates at the rear of the dais.

Verin chose her gift quickly. She raised her hand toward the Gifting Mistress; a golden chain wound through her fingers. From it hung a gem like a drop of blood.

Again the Gifting Mistress nodded her approval. "The

A SCHOOL FOR SORCERY

greatest of healers must sometimes fail. But when you are called to tend one who, in the prime of life, lies wounded or ill past all your skill to save, collect the tears of those who weep for the dying. Pour those tears on the gem and touch it to the lips of the dying one. If the tears come from hearts which truly grieve, the gem will restore life."

Verin slipped the chain around her neck and followed Salor to the rear of the dais.

Wilce and Taner advanced to kneel before Headmistress and, after she blessed them, rose and moved on to the Gifting Table.

Wilce selected a large, heavy staff, its sturdy wood carved with geometrical patterns. Mistress Blake glowed; her eyes reflected the soft-hued light streaming through the stained-glass windows.

"That staff will bear your weight as you walk the world, bringing peace to troubled lands. Suffering has taught you great wisdom; your voice will avert wars and bring accord and reconciliation. But powerful forces will oppose you—all the evil things which feed on hatred and discord. This staff is carved with powerful warding signs; it is your defense against those evil ones."

Leaning on his staff, Wilce went solemnly to join the rest.

Taner snatched up a dagger with a curved blade and jeweled hilt. Her eyes glinting, she held it high.

Shadows flickered over the Gifting Mistress's face.

"Taner, you have a quick temper and a haughty spirit. You wear scars on your soul as well as on your face. Yet you have learned to curb and channel your wrath. We send you forth to avenge wrongs against the innocent. You know potions and spells to bring sorrow to those who have caused sorrow, and weakness to those who have preyed on the weak. You have no need of a dagger, yet you have desired one. You have attained your desire." She paused. Taner averted her eyes from the Mistress's piercing gaze. "It is meant to defend and preserve life; let it be an emblem of victory, not an instrument of death. Use it wisely."

Taner bowed her head. "I promise to do so," she murmured.

The rear of the platform was full; Nubba and Tria alone remained in front. They knelt before Headmistress. Tria scarcely heard her charge. As she had climbed the steps, a glance at the Gifting Table had shown her only one gift lying on the dusty black marble.

"Receive your gifts, my daughters," Headmistress concluded.

Tria preceded Nubba to the table. Her dismay was tempered with relief. The solitary gift, a spyglass, must be hers, designed to complement her cross-dimensional vision.

She reached for the glass, hesitated, glancing at Mistress Blake. A frown puckered the Gifting Mistress's forehead. Tria drew her hand back, and Nubba grabbed the glass and clasped it to her bosom with a defiant look.

"You have the gift intended for you, Nubba." Mistress Blake's voice was stern. "No one will take it from you."

A deep flush spread over Nubba's features; her chin quivered. Watching her, Tria set her jaw, determined to hide her disappointment.

The Gifting Mistress sighed. "We have taught you so little, Nubba. You must learn how to use your gift. Look through it."

Nubba brought the small end of the glass to her eye and adjusted the focus while inscribing a wide arc with the large end of the glass.

She froze. The glass pointed toward the floor at the foot of the dais steps. A violent trembling seized her.

A SCHOOL FOR SORCERY

"The Shalreg!" Echoes of her scream bounced off the vaulted ceiling.

Tria followed the aim of the spyglass but saw nothing. Nubba, screaming, backed against the Gifting Table, her face contorted with terror.

Tria concentrated her vision on the spot where Nubba looked. Was that, perhaps, *something* on the floor? A barely visible insect? A speck of dirt?

She closed her ears to the sound of Nubba's shrieks and shut out the sight of the bewildered spectators. Most of all, she banished the thought of the empty Gifting Table. Her mind centered on the speck, enlarging it.

She shrank back in horror, recognizing the hideous apparition from Nubba's interminable descriptions: the whirling, multifaceted eyes, the dripping fangs, the body armored with tight-fitting scales, the spiked legs ending in sharp pincers.

The monster lunged toward her, pincers clicking. Tria snapped the cord of her concentration. The creature sank back into near invisibility.

Tria snatched the spyglass from Nubba's frozen hand, reversed it, and pressed the large end to Nubba's eye. "Look, Nubba. Look at the Shalreg again."

Fearfully Nubba peered through the glass. A confused expression spread over her face. Hands shaking, she moved the spyglass around, searching for her nemesis. Tria grasped the spyglass, pointed it toward the minuscule monster, and held it steady.

Nubba's mouth fell open; the arch of her eyebrows imitated the vaulted ceiling. She stared through the inverted spyglass for a long moment. With a shout, she bounded off the platform, spyglass to her eye, and stomped hard on the floor, dancing a jig around the spot at which the glass was trained. She ended the bizarre performance with a triumphant song.

E. Rose Sabin

"The Shalreg's dead. I killed it. By myself I killed it. I've won; I'm free. The Shalreg's dead."

Spectators stared in openmouthed puzzlement. The group of graduates reacted with embarrassed sniggers. Nubba danced up the stairs and made a jaunty curtsy to the Gifting Mistress.

Mistress Blake smiled. "You've discovered how to use your gift to shrink your own fears to a conquerable size. Your glass will reduce fear; it will magnify opportunity. It does not lie; it restores objects to their true proportions. Many are like you, Nubba—imprisoned by their own distorted perceptions, needing a corrected view of reality. Seek them out and share your gift."

Beaming, Nubba joined her classmates.

Tria stood alone before the Gifting Mistress. She trembled, conscious of her soiled and torn dress, recognizing her unworthiness.

Mistress Blake's clear gaze swept over her. "You come late."

Tria hung her head. "I'm sorry. When I was leaving the school, halls and doors and stairways opened to me, and I had no time to explore them. I tried to come straight through, but I got lost." With a deep twinge of regret, Tria added, looking at the empty table, "I guess I should have stayed and traversed them all."

Mistress Blake gave an enigmatic smile. "You've journeyed farther than you realize." Holding her palms downward, she spread her hands wide over the empty table. The motion sent dust motes whirling in the rays of colored light. "Each of your classmates has selected his or her gift; all that remains is yours."

Was the Gifting Mistress mocking her? Tria's shoulders slumped. Her eyes swam with tears at the sight of the black marble table, its emptiness accentuated by the thin layer of dust.

A SCHOOL FOR SORCERY

The organist sent the strains of the recessional echoing through the hall. Numb with disappointment, Tria stood immobile while the graduates followed Headmistress from the platform. Most averted their gaze as they passed Tria, but Verin brushed her with a pitying glance. Nubba hesitated, but gripped her spyglass and hurried after the rest.

Mistress Blake took her place at the rear. The procession swept down the aisle and out of the assembly hall. The audience filed out. Many cast curious looks at Tria, but none approached her. The organ music ceased.

A tear spilled down Tria's face and splashed onto the table, inundating a mote of dust.

Her sight blurred, then cleared and focused on a tiny, water-cloaked world spinning in inky blackness. She knelt and breathed on it, blowing off some of the water, stretched forth one finger to touch it, watched it swarm with life. With gentle care, she flicked it upward to join the galaxy dancing in a gleam of golden light.

Tracing its spinning progress, her enhanced vision saw oceans and continents, swirling clouds and belching volcanoes, blistering deserts and steaming jungles. Beneath her nurturing gaze, creatures of the teeming seas blundered out onto land and established themselves, sunning on rocks, slithering through grass, bounding up mountains, swinging through trees, spreading wings and soaring into the clouds.

"The worlds are born of dust and the tears of the gods."

Startled, Tria looked up. Veronica stood on the other side of the table. "You already know the loneliness of the life to which you are called," she said. "Your gift shows you its beauty and power." She smiled and held her hands toward Tria. "Welcome to the Seventh Level."

E. ROSE SABIN

# EPILOGUE

Tria wept at the appearance of the tiny world she had set in motion. For no more than a few moments, she had forgotten it. In those few moments, forests had turned to desert, mountains had split asunder, sending lava and ash over all the surrounding land; rivers and lakes had dried. The oceans stank. Creatures fought and tore at one another until few remained alive.

Her tears sweetened the oceans and filled the rivers and lakes. Her breath calmed the warring creatures. New growth appeared and nibbled away at the deserts.

She sighed with relief. This time she had saved it. But there would not be many more such times, she knew.

"Is it real?" she asked Veronica.

"What is reality?" the Adept answered. "The world is as real as you are."

"How real is that?" Tria asked with a touch of bitterness. "I'm still not sure who I am. I was only a reflection—until, suddenly, I was the only one left. Did that make me real?"

"You were always real. If the word has any meaning." Her eyes twinkled. "When you can define 'reality' you will have surpassed me. When the other selves died and reunited with you, it made you no more real than you already were, or than they had been. What it did was increase your power, because they added their levels to yours. Now see to your charge. You're neglecting it again."

With a guilty start, Tria turned back to the tiny world. Again it needed extra care to recover from her brief inattention.

"What will happen to it when I sleep?" she asked. "Or eat? Or even think of something else for longer than a minute or two?"

"It will perish," Veronica said. "It is destined to be short-lived. Your first test as an Adept is to see how long your care can sustain it. The effort will hone your talents. When, despite all you do, it dissolves into nothingness, your grief will teach you wisdom."

"And then?" Tria cupped her hand protectively around her tiny world.

"Ah, then." Veronica chuckled. "Who knows? The school could use another maid."

Sabin, E. Rose

A school for sor-
cery / E. Rose
Sabin.

DUE DATE

| | | | |
|---|---|---|---|
| | | | |
| | | | |
| | | | |
| | | | |
| | | | |
| | | | |
| | | | |
| | | | |
| | | | |
| | | | |

17.95